The Phantom Queen Awakes

Published by Morrígan Books
Östra Promenaden 43
602 29 Norrköping
Sweden
www.morriganbooks.com

Editors: Mark S. Deniz & Amanda Pillar

ISBN: 978-91-977605-9-1

Cover art by Reece Notley © 2009
Internal Artwork by Cecily Webster © 2009

First Published February 2010

Edited by
Mark S. Deniz & Amanda Pillar

MORRÍGAN BOOKS

Available titles from Morrígan Books:

THE EVEN
by T. A. Moore

HOW TO MAKE MONSTERS
by Gary McMahon

VOICES
Edited by Mark S. Deniz & Amanda Pillar

GRANTS PASS
Edited by Amanda Pillar & Jennifer Brozek

DEAD SOULS
Edited by Mark S. Deniz

Dedications

Amanda:

Love: For Tom Bicknell, fiancé extraodinare.

War: To my grandfathers, survivors of war: Jack: the soldier, and Stan: the POW.

Death: For my stepfather, Boris, who is fighting it.

Mark:

Love: For Etina Deniz, my life, my love.

War: To all those brave women; waiting and hoping that their husbands, lovers, brothers, fathers, sons and friends would return: keeping hearths warm, children fed and schooled. And to those who have fought/are fighting for their beliefs.

Death: For my mother, Lesley and grandmother, Christine; women who taught me the value of life before their journey to the undiscovered country.

Mark and Amanda Would Also Like to Thank:

The editors would like to thank: Katharine Kerr, Elaine Cunningham, C.E. Murphy, Anya Bast, Michael Bailey, Peter Bell, Linda Donahue, Lynne Lumsden Green, L. J. Hayward, Jennifer Lawrence, James Lecky, T. A. Moore, Mari Ness, Sharon Kae Reamer, Martyn Taylor and Donald Jacob Uitvlugt, for sharing their wonderful stories with us.

Reece Notley and Cecily Webster, for their amazing artwork, inside and outside the book.

Tsana Dolichva, Sargon Donabed and Heather Snow, for their selection work.

Michael Bailey, Kym MacFarlane and Sharon Ring for their invaluable proofreading assistance.

An extra special thanks goes to Ruth Shelton: contributor, selector and proofreader. You made this journey three times as enjoyable and we are honored to have your presence so apparent within this book.

The Morrigan.

Interesting, vital, violent, charismatic, alluring; there are many ancient deities that may be able to inspire such description, but few who linger in the modern mind. The Morrigan — Morrígu, Morríghan, Mor-Ríoghain — otherwise known as the triple goddess, was a deity of war, fertility, prophecy and death.

Her name led scholars to translate her title as 'Sea Queen', 'Great Queen' and, of course, as 'Phantom Queen'. Within the Ulster Cycle and other texts, she appears in various guises; as a crone, maiden, mature woman, eel, cow, wolf and a crow or raven. Her sexual love aspect was also related to fertility cycles (this is also shown through her link to cattle) and luck; when she slept with a great hero or god, it helped ensure his victory in an upcoming battle.

The triple goddess included many aspects, and Badb, perhaps the most well known, was but one of them. Badb was a goddess in her own right, but was related to the battle crow. Badb was also associated with the *Bean-sidhe* (fairy woman); the *Bean-sidhe* later became linked to the Banshee, a foreteller of death. Macha was another aspect of the triple goddess, as were Anann and Nemain, among others.

It is clear that the Morrigan was a goddess created for story-telling; there was little she did not control or influence. Thus, when Mark S. Deniz decided he wanted to create a publishing company that promoted a darker brand of fiction, he looked no further than the goddess who spoke through his own writing. Thus, when it came time to produce the next Morrígan Books' anthology, where else was he to turn but to the namesake of his company and his inspiration?

Then, when Mark suggested the idea of his anthology to his in-house editor (that person being me), I waved my arm around enthusiastically — although with a shred more dignity than a child waiting to be called upon in class — and put my name down for the job of co-editor. Wisely, Mark decided I would be a valuable addition to the book.

Why me? Well, apart from being the in-house editor (contrary to what you might hear, it really is all about who you know), I have a university degree or three in archaeology. And I've always had an interest in Celtic deities — all ancient gods, for that matter.

In fact, I specialize in Near Eastern religion, and have come to dance a time or two with the gods of Briton through studying the Roman Empire. So, when it came to proposing the guidelines for this collection, Mark left it all in my 'capable hands'.

I knew what I was searching for and so did Mark. We hoped to see stories that encapsulated the nature of a goddess who failed to fit into any one mold. We didn't want stories that focused on a 'Mother Goddess', nor tales that were solely gore-splattered renditions of war. No, we wanted stories that spoke of the Morrigan's various aspects, from death to love to hate and hope.

We wanted stories that spoke of the nature of man...and god.

Amanda Pillar & Mark S. Deniz
December 2009

Contents

RISING TIDE 1

Ruth Shelton

KISS OF THE MORRIGAN 3

Anya Bast

I GUARD YOUR DEATH 19

Lynne Lumsden Green

RAVENS 25

Mari Ness

GIFTS OF THE MORRIGAN 35

Donald Jacob Uitvlugt

CAIRN DANCER 45

C.E. Murphy

WASHERWOMAN 63

Jennifer Lawrence

THE RAVEN'S CURSE 69

Sharon Kae Reamer

THE LASS FROM FAR AWAY 97

Katharine Kerr

THE TRINKET 127

Peter Bell

THE DYING GAUL 147

Michael Bailey

THE CHILDREN OF BADB CATHA 161

James Lecky

THE PLAIN OF PILLARS 179

L.J. Hayward

THE SILVER BRANCH 207

Linda Donahue

THE GOOD AND FAITHFUL SERVANT 231

Martyn Taylor

THE WHITE HEIFER OF FEARCHAIR 253

T.A. Moore

SHE WHO IS BECOMING 271

Elaine Cunningham

Ruth Shelton

Rising Tide

A thousand tiny tidal pools shimmered in the afternoon breeze, reflecting the sun overhead, while the last of the storm clouds blew away to the south. I walked amongst them, barefoot.

I picked my way slowly, careful not to disturb the minute things swimming within, each little life clinging desperately to the sides of the shallows or floating to the bottom to lie still in the silt. I thought about the lifespan of those frail beings — so dependent upon the pull of the moon and the seasons — and I marveled that anything might find reason enough to live when life itself was so short.

There was a rumble of thunder in the distance. Across this low flat of land and water, the tide was rising. Looking around at the shining pools of blue and green and brown, I knew I hadn't much time to work before the fresh tide washed them all away.

And so, I reached down to the closest and dipped gently into the iris with my beak, breaking the surface of the now-still eyes of a warrior.

They would reflect the sun no longer.

Afterword

'Rising Tide' was an attempt to describe something felt and seen that blossomed fully-formed inside me. One moment, I was washing a tile floor; the next, I was surrounded by corpses on the sand and salt spray stung my face.

I hadn't planned on writing a story. In fact, I had no interest in even trying and nothing could have been further from my mind, until about two minutes before the vision grabbed me and my fingers hit the keyboard.

Biography

Since she's far more accustomed to wielding a red pencil than having it pointed in her direction, Ruth found herself taken by surprise to be included in this anthology. Maybe she'll take a whack at writing fiction again in another fifty years or so. Meanwhile, she's content to read other people's work, chase down cat hair dirigibles, ride motorcycles, cook, and poke into things which are both unknowable and ephemeral. Ruth shares some of these hobbies with her sweet geezer in a home they share in Louisville, Kentucky, US.

Anya Bast

Kiss of the Morrigan

Severus looked down at his hands. They were roughened and dry from the handle of his sword, and blood had filled the long cracks made from the cold, drying to a rust color. *Blood*. It was a familiar sight. He just wasn't accustomed to seeing his own.

The sounds of the camp swelled. Fires crackled and snapped in the wintry air. Male voices rumbled and boomed: men telling tales of battle, occasionally punctuated by the wails of the dying.

They were familiar noises.

The sweet, sour stench of rotting wounds filled the air. Not even the cold could banish it completely.

It was a familiar scent.

But, if he concentrated, he could see the wheat that grew tall and golden around his home in the summertime. He could remember the color of his wife's hair that almost matched it. If he closed his eyes before sleep, he could sometimes hear his eldest son laugh and almost smell bread baking.

Almost.

"It was a good battle today." His friend, Paetus, sat down beside him, now stripped of his gear. Almost all the blood that had spattered Paetus' forearms, face and hands had been wiped off, though his close cropped, light hair still showed a dried spray of it. He'd changed his clothes, but his eyes held the shine they usually did after they fought the Britons.

"A good battle?" Severus ran his hand over his jaw, feeling rough stubble. There was no such thing in his mind, but Paetus thrived on taking new lands for the Empire in a way he never could, though he did not express his true sentiments. "I suppose it was."

Paetus looked into the crackling fire and shook his head. "These Britons have a spirit like I've never seen."

"They're fighting to protect their way of life; we would do the same."

"It may mean an end to us both."

Severus nodded. "It may. No one can foretell the fates of men but the gods."

"So accepting of destiny. You've always been that way." Paetus rubbed a hand over his scalp, bowing his head a little. "You and I have traveled together, fought side by side for a long time now. I can see you slipping away within your head more and more, Severus. Where do you go to escape the blood?"

Severus lifted his gaze to Paetus' and allowed a smile to flicker across his lips. "I go home, Paetus, home."

Paetus looked past the fire and into the forest beyond, the slight smile he wore dropping away and his eyes losing a bit of their shine.

At the beginning of their journey together, they'd agreed to watch out for each other and to look after the other man's family should one of them fall to a Briton's spear or sword. It was a good pact, an honorable one. One born of pietas. Paetus had four children, a wife, and a farm not far from

Severus' in Rasenna. Both he and Paetus were Etrusci. It made them brothers.

Severus' wife had borne a daughter that hadn't lived, but his two sons were robust. His older son was six and his younger would be close to two by now. The child had been but a tiny infant when Severus had left the farm. If he fell in battle, his friend would care for them.

"Home would be a good place to be, my friend," answered Paetus. "Gods willing, we'll soon be back there tilling our fields." He glanced at Severus. "I will keep you from slipping over the edge of insanity until then." Paetus clapped Severus on the knee, laughed heartily, then rose and walked toward the cooking fires.

The spitting fire he sat before warmed the front of his body and left his back icy. Pushing up from where he knelt, he made his way to the edge of the camp and into the dark woods. He needed to be away from the men for a moment.

Twigs snapping under his boots and cold dry branches caught his leather bracae — one of the items of clothing the Romans had adopted from the Britons — as he made his way to a half frozen river not far from camp. Here, the naked winter tree limbs dipped bony fingers into the dark water. Camp noises could be heard even here, but they were muffled under the heaviness of the silent, dead forest. Ice cracked beneath his feet as he knelt and pressed his bloody palms to the river, letting the cold leach into his skin and blood swirl with the current.

He'd been fighting for so long now, too long.

The tribes they fought were courageous and bold, their battles hard won. Sometimes these people turned up in naught but thin tunics and bracae, other times they wore nothing but paint. But always they fought with their hearts to defend their lands and families — just as hard as Severus would fight to protect his.

Severus looked up at the stars and quickly figured out what direction home lay. Bowing his head, he raised his near frozen hands to his face, welcoming the bite of the cold to temporarily numb the longing for his hearth.

Water sloshed to his left and he glanced over. A woman in a black hooded cape knelt at the river with a pile of laundry beside her.

Severus blinked, wondering if it was an apparition he saw. It was nighttime and they were near a battlefield, not to mention his legion's encampment. It was more than passingly strange to see a local woman here; she had to be from one of the nearby villages.

He stood. "What do you think, old woman, coming out here so late at night?"

There were some men at camp who were riled by the battles they fought, others had simply gone half crazy and were lost in lust for violence and death. A frail, elderly woman like this one would be in danger if her path crossed one of theirs. Luck was with her this evening, that it was he who'd encountered her.

She rocked back on her heels and turned her face up to the moonlight. She wasn't old at all. She was young and very beautiful. Pale skin and long dark hair. Well formed features. Slight of build. She wore a coarse black cloak, the hood halfway over her head. Her narrow hands gripped a piece of clothing plunged into the icy water, but she didn't seem to feel the cold.

She didn't answer him. No great surprise. He spoke in Latin, not knowing the dialects of these local tribal people, and she likely didn't speak his tongue. Still, it was odd she should not react at all. She was clearly a woman of the area and he was the enemy — an invader and conqueror. The mere sight of him under this full moon should have put the fear of the gods within her breast.

The hair on Severus' neck rose and a chill that had nothing to do with the weather stole over him. What was wrong with her?

"Did you not hear me address you?" he asked, again in Latin since he couldn't question her in any other language.

Finally she turned to look at him. It was more of a glance, really, a cool dismissal. "I am not deaf."

So she did speak Latin. It wasn't unheard of, but it was unusual. Everything about this encounter was unusual.

"You're endangering yourself by being here. A woman cannot venture this close to our camp under these circumstances and not expect to be raped or worse."

A smile flickered over her full mouth. "I can take care of myself."

Severus shifted, studying her. The women in this part of the world were unlike those of Rome in many ways, but not unlike his own wife. His wife held the fury of the gods within her and he dared not anger her. Here, the females were even more so. Here, they came from warrior stock and it was common enough to find women who believed they could hold their own against a stronger man, but generally they were mistaken.

As this one was. Such a delicate, lovely creature wouldn't stand a chance.

"What are you doing out here so late?"

She held up the item of clothing she washed — a coarsely woven green tunic with the likeness of a hawk embroidered with care near the hem — and pushed it under the water again. "It's clear what I'm doing." Then she wrung the water from the tunic, placed it on the pile and stood with the laundry in her arms. She turned toward him and tipped her face to the bright moonlight again.

The breath rushed out of him in the full face of her exquisiteness. Her cheeks were rosy against the perfect, pale skin of her face. Her eyes — in contrast to his wife's cornflower blue — seemed nearly black, fathomless. Her hood had fallen with her movements, revealing long, silky dark hair. Her lips were as pink as her cheeks and her chin contained the slightest cleft.

Never in his life had Severus encountered a darker, more superb beauty.

Her expression was unreadable as she murmured, "You have your job and I have mine." Then she turned and walked into the forest in a direction that led away from the camp.

Stunned, Severus stood for a moment, and then went after her. He told himself he was following her to make sure the fool female made it back home unmolested, yet the truth was that he simply wanted another look at her. Her presence was almost intoxicating.

Yet once he stepped back into the tree line he could see no one. Only a raven sat silently on a tree limb above his head, watching him with eyes as dark as the woman's.

The roar of dying men filled Severus' ears. His horse leapt over a dead Roman, a spear still clutched in Severus' bloody hand. The man had not even had time to release it before he'd been cut down by the sword of their enemy.

One couldn't tell mud from blood now.

Across from him, Paetus swung down from his injured horse and entered the fray. Digging his heels into his mount, Severus surged forth past his men and the enemy tribesmen who fought so passionately to defend what was theirs.

They hadn't a prayer.

Not against the Roman battalion of archers who had already laid a carpet of bodies for his mount to dance around. Not against the first wave of spear-wielding soldiers who, more often than not, laid down their lives and took one or more of their enemies with them. Surely not against the cavalry who cut a bloody swath through them, all the while mounted far above them.

A bearded barbarian came from his left, teeth bared and sword cleaving through the air. It bit into his mount's flank and Severus went down with equine screams echoing in his ears. He hit hard, narrowly missing the heavy weight of his horse and rolled away, colliding with the dead body of a fellow Roman. A blade ripped through the air above him and Severus leapt to his feet, dodging the tip and swinging his shield around to catch the man in his throat. The edge of his shield connected with soft flesh and the man made a gagging sound, falling backward with blood coursing over the hands he held to his injured neck.

Severus only had a moment before the next barbarian was upon him. A blade hit his cuirass and sent him stumbling forward. He touched a hand to the ground, pushed up and whirled around, cutting upward with his sword in a deadly arc and slicing through the muscle and tendon of the man's unprotected throat.

The lifeless body of the attacking barbarian fell to the ground and Severus stared down at the half headless man, at the pool of spreading blood. There was something familiar about him, something...

The tunic.

He'd seen it the night before. It had been the article of clothing the beautiful woman at the river had been washing. It was a deep green, woven with the pattern of a hawk at the hem. He remembered it well, because it seemed as though a woman had spent much time on the piece, someone who had loved the man enough to make it for him.

Had it been the same woman he'd encountered last evening? Had Severus just killed her husband?

Severus only had a moment to wonder at the coincidence before the battle forced his mind away from the river's bank and back to the field.

Severus stepped up to the river and knelt, plunging his hands into the water and bringing it to his face. The cold woke him from the stupor he'd found himself in after the battle. He'd slipped into the forest as soon as he could, as the slaves rushed around tending the wounded and dying, fetching water and keeping the fires stoked.

Paetus had returned to the camp victorious and flushed with the power of a conqueror. The day had been a rout. They'd squashed their opponents into the bloody earth with the heels of their sandals and were that much closer to taking this entire region for the glory of Rome.

He tipped his head toward the star strewn sky. Mars Gradivus. "Forgive me," he whispered.

The man with the green tunic he'd killed today had been the husband or the brother of the woman he'd met at the river the night before. He could find no other explanation for what had happened.

Severus killed because that was what was required of him. At first, he had always come back from battle flush with triumph and pride of his country, a quality that Paetus had not yet lost. But now, after seeing the bravery of the barbarians they had come to slaughter, seeing the honor and passion with which they defended their hearth and home, now...

Suffice to say that he'd never wished for nor wanted any sort of a personal connection with those he slew. He lowered his head and plunged his hands deeper into the water, atonement for being one of the deadliest warriors in his legion. He was their pride, but he took no joy of it.

A soft weeping met his ears and he opened his eyes, looking for the source. The washer woman knelt not far away, a pile of clothing on the icy bank next to her and that same dark shroud-like hood half covering her beautiful hair.

Severus had not expected to encounter her again this evening. He'd only been seeking serenity and quiet away from the camp. Seeing her again and knowing what he'd done, made him repeat his words. They came out ragged and low. "Forgive me."

She turned her face toward him for only a moment. "There's nothing to forgive. It is what it is. Bad men must die and so must good men."

"I killed your man today. I know it because I saw you washing his tunic last night."

She took a piece of laundry up and calmly dunked it beneath the black water. "So it was you who killed him." Her tone of voice was eerily calm. It had to be from the grief.

He made a low sound of misery and turned on his knees to face her. "I cannot sit here on this beach near you and say other than the truth. It would dishonor us both." He paused. "Who was he to you?" He wasn't sure why he asked. Perhaps it was better if he didn't know.

The woman continued to wash her clothes without a word, until she finally put aside her work and stood. "What does it matter? He was my brother, son, husband, father. They are all my men."

Severus pushed to his feet, feeling his gut clench with the agony of the thousand deaths he'd caused her people.

She took a step toward him, her eyes shining bright with tears. "They are — all of them — mine."

Dear gods, she was so beautiful.

She walked up to him boldly, her face tipped up, the gentle curve limned by silver moonlight. "Do you want to kiss me?"

Severus blinked. "I don't deserve a kiss."

Her face drifted closer to his. "I didn't ask whether or not you deserved a kiss. I asked if you wanted one."

He hesitated only a moment, his mind filling with thoughts of his wife. Sweet Aelia with her hair so long and thick like honey, her eyes such a pleasing, light shade of blue. Physically she looked nothing like this woman, yet they shared a strong common quality. It was almost as if he faced Aelia on this river's shore. This woman seemed suddenly like home. Like everything he wanted and needed. He melted into her presence the way he would melt into his wife's, took comfort in it.

Her lips touched his and brushed. She didn't seem to care that he was covered with other men's blood, perhaps even her kin's. Instead, she seemed to revel in the taste of it on his lips, running her tongue slowly over his mouth. In acceptance of him. In his head it was like forgiveness.

Absolution.

He needed more. Making a low sound in the back of his throat, he pulled the woman against him. Crushing his mouth to hers, he forced her lips to part and slid his tongue within. He wanted to drink her, consume her, take all she offered him and then more. He wanted to sink himself into the feel and taste of her and forget the events of the day. She was seductive darkness, the kind he could lose himself in — dangerously addictive, but hopelessly alluring.

If he could, Severus would have lowered her to the icy bank of the river, lifted her skirts and lost himself even further. He would have slaked his guilt between her pale thighs and spilled his sorrow within her womb.

Instead, she pushed away from him.

Shadows hid her expression. Severus could only see her mouth. A smear of blood from his kiss marked her lower lip. "You are one of mine too, warrior."

The woman turned and scooped up her laundry. On the top of the pile Severus glimpsed a muddy colored *lacerna* that looked familiar to him. If the woman came from one of the local tribes, what was she doing with a Roman soldier's cloak?

Especially one that looked like it belonged to Paetus.

She could not have plucked it like a vulture from the dead man on the battlefield since Paetus had not perished in the day's fighting. Severus had seen him in the camp before he'd left for the river.

Severus started toward her as she disappeared past the tree line, but by the time he reached it, she was already gone. Only the night misted through the leafless trees.

Severus stayed closer to Paetus than usual as they entered the fray. A damp chill had clung to him ever since he'd glimpsed his friend's *lacerna* by the riverside. Foolishness on his part, surely. The constant battles were finally breaking through the iron-strong grip he'd kept on his emotions, that was certain enough.

Still, he had an uneasy feeling about the skirmish today and the fate of his friend in it. Severus would stay close to his comrade and watch out for him, as Paetus had always done for Severus. It was what brothers did.

The hooves of his new mount pounded the ground as they entered on the second wave of the attack, battling Britons that seemed to never give up and never seemed to dwindle in number. They were less numerous than the

Romans, yet they fought with a passion that made up for the difference. Never in Severus' life had he met an opponent as worthy as these uncivilized people and that earned them his grudging respect.

Paetus' blade soared through the air in a bloody arc out of the corner of Severus' eye. Together they cut through the foot soldiers, taking down one after another. The Britons had charged their chariots through the cavalry line, leaving behind a cluttered mess of overturned and half-shattered vehicles that Severus' horse danced to avoid.

"Watch out!" Severus yelled as Paetus' mount backed into the broken end of a spear lodged in the ground.

His friend's horse bolted, throwing Paetus to the ground. He let loose his shield and it rolled away, though he kept a tight grip on his sword handle. Not far away, a Briton spotted Severus' brother. The barbarian ran toward him, arms flailing and a cry tearing from his throat.

Severus leapt from his mount, scooping another shield as he did so, and stopped the man with a heavy clang of blade on blade. The lengths of metal kissed and locked at the grip. Severus swung his shield around and took the man in the head with the edge. He fell to the ground with a yell of pain.

By then Paetus was up, but they were quickly surrounded in a pocket devoid of Romans. His sword swinging hard to the right, Severus connected with a heavy bearded Briton, catching him in the stomach with the tip of his blade and spraying blood. Pivoting on his foot, he blocked another blow, the force of the hit reverberating down his arm and through his armored chest.

Sweat pooled in Severus' navel and coated his face and neck under his helmet as he and Paetus took on the barbarians around them while standing back-to-back. Three Britons approached from their right, hands tight on their sword grips and ready to strike.

Paetus let out a roar and attacked, sword and shield flashing in the sunlight. One of the Briton's launched toward Severus, who slashed downward, penetrating the barbarian's thigh, before pivoting to meet the next-comer. A tall, well-muscled Briton struck Severus' shield, clashed with his blade, and then pushed him back.

Severus stumbled, tripped over a body and went down hard. The Briton loomed over him. Then Paetus was there, beating the Briton back before he could pounce. The Briton pivoted at a crucial moment, and went for the unprotected area of Paetus' neck, where his helmet did not touch his cuirass.

"No!"

Severus lunged to his feet and speared the barbarian in the stomach. But it was too late. Just as the barbarian fell, so too did Paetus, his eyes wide and surprised as blood poured forth like the dark waters of the river, over his hands and down his chest.

Severus stared at the fallen body of his friend, numb to the core of his bones, while the fighting raged on around him. He plunged the tip of his sword into the ground beside Paetus' head and knelt beside his brother in the war-churned earth.

Paetus' black eyes stared at the sky, seeing not clouds but the Afterlife.

Severus lurched toward a tree and rested heavily against the trunk, bloody sword falling from his lax fingers. He'd crashed through the forest to the river as soon he'd returned from the battle. She was there, just as he'd known she would be — kneeling at the water's edge and washing her laundry.

Was he going insane? Had the battle finally grasped him in its clutches and was it pushing him towards madness?

Or maybe it wasn't madness at all. Perhaps the gods had sent him a messenger in the form of this woman. Perhaps he was being punished for something.

"You!" He stumbled towards her and came down heavily on his knees, ridges of frozen earth piercing through his blood stained leather bracae. He couldn't get the sweet, sick smell of death to leave his nostrils, not even long draughts of the frigid night air could banish it. "Tell me who you are."

She only continued to dunk and scrub a tunic under the swirling cold, black water.

He reached out to touch her shoulder, to whirl her toward him so he could see her face, but some unknown impulse stopped him. Like a primal instinct. Fear welled, as though it wasn't a simple woman kneeling before him, but a wolf.

In his mind, suddenly she was the warrior and he was the prey.

He made a fist, the skin cracking, causing the blood to well and drip to the shore of the river. "Please," he entreated, his voice a low rasp. "Tell me what you are."

"I am nothing but a woman," she answered, continuing to wash the clothes that lay in a pile beside her.

"You lie. You are more than that."

"I am woman and I am everything you should fear. I am fate. I am prophecy. I am war. I am destruction. And I am death."

Severus could feel that she spoke the truth.

"He's dead: the one who wore the woolen *lacerna* that you washed on this river bank last night. His name was Paetus and he was a good man, a man with children and a wife."

"So many of them are good men, the ones who fall."

The incessant washing made anger pound in his head in a low staccato. Still he didn't touch her, every survival instinct he had kept him from doing it. "Why did you kill him?"

She stood and looked at him with eyes darker than the cloudless skies above and just as cold and unreachable. "Death is a part of life. Everything that is born and all that thrives will one day pass away. It will go better for you if you simply accept fate, Severus." She looked down at her laundry and his gaze followed.

There, in the cold black water, floated the same tunic he wore. It had the same tears, the same rust-colored stains. His blood icy and his limbs paralyzed, he watched it swirl for a moment and then disappear, pulled under by the inexorable current.

Afterword

I was immediately intrigued with the idea of writing a story about the Morrigan, a figure in Irish myth that has long captured my imagination. I have always seen the Morrigan as having a lot in common with, say, the vulture. She's doing a dark job that needs to be done and she's got a bad rep for doing it well. I chose to depict her as the *Bean-nighe* — the washer woman — in my story, because I love the idea of her as a harbinger of death, especially as it is such a seemingly innocuous guise.

Biography

Anya Bast is the national bestselling author of numerous works of romantic fiction, mostly all paranormal and mostly all scorching hot. She lives in the country with her husband, daughter, and an odd assortment of rescued animals. To read more about Anya and to find out more information about her books, please visit http://www.anyabast.com/.

Lynne Lumsden Green

I Guard Your Death

Maiden

Hidden, Pwyll watched a young woman as she washed clothes in the stream. Her hair was the color of a newly-forged copper shield, with deep crimson shadows. Every time she bent forward to scrub, her tunic gaped to reveal her perfect, pink-tipped breasts. Her skin was a smooth, lustrous cream, and her wet hair draped across her thighs, making the cloth cling.

The singular beauty of the washerwoman stirred his blood, tugging at him; he was the compass and she was the North Star. Pwyll made certain the girl was alone before he stepped out from behind the rock. The woman stopped scrubbing when his shadow fell across her and she looked up, but her eyes held no fear. "Who are you?" she asked.

Pwyll didn't answer. Instead, he bent and grabbed a double handful of her hair, pulling her to her feet. She didn't scream or struggle as he dragged her from the stream to a grassy cleft. He nudged her behind the knees with his leg, while pushing on her shoulders, and together they fell to the ground.

With one hand firmly entangled in her hair, Pwyll reached into her tunic and groped her breasts. Still, she didn't fight but remained strangely, regally calm. He shoved her onto her back and slid her skirt up to her waist, and their eyes met. For a moment Pwyll hesitated, for through her eyes he could see past eternity and into the infinite. Momentarily dizzy, he dropped his gaze and his desire was renewed.

"I wouldn't, if I were you," she warned him. Pwyll ignored her. Her thighs were as rounded and ripe as he had imagined them and his need roared through him, stronger than before.

"I warn you again; I am not what I seem." Her voice was low, and if he had been listening, he would have sensed the impatience. He looked into her eyes and saw the skin around them pulled tight by her trapped hair. Her expression was still unreadable, but she remained limp. Somewhere, a less primal part of his mind was disturbed by her lack of fear, but he could not focus beyond her soft flesh. She drew in a breath as he forced his way into her body, and remained motionless while he sought his moment of ecstasy within her. Her flesh was very sweet.

Once spent, he collapsed on top of her, crushing her. He tugged his hand from her hair, not caring that strands of it came away with his fingers, not caring that he had hurt her.

His ear was next to her lips. "Doom and triple doom, upon you and your clan," she whispered.

She vanished from beneath him.

Pwyll clambered to his feet, suddenly afraid. He had ignored her warnings, and now he knew it was no mortal he had taken. He scrambled to where he had first seen the washerwoman, hoping to see her back at her task. He knew there was little chance of asking for forgiveness, but maybe he could offer restitution, for he had inherited a wealth of weapons and jewels. The clothes were still beside the stream and seeping water; a pink-tinged trickle that dripped steadily.

He picked up one of the items and stared at it. It was a cape, twin to the one around his own shoulders. It even had the same brooch; a gift from his father, except the stone was black instead of blue. With growing horror, he held the other clothing up and saw his shirt, his tunic, his trews, all sodden and stained.

The girl had been the *Bean-nighe*, the little washerwoman who would foretell your death. Sometimes, you could escape your fate and it was even possible to ask the washerwoman for a blessing. Pwyll had ruined any hope of a reprieve from his death. However, there was still a chance he could avert the doom he had placed on his clan *and* retain his honor. He fell to his knees. He called up to the sky, "Oh great Morrigan, I beseech thee. I will make restitution."

Three crows started to circle overhead, a wreath of dark feathers, their harsh cries a litany of accusation. One flew down to land at his feet. The bird seemed to shimmer for a moment, before it formed into a naked woman with hair as black as a crow's feathers, her belly swollen with a ten month child. Tattoos covered every square of her skin in a complex pattern of dark blue plaits, triquetra, knots, spirals, triskeles and wyrms; most of her skin was a puzzle beyond the knowing of any man. However, Pwyll did recognize the pattern on her stomach, a highly detailed tree of life, its fruit and leaves twisting into runes. The tattoos made it hard to read her expression, but her voice was hard and cold. "There is no way you can avoid your doom, lad."

"I know that. I accept my fate. But please, my Queen, I would beg that you set no doom upon my kin."

"It's a little too late to be asking any favors from me, isn't it?" For one instant, she was again the little *Bean-nighe,* and her hands gestured to the bite marks on her neck, and the bruises on her breasts and thighs. There was a trickle of dark blood on the inside of her legs, snaking its slow way to the ground. Then, the goddess was back.

Pwyll groveled, holding his hands palm up towards the goddess. "It was only I who committed the crime."

"Your clan raised you. They taught you the manners of a man. They taught you poorly, and deserve part of the punishment." The woman was grim. "They must share your fate."

Pwyll pulled out his knife. "I'll kill myself right now, if you will forgive them. Will you accept a blood price as payment for my great wrong against you?"

The goddess' severe expression softened a little. "You are prepared to make that sacrifice, and restore my honor with your life?"

Pwyll shuddered, but he whispered, "Yes. If I must."

"So be it. I will accept your sacrifice, and if you die like a warrior, I will bring no doom down upon your clan or kin."

Giving himself no time to dwell and despair, he drove the knife deep into his chest. A gout of blood spurted forth, painting a red crescent across the throat of the pregnant woman. As though the blood were magic, she changed form.

The woman became a gray-haired crone, with a battered green shawl enveloping her bony chest and shoulders.

Rusty blood dripped from the hem of her black dress, and the bright crimson stain around her thin throat was now a copper torc. Her face was both savage and sad as she watched the man bleed away his life.

Pwyll's vision grew dark and then his body weakened and he fell to his knees. He refused to make a sound, and he valiantly tried to remain upright.

The ground about the woman's feet was a tapestry of the rich red of his sacrifice.

Pwyll swayed, and the goddess caught him before his head hit the ground. She held him to her chest, and muttered, "You poor boy. You poor, stupid boy. I guard your death." He died in her embrace, his last breath rattling against her neck.

The twin crows that had remained overhead swooped down to land on her shoulders, their wings setting her wispy hair fluttering like a battle flag. The crows pecked at his eyes as Pwyll gazed blindly into the clear sky.

"What a waste," said the Morrigan. She abandoned the body and rose to her full height, the crows flapping to keep their balance. For a moment, three women stood by the stream, before three crows rose into the air, flapping determinedly away.

I am drawn to the knotted darkness of the Celtic Twilight. Fairy tales were never meant to be politically correct; they were originally about the dangers leering in the shadows beyond the glow of the hearth, at the bottom of a loch, behind that smile with the too-sharp, too-white teeth. I like to walk into those mossy shadows and bring back the stories lurking there, armed with my word processor and a pure heart. As a mythogynoclast, it is my destiny to bring back the histories of all the old goddesses, including the Morrigan. You asked to see the Phantom Queen awake after all. I didn't promise you that she would be a tame goddess.

Lynne Lumsden Green is just about to finish her second degree and embark on a further academic adventure: Honors. Her topic will be firmly based in the genre of the Fairy Tale, but not the sweet and twee sort; she prefers the older stories still rife with sex and blood. (And if you want to know what a mythogynoclast is, go look it up.) This year saw her helping judge the Aurealis Awards for the third time, and working as a volunteer for the Reality Bites Literary Festival and Voices on the Coast Festival. If you run into her, give her a big hug...she needs all the support she can muster.

Mari Ness

Ravens

She crawled along the roofs, harvesting black feathers.

The first raven had fallen from the sky at dawn, crashing upon a rock in front of the tanner's cottage. The fall had cracked its skull, and it bled while the villagers stepped around it. The second had fallen but an hour later, landing outside of the small chapel, hand built by one of the monks, a chapel many of the villagers still avoided. The third fell as the sun reached its peak, landing on the crossroads at the village center. By late afternoon, clouds of ravens fell from the sky, their feathers and blood blanketing the three small streets. By midnight, each straw roofed house was littered with ravens.

The villagers shook their heads, and pretended they did not know what this meant.

Maire knew. But still, she gathered the feathers, soaking her hands in blood. The others stayed beneath the roofs with their children, their mouths forming prayers in a mingle of languages.

The first to die was a child, also at dawn. Maire gathered feathers as she heard the cries of the mother; tried to shut her ears against the father's sobs. The monk emerged to comfort them. They wrapped the child in rowan and rue, and sang the old prayers over her.

The second to die was an ancient man, in the evening, clutching at his heart and then falling to the floor. Fewer wails this time, and stronger songs. He was buried under the light of stars, over the protests of the monk, who wanted to say more prayers.

The third was a young woman, just married, who had never learned to bake decent bread.

Three days passed.

And then another raven fell.

"I'm going to the mound," Maire said to the villagers who had gathered around to look at the fallen raven.

"That will do us no good," said the miller.

"We have only the songs," said Una, whom Maire did not like.

"They will do no good either," muttered Sorcha, whom Maire did like. "The Raven Queen weakens."

Maire listened for the hiss that should have followed those words, but heard nothing.

"You might try praying there," Maire said, waving towards the chapel. "If the Raven Queen—" she said the name coolly, but no one stopped her "—has lost all power, there's a magic there that might protect you."

"Or it might be she needs their blood."

"Blood to restore the ravens."

"Blood to restore her sight."

"Blood to restore her flight."

"Three deaths she's had, three and three more she needs," crooned another.

Maire's hands whitened around her walking stick.

"Might be," she said. "Might be. And I'll be going to find out."

"And how will you see?"

Maire smiled. "I won't need to. I'll feel."

"And how do we know you will have the strength?"

Maire held up her bag. "I have her wings," she said.

She ignored the hisses of the village women as she left, along with the well meant prayers of the monk who called out to her as she left; bag over one shoulder, a stout staff in her left hand, tracing out the old road from the village that passed by the mound.

In truth, it could hardly be called a road, that path, though it led to other places; other villages, even fabled cities and towns that Maire had never visited, but had heard of from the few travelers and monks that entered their village in search of bread or other goods. She did not think of those cities now as she used her staff to push her way along the path.

It had been a true road once, she'd heard, and then the ravens had come, not dying. Her hands whitened again, and she thought of the two babies still in the village, the other small children playing in the fields.

She felt the first drops of rain touch her face; felt an odd tug to her left, then her right, then her left again.

She took three deep breaths, turned about three times and followed the pull, feeling her feet walk up a mound—

—and then felt the earth slide away beneath her, felt herself falling, falling, wrapped in sudden chill, almost thinking that she heard the feathers screaming...

She awoke in the cold and the utter stillness.

She did not move for a long moment. This was wrong, she thought; the underworld was supposed to be filled with whispers, with music. She remembered the tales of the shadows that pulled men into the mounds for dancing, of the little red capped creatures that promised wealth and beauty to women.

No tale had mentioned silence. Or the cold. For a moment, she heard the voices of the village woman — *the ravens are dead*. She shook herself, and reached behind her for the sack of feathers. She pulled one out and stroked it.

She thought she felt a faint touch of cold wind.

Sitting here would do no good. She raised herself up, adjusted the bag around her shoulders, and stepped out into the darkness, clutching the feather.

As she walked, she sometimes thought she heard half whispers, or half snatches of songs, hushed before she could catch a word. She was certain, however, that the cold kept deepening. She had brought with her a cloak of double woven wool, but it did little against the chill.

The path — and it was a path, marked with rough walls on each side, which to her fingers sometimes felt like stone, and sometimes had the slippery feel of what might have been bone — followed, she could feel, a slow downward spiral. After what seemed hours of walking, she wondered if she was heading in the right direction, if perhaps she should head towards the top of the mound. She paused, turned around on the path, and stepped forward—

—only to feel herself heading down again.

She reversed herself, hardly knowing why, and continued in her original direction.

She lost track of time, of her steps, of the depth, but felt she had travelled the lengths of many raven wings when she heard the distinctive sound of raspy breathing.

Her footsteps froze.

"Who comes?" asked a voice.

Maire thought her hands had changed to solid ice. Her throat hurt. "One who has summoned the raven."

The cold, if possible, deepened. She reached behind her, to the bag she carried, trying to draw out a second feather, but her hands were too cold to move.

"Who comes?"

"One who has used the raven's feather."

"Who comes?"

"One who would speak with the Raven Queen."

Something dry and cold brushed her cheek. She held herself still. The cold dryness reached up to cup her face in ten narrow, rough points. She suddenly knew what her cheeks felt: fingers of dry bone. She swallowed to keep from screaming.

"And what would this one speak of to the Raven Queen?"

"Ravens fall into our village."

"Lives for a life," said the Raven Queen.

"You have had four," said Maire. "Four for the death I asked. The death I asked and three."

"And still I am unpaid. Three and three and three again: that is and was and will be the price."

Maire remembered the fists slamming into her back, the shouts, the nights she spent huddled in the ashes, wondering if she dared kick a coal into the wall. She remembered the woman, now dead, who had never learned how to bake.

"Do you touch them, and I shall take your wings."

"Do you take my wings," the Queen hissed, "and I shall take your eyes."

"You cannot," said Maire. "For I am already blind."

Silence. Then the Raven Queen laughed.

"Yes, I remember you," she said, her voice seemed filled with a thousand screams, the cries of songbirds and the shrieks of ravens. "The blind one, crying in the night, weeping over her tender and torn skin — without the courage to bend her fingers around his neck."

But she had dreamed it, dreamed of choking him, of beating him, of wrapping her fingers around his neck and hearing his breathing cease and—

"I had the courage to call your name, and call upon the raven song."

"To have another kill him. For cruelty."

She remembered the blows striking her cheek, remembered the—

"No. Because I could not see."

"And now refuse to pay my price."

"I did not know your price."

"You did not see."

"Three and three and three again? For but one death?"

"A price of kindness, not of cruelty."

Maire thought of the child who had died. "You name that kind?"

Another whisper of frozen touch across her cheek. "The child plays beneath my mounds. And her brothers may waver now before they call my name. And think upon it. What would it mean, if any could call upon my name, and have no cost to pay?"

"And why should they be the ones to pay my price?"

"A point. A point."

Finger bones caressed her cheeks again; this time Maire did not suppress a faint moan. "Indeed, a most fair point. And I could, I think, spare your village, yes. Spend my nights in the shadowed hills, and think no more of ravens, and let its children grow in peace."

Maire found herself breathing again.

"But then no other could call out my name, for aid at home and war."

Maire thought of her own dark nights in the straw bed; thought of the women with arms bruised from their husband's love, thought of the men who sobbed at the deaths of brothers and friends. She thought of the tales she so often heard, of ravens shrieking during war.

"You lie," she said.

"Without the blood, I cannot answer another call. And I am too weak to journey far." And now the voice was a rich caress, "Your words brought me to this hill. If not your village, where else can I sip my blood?"

"Our cows—"

"Do not pulse with a human soul."

"Your wings—"

"Beat only when filled with human blood."

She remembered her mother, weeping over her when she was a child.

"Your choice," the voice said, and it was filled with gold; "Deny me your promised price, and deny all others the power to call upon my name, or give to me my feathered wings and step aside, and know the helpless have a shield."

"Too heavy is your price."

"Three and three and three again," the voice said, now filled with the calls of ravens. "That is the price. But perhaps we can bargain; you and I."

Do not bargain with those under the hills, for they are full of treachery and deceit. The song said nothing of nine deaths.

"I make no bargains," Maire said. "Not with tricksters."

She knelt, and pulled a flint and stone from beneath her robes, and set the feathers alight.

The Raven Queen spoke not a word, though Maire choked in the billowing smoke and stretched out her hands towards the fire's warmth. But still her hands remained icy cold, and she shook upon the spiral path.

"Farewell," she said, after she sensed that the smoke and flames were nearly gone, and turned to walk back up the stairs.

"Alas," said the Raven Queen, and Maire thought she could hear regret in her voice. "No mortal can step beneath these mounds and return to her sunlit home. Not without a dance or two; not until many turnings of the sun."

"Then I shall stay here and dance," Maire said, allowing her flint and stone to drop, waiting for another touch of bone.

It did not come. The Raven Queen laughed. "Farewell, then," she said, and Maire heard the footsteps leaving, walking up through the mound.

"Where do you go?" Maire shouted.

"To collect my price, of course."

"You have no wings!"

Laughter filled the frigid air. "Aye, I do not," said the Raven Queen. "But birds can walk upon two feet."

The tears upon Maire's cheeks felt like ice. Her voice seemed caught in her throat.

"Did you truly think you could hold ravens so easily?"

Three and three again.

"Take my blood instead," Maire cried.

More laughter. "You would bargain then?"

"I would," she said.

Maire felt icy hands upon her breasts; felt herself folded into a cold embrace. "You will need your sight for this," she heard. And the Raven Queen pressed her lips to Maire's eyes.

Light: gray, the early gray light of morning, but light. She could see before her the shadowed forms of houses and grasses and weeds. She blinked, feeling dizzy with radiance, and blinked again. She hardly knew how to handle vision.

It was not her village. She knew that, although she had not seen her own village since the fever. This place felt different, smelled different.

A raven swept over her head, calling out. She hesitated and stepped into the house that stood before her.

A small place, like the houses of her village, with three people huddled in the great room near the fire. They did not stir as she approached, and she did not look at them, drawn to the cloth hanging in the rear. She drew the material aside, and stared at the flushed and sweating face below.

She bent down to kiss the girl upon her forehead. From above, she heard the ravens shriek.

Afterword

It's probably best not to bargain with tricksters.

This story grew from the old tales of journeys beneath the fairy mounds, from the warnings about bargaining with fairies and gods, and three black feathers I found on a parking lot, with a hint of blood on one.

We have cats and alligators and eagles and hawks here; it is not always safe to be a black bird. No safer, at least, than travelling in other realms.

Biography

Mari Ness lives in central Florida, near bike trails haunted by old trees, new mansions, half crumbling homes, the occasional ostrich, and the not-so-occasional alligator. Her work has appeared in multiple print and online venues, including *Fantasy Magazine, Ideomancer, Hub Fiction* and *Farrago's Wainscot*. She blogs about bad movies, evil squirrels, and other inconsequential and important things at mariness.livejournal.com.

Donald Jacob Uitvlugt

Gifts of the Morrigan

Badb

The third night the youth dreamed of her, he awoke in a cold sweat. He remembered little of his dream. Hair the color of a moonless night or a raven's wing. The heat of his arms around her, the pressure of their bodies together. A wordless, bestial cry — of fury or of passion, he did not know. A struggle, a clash of bodies for supremacy. A contest he had been losing, and to his horror, the losing had been pure ecstasy.

Thus he awoke, sweat cold on his skin, but blood hot and pulsing in every vein. He felt as lathered as a hard-ridden mare, and there arose in him the desire to wash the too-pleasant nightmare from his body. He made his way to the river by the light of the stars and of the crescent moon. The cold waters soothed but did not extinguish the internal fires kindled by his dreams.

As he bathed, a maiden came upon him, hair so dark it seemed to be one with the night itself, cloak billowing behind her like wings, though there was no wind. She brought her own cold from the north, with the burn of ice. Her beautiful face strained under a ferocious passion.

"I have found you at last." She drew a sword and pointed it at his neck. "I would slay you, if your fate permitted."

He gathered as much dignity as could a man floating naked in the water. "Why would you slay me? What crime have I committed?"

He knew he should make away. Swim to the opposite shore and flee. But he was young and she was beautiful, and the spell of his dream was still upon him.

"I have dreamed of you these past three nights. You have made me fall in love with you, my brave and beautiful youth. And for that, you shall die."

The words were spoken not as a curse. The maiden's anger had faded. More like a prophecy or a terrible truth did they drop from lips red as apples. The young man rose from the water. The tip of her sword dropped. A hand went to the pins that held her garments in place.

She was indeed lovely, and her wildness only added to her beauty. She grappled with him, and they fell on top of her garments, and the passion of their coupling was sweet as battle and bitter as love. The moment of ecstasy was like the cry of a bird taking flight.

For a long while they lay in each other's arms. Then horror descended on her face. She pulled her soiled garments from under him, gathered them about her. When he tried to stop her, tried to plead with her to be his forever, she slapped his face. Her nails scratched him, drew blood.

"I will hate you forever, for I was a maiden and will be a maiden no more. I can never forgive you for making me love you. Pray that we never meet again."

She flew off into the night, disappearing as she had come. Her sword she left behind and he claimed it as his own, and well it served him as he went from triumph to triumph. The nail mark on his cheek scarred. And try as he might, he could never bring himself to pray the prayer she wished on him.

Macha

The warrior could not sleep. For two nights he had dreamed the same dream. Though he remembered little of it, he feared to sleep this third night. Instead, he girded on his sword, threw open his tent flap, and went out beyond the camp. He inspected the field of war by the light of the full moon.

The smell of the previous day's battle was rich and heavy in the air. Blood. Bodies. The excrement of men and horses. The war-stained land sang to him, string of harp and wail of pipe and beat of drum. If tomorrow it was fated that he die, it was well. If tomorrow saw victory for kith and clan, so much the better. Certainty reigned like peace in his soul.

She came up from the earth, a dark shadow taking on solid form. As beautiful as before. He thought he was dreaming. Mayhaps he was.

"I have found you again. How I wish that I had slain you under the crescent moon."

He was ensorcelled by her beauty, but he found his tongue at last. "How can you speak thus? Since that night you have burned in my heart. No other love have I enkindled there. I love only you."

Tears fell from her eyes, two dark rivers in fields of white. "You know not whom you love."

He took her in his arms. "My clan decreed that I must sire children, and I have done my duty by my wife. But I love only you."

He had misunderstood her words, and it enflamed her. She fell upon him in a passionate fury. Their limbs entwined. A hand removed the pins that held her garments. The sweet, sad struggle resumed and continued until the moon was sinking in the west. They rested in each other's arms.

From her fallen garments she took a golden torc. Like plaited rose stems it was, and when she placed it around his neck, the thorns drew blood. On his brow she placed a hawthorn crown.

"A bride of blood, I birth in pain the nation given you. I can never forgive you for making me love you. Pray that we never meet again."

She collapsed into the blood-soaked soil. A dark shape passed over the setting moon and a tremor shook him. He felt for the crown and laughed as he touched naught but his hair. Then he rubbed at his neck and pricked his finger on the golden torc that rested there. His clan won the battle that day and soon made him their chief. But try as he might, he could never bring himself to pray the prayer she asked of him.

Morrigan

The old man did not sleep much anymore. His hands trembled and his eyes were dim and he knew they plotted to take the clan away from him. He did not care. The night before, she had come to him in his sleep and he knew happiness, if only the happiness of dreams.

That evening he sat on a chair in the garden under a waning moon. He smiled at the apple trees his long-dead wife had planted. She had been a good woman, but she was not her. No one was. A god or mortal, he knew not. He only knew she had been his one and only love. He would give his life for one more moment with her.

And there she was, perched in the branches of the apple. She had not aged since last he had seen her, she was more beautiful than ever, and dark passion smoldered in her eyes.

"I have come for you a last time, my love." She slid down to the ground, walked to him like a she-wolf stalking her prey. "Would that I had slain you the first night we met."

She removed her garments and laid him upon the soft grass; they made love under the stars. He had not been with a woman in years; tonight it was like he was a young man again. Their love was a gentle and beautiful thing. And yet he wished for the wild maiden he had loved on the river bank.

When they had finished, she stroked the scars on his cheek. Her touch still burned. He kissed her fingers. "Please, my love. Tell me your name."

Her smile held the sadness of the grave. "I am called by many names. Those whom I love may call me Anann."

He stroked her long black hair. "I have known no other like you, Anann."

She kissed his cheek. "A boon you may ask of me, Mabon mac Lugh, as I love you."

He spoke without reflection, in an instant, the words spilling out of his mouth. "Make me as I was when we first met. Let me never taste death. If such is in your power to grant, this is what I wish."

A wailing cry escaped her chest. She shook with silent sobs, tears falling like rain. "Please, ask for something else."

She pushed herself away from him, but he clung to her. With all his strength, the old man held her to himself. "If you can do this, you must grant me this boon. As you love me..."

Her fury blazed in her eyes once more. "I can never forgive you for making me love you. You will regret such a gift. I pray you, ask for something else."

He shook his head. "Eternal youth, nothing else."

She pulled her garments about her, raising the hood of her cloak over her head. From her garments she drew forth a chalice. At her command, it filled with a wine that smelled of wormwood and apple blossoms. She held it out to him. Her tears fell into the chalice.

"Do not weep." He took the cup from her and drank deep. "Now we can be together forever."

As he spoke, the bloom of youth had already returned to him, his white hair turning brown, his week limbs growing strong, vigor coursing throughout his body. He smiled triumphantly, only to have his heart break as she ran from him.

"For you!" He chased after her, arms outstretched. "I live only for you!"

Her face stopped his chase. "You fool. You lovable, insufferable fool. How could you have asked for eternal youth? Had you died, I would have been yours forever. But I am Death. Now you are immortal, and never can we meet again."

The youth sank to his knees and let out a wordless, bestial cry that found its echo in the croaking of the raven that flew off into the night. Flew off, never to be seen by him again. Tears fell to the earth as he cursed himself and wished he had prayed the prayer she enjoined on him the first night they had met...

'Gifts of the Morrigan' is a meditation on what sort of man might fall in love with the triple goddess. The three scenes show the male counterparts to the three aspects of the goddess: youth, warrior, old man. If the Morrigan was ever fated to love a mortal man, what could she give but herself? Love, success in battle, death. And being a goddess, she would also know how a mortal man would respond to such gifts...

Biography

Donald Jacob Uitvlugt grew up in western Michigan and now lives in central Arkansas with his wife and dog. His short fiction has previously appeared in a number of print and online venues including *SpaceWesterns.com, Renard's Menagerie, ChiZine,* and the anthologies *In Bad Dreams, Malpractice,* and *Cinema Spec.*

C.E. Murphy

Cairn Dancer

Moonlight flowed down the river like ice, turning the water to a smooth, unbroken promise of power and danger. Even as a child, Mairaed had broken from other tasks to wander to the water's edge, there to stand silent and unmoving until someone came to fetch her. Shouting her name was not enough: she couldn't hear her parents, she once explained; not over the voices that sang down the river.

They exchanged glances, then, her mother and her father, and after that it was always one of the wise women or the old men of the village who took her gently from the river's side.

The night her first woman's blood came as a stuttering black smear on her thighs, Aine, the eldest of the wise women, visited their small stone home. She dressed Mairaed in the druid's white she herself wore, and took her away. Mairaed, too blurry with sleep for excitement, stumbled in Aine's wake until they reached the river, then came alive with a shock that still took her breath, even in memory. The water that cold night felt peppered with vitality, as though living blood prickled under its wet skin. Need coursed through her, stronger than even that which had sent her to the river's edge so many times.

It came as music; as a lament, an ancient tune whose words were lost to time. Only sweet harrowing notes remained, rising from within her and bursting toward the sky. She stood ankle-deep in the river, face turned upward as she sang with all her heart, and without a sound.

"So it's in you indeed. A blessing and a tragedy both," Aine murmured, drawing Mairaed's gaze to her. She was aged sixty summers or more, and Mairaed only a woman that night but for a heartbeat, it seemed the silver-haired elder was the girl, and Mairaed herself an ancient crone. In that brief window, Mairaed saw who Aine had been: the child, the wife, the mother, all long before Mairaed's birth.

She saw, too, a darkness in Aine's breast, and saw the first thinness of strain come over the woman as a promise of hardship yet to come. A season: no more, and Aine would be gone from this earth, and from the brief spasm on the older woman's face, Mairaed saw that she knew it. Knew, too, that Mairaed herself had seen it, and the woman's hand was gentle on her hair for an instant. "A blessing and a tragedy both. Your eyes will see too much, for now and ever. Come, girl. The river is waiting for you."

It was not, in the end, the river which waited, not at all. It was instead the cairns, rough tall stone piles which housed the dead, and honored them. It was their song calling her down the length of the river, inviting her to their sacred place.

"I didn't know," she said, that first night amongst the tall stone cairns. "I didn't know they sang to us."

"Most don't. It's easier to let them go if you don't know," Aine replied. "Easier to think the spirit goes on, joins the world again, when almost no one hears the song. I don't," she added, and Mairaed turned from the cairns in surprise. "My aunt did, and when no one in my generation heard the call, she taught me the dances so they might not be lost. My own daughter knows them for the same reasons, but it's yourself they're meant for."

A fist made itself known around Mairaed's heart: a squeeze that took her breath and sent an ache through her body. Her palms cramped; the soles of her feet shuddered, and she sipped barely enough air to whisper, "The dances."

There was a need in her body, an answer to a question not yet spoken. Something crossed Aine's face, not regret and not envy, but some cousin to them both, and a deep-set gratitude besides. Mairaed glimpsed understanding even as she looked back to the cairns: power called her here, a heady and exciting gift. Perhaps she could master it, but even so, she would always be its thrall. Her feet were moving already, called to the steps of an ancient dance she had never learned, and she kept only half an eye on Aine as the older woman moved ahead of her, showing her what her heart already knew.

Like the music, it was a thing of more freedom and more constraint: it was what the wind might be, if it could be trapped in a box and followed. Moonlight made a path to dance on, leading her from one tall pile of stone to another, certain as the stars. Runes burned from the hearts of stone where she brushed them, the names and shapes of the dead carved into the earth's bones, for all that no man had ever laid down any such markers. Each new step brought a howling from both within her and without, though neither had a voice she could hear, nor did she have breath to sing with even if she wished. There was only the lament, and the dance, and the dead.

There had been no cairn dancer for a generation and more: no woman or man to take flight from mortal senses and guide the dead beyond their earthly flesh. They had waited patiently; they knew nothing of time or restlessness. The fever growing in Mairaed was a thing of her own, a need to discharge a duty that had gnawed at her since childhood. Her steps came quicker, her hair sticking to her cheeks as sweat dampened her against the cold night, and her chest ached with the icy air she drew in through her mouth, too hungry for it to warm in her nose.

When the dance ended, it ripped the sky asunder.

Starlight spilled from the darkness, and moonlight made shadows and shapes in scattered clouds. A black-haired woman with ravens on her shoulders stepped forth, with her two sisters identical in all ways only a breath behind her. They wore gowns of spun midnight, their seams glittering with light as white as the sun, and they gathered the eager dead in their arms. The lament was ended, replaced instead by warbling coughs and curious hollow pops from the ravens, who left their mistresses' shoulders to herd souls along the starlight path.

Only when they were gone, ravens and souls alike, did one sister turn away from the others, and come down amongst the cairns to tilt Mairaed's chin up with a fingertip. She studied her with bright black eyes, then pressed a soft, cool kiss to Mairaed's lips. Mairaed made a sound in her throat, as curious and startled as the ravens. The woman paused as she withdrew, then smiled a bladed smile that named her no friend to the living, and drew Mairaed close again.

The kiss this time was deeper, hungry mouth parting to explore and taste and claim. Mairaed's woolen shift was no barrier to the icy hand creeping within, curving the weight of her breast in its palm and closing scalding cold fingers over her nipple. It burned straight to her heart, faltering its steady rhythm, and the heat that spilled between her thighs had nothing to do with the blood that had come that night.

The woman withdrew again, her sharp smile filled now with possessive certainty. She turned and walked away, joining her sisters, and starlight folded up to leave darkness behind.

Mairaed, without looking, without ever wanting to look, knew a handprint red and strong as a birthmark lay on her breast.

That night had passed a dozen years ago, and never once in the years since had the transition been so intense, so intimate, so sweet. Reasons upon reasons answered as to why: the dead she had given passage to that night had been strangers to her, nearly all of them, with no recent loss or sorrow to temper the power of the dance. There had been so many of them, too: a generation of villagers all at once, and the worst loss Mairaed had danced since then had been four children struck down together by illness.

The Morrigan had come that night, for the first time since her first dance. They were called by a feast of souls or untimely death, were the three-fold goddess of death and war and blood, and the small cairns offered both. Mairaed had stood frozen, captivated by their presence, but none of the sisters had looked at the woman one of them had marked as a girl. Disappointment and relief had twinned inside her: even a dancer for the dead didn't want the goddess' gaze on her too often, and yet to be ignored left a space around her heart.

Those things came back to her now, in the dark of a night she didn't want to face. Before dawn, she would know —

they would all know — the Morrigan's cool touch again, but it would be Mairaed herself who bore the weight of it.

"Mairaed." A man pushed open the door to her rough stone house, letting moonlight make a bright path across the floor. The only light had been banked coals: Mairaed closed her eyes against silver brilliance, then came to her feet as Sion ducked his head and stepped across her threshold.

He was handsome, was Sion O'Connail, with light eyes and a broad face beneath hair dark with moonlight. He'd worn the druid's white before Mairaed came to it herself, and had been a solemn child who kept his robes clean. She'd been an adult before she realized the robes were themselves a test: it wasn't easy to keep clean in a life of farming and digging and animal husbandry. A child determined enough to keep wool pristine was a steady soul, likely to age into a calm mind capable of holding clear thoughts: ideal for the wise folk of the village.

Mairaed's robe was, even now, rarely clean. But then, she played a different role, and on her, the white meant a transition to another world.

"Are you ready?" Sion asked, and under his words came the sound of drums and pipes; the sound of blades scraping from sheathes and of leather armor tested by thumping fists. The air through the opened door carried the scent of peat fires and new-cut hay, rich and sweet while they lasted. Soon enough they'd be drowned by blood, and for a while not even her beloved river would be able to carry the sticky flat smell away.

"I am." There was no other answer she could give, hadn't been since the night her blood came; hadn't been, in truth, since she was old enough to toddle to the water's edge and listen to the voices that called her down the river.

Tempered sympathy darkened Sion's eyes and he retreated into shadow, gesturing her out of her home with the respect due one far older than her years. They might have been a pair, once, gentle Sion and gods-touched Mairaed, but that, too, was a path closed to her in childhood.

The drumming stopped as she stepped outside. All the noise did, as though wool had been stuffed in her ears. Dozens of faces turned to her, alight with hope, with fear, with awe, and for a moment the river's song swelled and threatened to take her away.

These were her people, and she went to dance them victory in battle.

Aine's daughter had stories of such things, but nothing more: they had been at peace for generations, with no call to arms by a high lord. The wealthiest in the village, those who owned cattle and sheep and horses, sometimes took those horses to raid neighboring cattle; to steal fine bulls to cover their cows or to take the tenderest of new lambs when they needed their own to grow into breeding stock. That was sport, not war, and visited on them in return by others. Lives were sometimes lost, but mostly when a young man misjudged his horseman's skill, or an old one misjudged his own fading strength. There had been no blood debts to settle in Mairaed's lifetime and longer.

But then the dreams had come, first to the druids, then to Mairaed, and finally to the people themselves. Dreams of war: dreams of small warriors with black eyes and black hair; with olive skin and gleaming white teeth. Their swords were bright and sharp and their bodies glittered with impenetrable shells. Where those shells fell away, their legs were bared to the cold, as if they couldn't feel it. Their backs were covered in cloaks of blood, red and flowing, and no one in the village imagined they were men. These were the *Fir Bolg*, black monsters from under the earth who had once driven away the old gods and faerie folk of the land, and who came now to take it from the mortals who had settled in their place.

Dreams, in far too little time, gave way to stories flowing up the river: warnings of the *Fir Bolg's* attacks, and their ruthless prowess in battle. The dead were the lucky ones: survivors were chained and bound and taken away to serve in darkness, soft green shores and misty sunlight left behind. Those who bore the tales were those who had gathered children and elders and left, abandoning pride and home for a chance at life.

Most of Mairaed's village had gone with them, escaping toward the midlands and the rocky, barren west. Those who were left behind stayed to take up weapons, to slow the *Fir Bolg* and sacrifice their own lives that the children might survive.

Standing amongst them, in awe of their bravery and determination, a tightness slipped away from Mairaed and rose toward the star-filled sky, carrying with it her breath. It took a film from her eyes and it became tears, not of sorrow, but of pride. If it was not her fear that rose into the night, it was some part of it, and some part of her reluctance, so she could be filled with a lightness that slipped beyond the mortal world and showed her the steps to a dance she had never done.

"We ask a terrible thing tonight." Sion spoke from behind her, his voice loud only because of the silence: had a bird thought to whistle, his words might have been drowned beneath its tune. "We ask a terrible thing from one of our own, because an ancient enemy has come among us, and no mortal army is enough to beat them down. It's fortune that brings us a cairn dancer in our time of need, but the price to be paid is a mighty one. Mairaed O'Broin, will you dance this night for us?"

Silence fell again, words disappearing like weights in the river, without a ripple. What fear had remained transmuted within her, becoming frothy laughter that burst noiselessly in her throat and had more to do with release than delight.

"You think it's my strength that I draw on, my destiny whose path I walk." Mairaed closed her eyes, seeing the faces of the boys and girls she'd known in the image of the men and women burned into her mind. The earth still held her to the ground, her weight pressing against it, small stones round beneath her feet; she knew it, and yet felt as though she was carried upward, her chest filled with lightness that dragged her away, her soul no longer bound to her body. "You think it's my own power, but you're wrong. It's yours, and I'll dance that spirit and return it to you three-fold in the battle that you face."

She bowed to them without looking again, and let the aching draw in her heart lead her to the river, to the moonlight, and to the cairns.

Blood spattered, purple in the moonlight. A thin line of pain opened on Mairaed's cheek, burning higher with each moment that passed. The sword came again, pitted metal flecked with viscera that sprayed a vile arc. She countered this time, clumsy: she had never learned the steps to this dance, and no wellspring of unsought memory brought it to life in her as the cairns once had. Her hand, unused to the weight of a weapon, ached, but she lifted her sword again: again: again, each blow uncertain and each hit cleaving less deeply into the enemy than she might hope.

They were men after all, the little dark creatures she fought. Men, or the *Fir Bolg* had thrown off their monstrous forms to take on something more familiar, and were perhaps all the more frightening for it. Their shells were armor, better-made than the heavy leather plates her own people wore, but nothing more magical than that. It heartened her and she raised her voice, hurried her steps, made the news that the enemy were nothing more than men part of her dance.

Men, yes, but men who fought as one, in a way she had never imagined. Men who, when one fell, stepped forward to close ranks, so they seemed never-ending. There were simply too many, and that, too, she put into her dance, demanding everything from the cairns, from the dead, from the goddess who had marked her.

She was not alone. Her people fought with her, bright shadows amongst the cairns, as if they carried sunlight with them even while she fought beneath the moon. They had not followed her down the river, nor had they come to sing a song for the dead, and when she staggered back beneath an onslaught, she fell into Sion, whose robes were black and stiff with blood and whose oaken staff was matted with flesh and bits of hair.

Fell into, and through, as though he was a wraith.

Then, and only then, did battle turn to stillness around her. Only then did she see how the river ran red; how the very earth was thick and sticky with blood around the cairns — in her sacred place where the dead were meant to be honored and set free, not multiplied. Only then did understanding come to her: that she had danced to the edge of time to see what lay beyond it, and that come the morning, her people would die.

Rage boiled up inside her and spilled out, turning her vision to crimson and the moon to a bloody smear across the sky. Fury and hurt poured from her, a wall of dark emotion strong enough to fight the moonlight. Step by step it quailed and fell back, and step by step Mairaed advanced, red sword gripped in one hand, heartbeat surging black in her eyes, and a demand screamed through bared teeth. The scar on her breast burned, cold fire pouring into her body from that remembered touch, and she stalked onward, leaving the world behind.

Halfway to the moon, the stars split apart. Ravens poured out, glittering black in the night as they made a path of wings for the Morrigan. One sister walked with a hand curled to her chest, fingers working against her palm as her wrathful gaze found Mairaed and held her where she stood.

Triumph colder than even the Morrigan's eyes blazed in Mairaed, palm-print on her breast turning to ice: turning so cold that as she'd once known a red mark lay on her body, she now knew it burned silver, as bright and hard as the river in winter. Oh, there was a price, there would be a dear price to pay indeed, but now, and in this moment, it meant nothing.

Because not even a goddess can mark a woman and not be marked somewhat in return.

"I am your vessel," Mairaed whispered to the three-fold goddess's black gaze. "Fill me."

"You cannot command—" Three women spoke as one, the Morrigan's voice becoming the winter wind, cutting and sharp, driving ice into bone and stripping skin from flesh.

Mairaed spat, a hawk of sound from deep in her throat that cast away terror as much as it dismissed the idea that she was forbidden to command those she served. "There will be death. There will be blood. There will be war. These are your domains, Morrigan. Give me what I need to help my people survive and it will all be done in your name."

The sister who held her hand curled to her chest came forward, leaving the other two as black slashes against the night. "And if we do not?" Alone, her voice was a serrated thing, still full of power but shy of the implacability when they spoke together.

Mairaed's grip tightened on her sword as though her body thought she might fling herself into battle against the gods. The Morrigan smiled, showing teeth as pointed as her voice, the very expression inviting Mairaed to try, but words were the dancer's weapon now. "The *Fir Bolg* invade our land. Who will dance for you, Morrigan, if they take these green hills from us? Who will call on you in battle if godless monsters rule this island? Who will honor you, if we are gone?"

Thin lightning crackled between the three, starlight turned to a cutting edge, hissing with vindictive sound. Ravens warbled above that sharp song, their calls almost words, and between it all Mairaed knew she listened to how the Morrigan spoke among herself; how her thoughts were shared three to one and one to three.

"You are mortal," the one closest to Mairaed finally said aloud. "Fragile."

"All life is fragile. Even a goddess can bend to the whim of time."

"Not this goddess," the Morrigan said as one. "Not this time. Release your weapons. You will have no use for them when I am done with you. Come to me. Come to us."

Mairaed opened her hand, felt her sword's hilt roll free; felt the marks it left in her palm suddenly turn rigid and strong, as if tenderness had passed to calluses without blistering in between. She stepped forward, and the nearest Morrigan opened her curled palm to show a mark as red as the one on Mairaed's breast. Redder: blood oozed from it, thick and discolored in the moonlight, and pain shot through Mairaed's heart, stabbing deep enough to steal her breath. She faltered and the Morrigan caught her: all the Morrigan, three-fold goddess suddenly surrounding her, hands cool as ice and burning with fire as they lay on her skin.

"Lust," the Morrigan whispered, and the word ran like knives through their touch. Two held Mairaed's arms, and she ached where they grasped, pain rushing from her chest to her fingers until numbness was left behind. The third, the one who bled, slipped open Mairaed's robes and put her hand against the scar she'd left a lifetime before. Sticky blood warmed against the mark, and the Morrigan brushed her mouth against Mairaed's. "Lust for blood."

"Lust for death," her sisters murmured. "Lust for war."

Mairaed, trembling, whispered, "Lust for life."

The razor smile came again, this time more felt than seen. "Lust for us," the Morrigan said. "Take us in to you, cairn dancer, and we will give you the dance you need." Her lips turned hungry against Mairaed's, her hands cold and quick and searching, and where they touched they left behind heat that brought Mairaed's heartbeat to a roaring throb. Frantic for air, Mairaed threw her head back, and another sister covered her mouth with a deepening kiss. Lips and curious tongues tasted her breasts as knowing fingers parted her thighs and swept upward, inward, waking a need that had gone unanswered for a lifetime. Her heart would burst with it, would surely fail from the Morrigan's all-encompassing touch; from the desire for the three-fold goddess who was all, all, all that Mairaed could ever want.

And then in the moment of ecstasy the goddess was gone, leaving Mairaed white and spent and numb on a starlight stair.

Ravens guided her to the earth, stood clattering and clacking on the cairns, and giving the blade that lay between them bright-eyed glances of avarice. Mairaed crouched and lifted it: not the same one she had dropped, but one of far finer make, light and deadly sharp. Even as she wished it might be a weapon she knew better, it became one: a bladed staff, fast and easy to manipulate in her hands.

Her hands: her hands, too, were her own and were not. A glimmer of unknown strength lay in them; lay in the shape of her arms and in the length of her stride when she saw dawn was near, and that war would be upon her village with daylight. Her clothes were not her own, and neither were they the Morrigan's: she wore armor of silver and white, making her a banner in the coming light. It was the armor, the weapon, the stride of a hero; of a man out of legend, and not of a single young woman whose fate was bound to the river of death.

Bright-eyed corvids alighted on her shoulders, their wings half spread and black beaks open to cry go, go! Only when she began to run did they take wing again, the two who'd urged her on and an unkindness more besides, beating their way through winter air to keep promises, to meet destiny.

To make battle at the river's edge.

Blood spattered, crimson in the dawn's light. A thin line opened on Mairaed's cheek, but no pain rose with it. The sword came again, metal dull with viscera that mocked the rising sun. She countered this time, elegant: she had never learned the steps to this dance, but she knew them from within, as she had once known the cairn dances as though they'd been imprinted on her soul. Her hands were easy with her bladed staff's weight, swinging it, twisting it, smashing men aside with it, and each blow felling her enemy with more certainty than she might have hoped.

Each time one of the *Fir Bolg* fell, she crowed triumph, and her ravens spun in the sky around her, black-winged harbingers of death.

All around her — behind her, following her lead — came the people of her village; came Sion O'Connail, came Aine's daughter, came faces she knew and had once loved; faces for whom she had called the goddess Morrigan, so that they might live and fight another day. She saw in their eyes how they needed what she was, and so she plunged deeper into battle, turning the *Fir Bolg's* red cloaks to ribbons; breaking their small dark forms in half on her staff, cutting them to pieces with her blade. Her heart screamed with joy, every beat a thing of pain: no mortal form was meant to hold such battle lust, and the goddess of war hungered for more.

She was bloodless, unmarked amongst the soldiers, a slim creature of white and silver at the heart of the enemy, and even when their blades scored they drew no cry, drew no streak of red anger across her skin. Only their blood marred her armor, streaks and spatters that steamed in the cold morning light, and blackened as the day wore on.

Her people were weary: she could feel that in them as a remote and meaningless detail. They followed her still, but their strength waned, and she could not hold the field alone. Not alone, not even with the ravens, whom her people had feared until they saw the birds fed only on the eyes of the *Fir Bolg*.

"Hold!" Her voice was not her own: it was the serrated thing the Morrigan spoke with, but tempered by a mortal throat. "Hold until night, Sion! Hold until night, and then the land is mine!" She looked back as she called the rally, and saw new things in her peoples' eyes. Belief, yes, but worse than that, oh so much worse was the fear, for that was the price of calling a goddess to battle.

"Hold," she whispered again, and turned back to make war on her enemy.

At dawn the ravens feasted, gorging themselves on the slaughtered *Fir Bolg* and splashing red melted river water over their sleek black feathers. They clucked and gurgled over the dead villagers, but left them untasted, and one by one those bodies were gathered, and brought to the cairns.

Sion O'Connail was the first to see the broken body fallen amongst the tall stone piles. The first, and perhaps the least surprised: it was he who knelt by Mairaed's figure, who tested her skin for suppleness and found it frozen through and through. Dead a day, at least, and the spattered blood foamed at her mouth said perhaps her heart had burst. Her eyes were open, staring sightlessly toward the sky; her body was arched as though caught in a moment of rapture, and her skull and frame were cracked, as if she had fallen a terrible distance, when there was no high place at all that she might have tumbled from.

It was not easy, closing those staring eyes, and no one said him nay as he lifted her frozen body and took it some little way away from the other cairns and there began to shift the stones that would cover their dancer, and mark her place of rest as a spot of especial honor.

"No more cairn dancers," he said when her body was hidden, and because he was their voice of wisdom, the villagers listened. "No more," he said again. "Mortals are not meant to call on the gods. We have won the day, but we've asked too terrible a thing. This will not happen again."

Murmurs of agreement rose, the memory of Mairaed's twisted form too fresh to deny, and one by one the people of her village turned away to do mortal honor to the fallen dead, and to bury them properly. No more dancers, they said to one another, and when the last of the cairns were built, they slipped away, never to bury the dead in this place again.

And so no one saw a boy slip forth amongst the tall stone graves, and begin to dance.

'Cairn Dancer' was inspired by a watercolor painting I own of the same title. It's a wonderful, vivid painting of a beautiful woman swaying in front of stone cairns, and beyond that there's no resemblance whatsoever between story and painting. The painting's woman is quite modern; Mairaed's story was never imagined as such. But the woman in the painting did beg the question of why she danced at the cairns. Mark and Amanda's invitation to write a story for *The Phantom Queen Awakes* gave me an opportunity to explore the answer to that question, and I have to say I rather like it. Now, I can suppose my painting is Mairaed's spiritual, if not physical, descendant, still dancing for the souls of the dead after all these years.

C.E. Murphy is a fantasy novelist who makes occasional forays into short stories, comics and photography. Born and raised in Alaska, she now lives in her ancestral homeland of Ireland. More information about CE Murphy and her career can be found at www.cemurphy.net.

Jennifer Lawrence

Washerwoman

Perhaps because the wind was uncommonly bitter that morn, or because she could still hear the angry words Aoibheann had whispered to her husband, Treasa's son, in the darkness last night, Treasa spent ten minutes scrubbing at the laundry down by the stream before she realized that she did not know the other old woman washing her clothes on the opposite bank.

Treasa had long known her son's wife did not like her, wanted her gone so she could run the household in the manner she preferred, but it had still been a shock to lay there on her bed in the darkness and listen to Aoibheann whisper to Dallán about the tales she had heard from the last bard who passed through. About how the man had spoken of far lands where customs were different, and where, when a man or woman became too old to help the family any longer, they were led out into the wilderness in winter and abandoned to die.

Dallán had hushed his wife, but the damage was done. Treasa was thrifty with the house's resources, strict when it came to directing the work that had to be done — and there was always so much of it, cleaning and cooking and spinning and watching the children — but she had not thought that Aoibheann wanted to see her dead.

Little wonder, then, that her thoughts were elsewhere this morning as the cold curled round her shoulders, sharp enough to cut tough meat. Spring it might be, and the ewes in the fields with their lambs a full two months ago, but even the flowers in the meadow nodded their heads low and shivered as if they were chill.

"Rare frosty day," she said at last to the crone bent down over the clear water on the other side of the brook. The woman nodded and Treasa continued politely, hoping the conversation would take her mind off last night's shock. "Here's a prayer that the cold will keep the Northmen up in their own lands, where they belong."

"'Twill warm before an hour has passed," the woman croaked, her sticklike fingers scrubbing ceaselessly at a rusty stain on the length of an old, ill-mended green skirt.

"Good to hear," Treasa murmured, squeezing the water out of one of Dallán's tunics. She peered at the woman, belatedly realizing that the voice was not familiar. The hair under the woman's shawl was black as raven's feathers, with threads of white at the temples. "I don't know you. Are you Fearchair's kin, from his house over the hill?"

The woman was silent for a moment, wringing the water from the skirt, and then shaking the garment out to peer at it. It hung in wet folds, embroidered in black at the hem, and Treasa dropped the tunic in her hands. The skirt the woman held was identical to the one she wore, save for the vicious rent through the fabric over the hips, and the red stain around the tear.

That...cannot be what I think it is...But I'd know my own skirt anywhere. And that means she is...oh, Danu protect me.

"I am kin to all," the woman finally said. She tilted her head to listen and turned to look toward the east. "They are coming."

"Coming...who?" The basket at her side tipped over into the brook, and the clothes slowly floated downstream. The woman reached into her own basket and lifted out another garment, the swaddling clothes of a babe. There was a fresh stain of milk and oats on one corner, a stain matching the one on the identical wrapping that Treasa had gathered up this morning. Laoghaire spat up his gruel this morning, his belly would not settle...is he going to die? Am I? Seeing the washer at the ford is an omen...

A roar reached her ears from the beach to the east, and Treasa paled. She had heard the harsh, guttural sounds of the language of the Viking raiders only once before as a child. She had run and hidden then, burying herself in a hole in the ground in the forest, while the men of her father's village fought the Northmen and lost. She had been the only one to survive that raid, and still heard their voices in her nightmares.

She recognized it now.

"You could run, away from the coast, away from your home — west, into the woods," the woman across the stream said to her flatly. "You could hide, as you did once, and they would not find you. Your daughter-in-law would die. You would survive."

Treasa closed her eyes as the warming wind from the east swirled around her. "Aoibheann would die, yes. And so would my son, and his children, and the others in the village."

There was no answer, so she opened her eyes. The woman and her basket were gone. Only the bloodied, rent green skirt lay there, draped across the rocks, next to the babe's swaddling. Laoghaire...Maolán...Órlaith...Easnadh. She could see it in her mind's eye, those tiny bodies hacked and pierced by the Northmen's axes and swords.

And her own.

No! Let other old women prattle about omens. Yes, I have seen her and I will die, but it does not have to be today. She would not have spoken if there was no chance. I saw my clothes in her hands, Laoghaire's clothes...not those of the others. She spoke of a choice. There might still be time to run home, to fetch the babe — to save him from the axes and swords of the Northmen. I cannot save them all. The raiders are too close to flee. But if I can save just one—

She leapt to her feet and raced up the hill, running towards home as fast as her legs could carry her, tears streaming down her weathered, wrinkled features.

She crested the top of the hill, feet pounding along the beaten dirt path that led from the village down to the stream. She could see the boats nearing the shore, less than a mile away, where the ocean's waves beat against the rocks. Her heart slammed against the inside of her ribs like a blacksmith's hammer against an anvil, and her mouth had gone as dry as hanging herbs on the last day of August. The bell in the church built by the priests of Christ had not yet begun to ring; the men were out in the fields, leaving the women and children undefended.

Her lungs wheezed like a bellows in her thin chest as she ran, the pounding of her heart like the beat of a bodhran at a céilidh, and even as she neared the village, she had time for a prayer of thanks, glad she had not taken the Christian baptism, glad she had stuck to the ways of her gods, no matter how Aoibheann glared or how her son pleaded. If I had...would the Great Queen have come to bring me warning?

She thought not, snatching a quick glance at the shore as she moved around the rear of the family's hut. The first of the boats was being dragged onto the sand, but the shaggy, filthy warriors had not yet charged toward the village. She could see her people running, panicking, the women trying to gather their children and lead them to safety, the few men not in the fields racing toward their cabins to fetch their swords.

Treasa ducked into the cabin and forced her withered limbs to carry her back to where Laoghaire slept fitfully, bundled into his cradle. She grabbed up a blanket, spare changing rags, and then the babe himself before hurrying for the door. We may die of starvation in the woods; my dugs have been dry of milk for many a year now, and I dare not stop to try to leash and drag one of the goats along. But a chance at life was better than none at all. She paused only long enough to grab up a waterskin and a half-full basket of oats before ducking out of the cabin and dashing for the woods.

Treasa tried not to cringe as she ran. Her thin, papery skin was stretched taut across her shoulders, expecting to feel the impact of an axe with every step. The air burned in her lungs, the cold bit at her face, and as the branches of the trees gathered her in to the safety of the forest's shelter, she stifled a sob of relief.

Behind her, in the village, she could hear the first screams begin.

Afterword

A lot is made of the martial aspects of the Morrigan; her status as a goddess of war and death can hardly be overlooked. I've read stories in the past about her appearing to warriors and kings, and swooping over the field of battle as a raven. But she is also a goddess of prophecy, and aside from the passage in the *Táin Bó Cúailnge* where she appears before Cuchulainn as an old woman, washing his garments in a stream on the night before he dies in battle, I've never read any fiction portraying that aspect of her. What better protagonist for such a story than an old woman, already near death and seeking to find a way to escape it? This was the side of the Morrigan I wanted to share with readers, and I hope you all enjoy it.

Biography

Ye olde author likes the weird and the strange, which explains most of her friends. Married, with two daughters, she has earned a B.A. in Literature and a B.S. in Criminal Justice. Her interests include gardening, herbalism, mythology and fairy tales, theology, everything Celtic, role-playing games, horror movies, and the martial arts. She lives with her husband, her younger daughter, five cats, a dog, and a houseful of gargoyles somewhere near Chicago.

Sharon Kae Reamer

The Raven's Curse

Lys ab Gysell felt she had sat on a bumpy horse her entire life. After three weeks of riding along dry paths, she felt cloaked with the dust of high summer. It invaded every orifice and her hair and clothes were layered in grit. As some of her entourage and all the slaves traveled by foot, they had been forced to ride at a slow pace. They followed the trail north along the coast before turning inland to the estuary near the walled settlement that belonged to her husband-to-be and his people. The briny sea air assaulted her nostrils as they approached a small bay. She spied standing stones in the distance.

"What is that place?" she asked her escort. The individual dialects varied widely, but their respective tongues had enough in common that they could communicate.

"The *ar-men-hir* of Karnag," he answered. "The spirits of ancient heroes buried under the stones guard the *mor-bihan* — the bay — against invaders."

As they made the turn inland, she heard them before seeing them. On the hilltop in front of her, naked, painted men danced and brandished their iron-tipped spears. They welcomed her with loud blasts from long horns in the shape of pig snouts. Various sized dogs ran to and fro, barking wildly. She laughed with joy to see the men with their limed hair sticking up like frost-rimed sedges. She imagined that to an enemy, their demeanor would be altogether different and a frightening sight. In this case, it was a regal greeting. Fit for a queen.

Even before they entered the village, people lined the way on either side of her, eager to have a glimpse of her. She let her entourage lead her horse to where a tall man in a richly patterned tunic waited, surrounded by other noblemen. She knew instinctively it was her future husband. Unable to keep her eyes from him as one of his men helped her from her horse, she felt a smile form.

The rumors traded by the older women in her tribe were now confirmed. Iaun Reith was a handsome man, indeed. His loosely belted tunic did not hide a trim and muscular body that contrasted nicely with his thick mane of dark hair and a well cared for bushy mustache. He wore an astonishingly beautiful gold torc around his neck. Her folk had received hints of Veneti wealth — acquired through battle gains and shrewd trading — but Lys was in awe at the abundance of gold on the noblemen who surrounded their leader.

She could have done much worse, she thought, and hoped she would please him as well. She approached and knelt before him. His golden brown eyes sparkled like topaz as he held out his hands to her, and she rose to stand next to him. His answering smile as the throng of people cheered in front of them told her all she needed to know.

The joining of hands had been timed to coincide with the summer solstice. Two days before the fête, Iaun led her to the hut near the forest where the holy women of his tribe dwelled. Holy women were known to Lys, but her own people had none, so she was anxious about meeting them. Iaun explained that their approval of the match was a formality, but a necessary one.

"Why do I have to spend the night here?" she asked as they approached the two young women waiting patiently near the entrance to the woods.

"It's a necessary ritual. To make sure that we are fruitful," he said. "The holy women's blessing will fortify my seed."

His gaze as he said that had been rather easy to decipher. She knew he would not have waited to bed her under ordinary circumstances, but their handfasting symbolized a union between her tribe and his. Iaun knew the tradition required of a leader and was bound to honor it. Lys understood the hope this union meant to her own people. The Condrusi stood to gain more from it than the Veneti: protection, something her people desperately needed. They had already faced the Roman wolf at the door.

Iaun left, and the two women guided her through the wood to a willow bower they had already prepared. They sang softly to her while they bathed her with a fragrant mistletoe wash as she stood before them.

"How long have you been in training?" Lys asked.

One woman, not much more than a girl, Lys thought, shook her hair forward as she spoke. "We have just been adopted."

"It is an honor for our family," the other one said.

"Have you no holy men here?" Lys continued as they dressed her in a long tunic of white linen.

They smiled at each other before answering. "No. Not here."

Before she entered her bower, another woman approached her. The portions of gray in hair that hung in a thick cloud around her face, and ended in a long braid down her back, were in stark contrast to the dark hair of the other women.

"I am Uxía." She took Lys by the upper arms and then tilted her chin up, staring deeply into her eyes. "You have the eyes of a seer."

Lys started. "How can you know that?"

Uxía nodded. "Experience. I have enough of the Gift to recognize it in others."

Lys resisted the urge to look away and fought to keep her breathing normal. "I don't have any scrying talents."

"Seeing is not only scrying," she said. "Maybe I should have said that you have the Sight."

Lys looked away to hide her dismay. Only the most addled of old women in her tribe were attributed with the second Sight. "Those women are shunned among my people."

Uxía laughed at her reaction. "Do not fear. The Veneti revere their women, holy or not." She let go of Lys' arms and stood before her. "Do others of your tribe have eyes such a deep blue that the sea would grow jealous?"

Lys relaxed somewhat at Uxía's compliment. "No. My father has blue eyes, but of a normal shade. That is the reason why my people chose me to be the gift of our people. Blue is a color of good fortune."

"Your father is one of your tribe's holy ones?"

"No, but he is one of the village elders, one of the most respected among them."

Uxía nodded her approval. "In that case, the goddess will be pleased as well. She may visit you tonight. If she does, it is a sign of great favor."

The women had prepared a warm drink for her. It had a bitter, unpleasant taste, and she drank it all as they watched. It made her feel relaxed but oddly alert. She suspected they had laced it with the fly mushrooms her tribe's holy men used to prepare men for battle. Lys sat alert within her nest of soft grasses, her only company small snuffling creatures in the woods around her. She had not slept alone or outside since she was a young girl. Even the days of celebrating Bel saw her safely in her family's hut after dark. Her father had not wanted to risk the chance of her deflowering from one of the youths in her village. She was too great a prize to be lost.

A bright cusp of light appeared and danced in front of the bower. It settled in front of her, just above her forehead, and she looked into it for a time before she felt herself falling, being pulled into the light.

After a time that could have been five minutes or a year, the sky brightened. Only it was not the sky, but a small area around where she sat. She was naked and her long hair fell loose about her, providing her a scant but welcome covering. She felt neither cold nor heat. She could not see any trees through the light, only a dense white fog that pulsed forward and backward. It made her dizzy to watch it, so she looked instead at the ground.

"You are not known to us."

Lys raised her head at the sound of the voice. She gasped at the creature in front of her. It seemed to shift in and out of dense pockets of shadow that had formed within the fog. First one face appeared and merged before changing into another. One minute a proud young girl with a warrior's grimace and fierce eyes watched her, the next a motherly face stared out at her, less fierce but no less proud. Finally, a dark-haired woman with black brows and full lips looked her over.

"Tell us your name," she said.

"Lys ab Gysell."

Was this the goddess the women had spoken of? Curiosity warred with a feathery feeling in her stomach. Was she a tree spirit? Or a guardian of the sea? Lys had yet to meet such a being in human form. "May I know your name?"

A hand reached out to lift Lys' chin, much as Uxía had done, and the woman barked out a short laugh. "Well met, Lys ab Gysell. What would you call me?"

Lys tried to think. Her people paid homage to many deities who transcended tribal borders. "Are you one of the Valkyrie that the northern folk speak of?"

She frowned. "Some have called me that, but without good reason. The women here call me Cathubodua. But it does not matter. I have many names, and not all of them are favorable to me." The face changed to an ancient crone with watery eyes who appeared to wash clothes in an invisible stream. She seemed to watch Lys, although her eyes were unseeing. Lys shivered under the gaze. The crone was frightening in ways that the warrior woman was not. Lys felt as if she looked into the face of Death.

"You look young and strong. You will bear many healthy children," she said in a wheezy voice. "What say you, maiden?" Her cross expression puzzled Lys.

"Are you angry with me, respected mother?"

"Impatient for answers. Time moves too slowly. You move too slowly."

Lys did not want to vex her and hurried to give answer. "Our family has strong women. We do not shrink from hard work or the pain of giving birth."

The warrior woman returned, laughing. "That is good. What goes in must come out. Iaun's seed is as strong as his thirst."

"What do you ask of me, then? How may I serve you?" Lys bowed her head to wait for the goddess' commands.

"Ach, Lys ab Gysell." She spat to the side as if to frighten an enemy. "I would have you ask me for a boon. It is your wedding and your right."

Shadows danced around her. First one face then another flew in and out of focus. Finally, a motherly countenance appeared. Lys saw the moon reflected in her eyes. She turned her head, but could not find the light's source. She exhaled in a burst, unaware that she had held her breath.

"I can think of nothing other than long life for my husband and me and peace for our people," she said.

The woman smiled then. "I can offer you something else, a valuable gift for your folk and those of your husband."

Lys grew suspicious. She knew from the tales of the holy men that gifts from the gods were something to be wary of. "What sort of gift?"

"The ability to walk in *Ande-dubnos*. You may also pass it on to your children." Her beatific face radiated joy; it was meant to be a face to trust.

Lys knew better. "Do you mean the power to cross into the *Anderwelt*?"

She nodded. "Yes, child. A better boon you could not ask for. With this gift you may form the dreams of your people to guide them. You can rule them as you see fit."

"That does sound like a queenly gift. What do you ask from me in return?"

"Only this," the goddess beckoned her forward. Lys approached and knelt, feeling that it was expected of her. Hands touched her shoulders, a light touch. She felt long fingernails scrape over her skin. The feeling was not unpleasant.

"To Lys ab Gysell, should she choose to walk with me, I hereby grant the power over *Ande-dubnos,* to fashion the portion of the shadow realm it encompasses to her desires."

The hands clasping her shoulder tightened and Lys felt a reply was required of her. "I hear your words, my lady."

"This power has its responsibilities." She paused and eased her grip on Lys' shoulders. "The dreams of men need to be cultivated and nurtured against the threat of chaos. This requires a journey into *Ande-dubnos* each year to perform such tasks as are necessary."

Hands lowered to grasp her upper arms and urge her upwards. As Lys rose, she gazed into the unsmiling eyes of the warrior.

"I will do my best."

The goddess considered her carefully. "In addition to your gaining entrance into the *Anderwelt*, as you call it, the reward for this duty is twofold. I bestow on you good fortune and a fair countenance for you and your descendants from this day forward, as far as it is in my power to fulfill."

"That is kind of you, my lady."

"Kindness has nothing to do with it. I grant this not without purpose." The goddess smiled on her without mirth, but her expression, at least, was not unkind. "Prosperity and the beauty of the fée have their price, but that is something that is paid on demand and not beforehand."

Lys studied the face before her. Strong. Fierce. And merciless.

"Your fate and those of your children are from here on intimately bound, Lys ab Gysell, with the fate of Iaun Reith and his tribe, be it ever so small."

"We are to be formally joined. I see no problem with that."

"But your children might. Therefore, you must bind them to me now as well."

"I am willing to do this thing, but I would ask why."

"Because the descendants of the Veneti and the Condrusi will someday be all that remains of our way."

Lys considered the gravity of what she said and felt afraid. She knew the Condrusi did not have the might to overcome the powerful Roman warlord they called Caesar or the tribes to the north and east. Her folk had formerly accepted patronage and protection from the Treveri. The two tribes shared kinship bonds and many customs, but the Treveri had begun to suckle from Rome's teat, setting her people adrift.

Lys thought about the children she hoped to bear. Her children's word was hers to give as long as they were not yet out of her womb, and her pulse quickened at the thought of the great fortune she was receiving. "It is done," she said and lowered her head.

Lys bore twin sons to Iaun within a year of their binding. The women marveled at the ease of the birth in one as young as Lys and at the health of her babies. The Veneti rejoiced at the new arrivals and slaughtered lambs for the feast to celebrate Bel's return.

They renewed the handfasting a year and a day after the initial ceremony to much fanfare, another cause for the Veneti to celebrate. Uxía tied the double knot over their crossed hands, signifying the permanence of their union. Iaun's vigorous appetite for her sparked such a deep satisfaction in Lys that she vowed to return the favor by being a good wife and leader for Iaun's people. A few days after the solstice, Lys realized she was again pregnant. The fortune that the goddess had promised her seemed already to have come to pass.

"Why do you have to go just now?" Lys spoke to her husband as she finished suckling her third son, born just a fortnight before.

Iaun watched her with an admiring gaze as he stood in front of his weapons chest. "You heard the messenger your father sent. They need our help. The men have grown bored over the winter, and it will give them a chance to win some trophies. I would also learn the extent of the threat from the Roman wolf pack."

Her twins pulled themselves up on Nolwenn's legs. Lys had accepted the Veneti tradition that decreed the exchange of sons among noble families and entrusted Nolwenn, the wife of Iaun's brother Gwened, to care for her children. After Iaun looked at Nolwenn pointedly, she took the baby from Lys and left, herding the twins in the direction of her own hut.

"And why can't I go with you?"

He closed the chest and motioned for her to join him on their fur-lined pallet.

"I need you here in my absence, Lys. The people need you. Gwened will help you to oversee things while I'm gone. Trust him as I do."

Lys' third pregnancy quickly followed Iaun's triumphant return. Eager to capitalize on his tribe's support and the recent influx of artisans, he began to oversee the construction of his own small fleet of ships. They were to be low but fast wooden tubs with sails made of leather skins, capable of seaworthiness in both the shallow and deep waters that would be needed for a planned trading expedition to the West.

She looked up from instructing one of the craftswomen in the joining of hides for the leather sails as she caught a glimpse of the twins chasing each other through the shipyards. Lys' leatherworking skills had been learned at her father's knees, and she was glad she could put them to good use now. Gwened smiled approvingly at her work.

"The building is going well. Especially with their help," Gwened said. They both watched the twins as they handed fresh moss to the men who used it to seal the planking.

"I'm hoping it will take a while. I'm not looking forward to Iaun leaving again so soon."

"I'm thinking of taking the boys with me on a short hunt," he said, after Lys rose to stand next to him.

She laid a hand on his arm. "If you think so, Gwened."

Because of his fair coloring and steely gray-blue eyes, it was rumored that his mother had lain with one of the Northern slaves, although no one spoke about it in his presence. She valued his companionship and had learned to trust his judgment during Iaun's absence. His wife, Nolwenn, barren herself, had gladly taken Lys' third son into her care, leaving her free to handle tribal affairs.

The time of celebrating Imbolc was well past and Lys felt unwell as her term approached. She sought out the holy women for assistance to ease the birth. Uxía brought her into one of their huts, structures of woven reed walls and steep thatched roofs. She laid Lys on a bed of heather rushes softened by a covering of winter hay and gave her tisanes of willow bark. Uxía confirmed that the delivery was drawing near.

Her pain eased, Lys felt herself slipping in and out of dreams. During one of them, Cathubodua appeared to her. She came in her warrior aspect, accompanied by a black cloud of ravens winging about her head and shoulders.

"Three healthy, beautiful sons you have borne," she said. "I demand payment for continued good fortune." Based on her appearance alone, Lys would have guessed that the fierce maiden was younger than her by several years, but the eyes that bore into her contradicted the impression of youth.

Lys nodded for her to continue.

"I would have these first daughters, both of them. They will be mine."

Lys shrank back and held her hands over her belly. She felt the first contractions that signaled the impending birth. "You wish them to enter into the care and training of the holy women?'

"No. Mine. Given. You will sacrifice them to me the year they come into their maidenhood."

Lys' breath came rapidly as her chest tightened with dread, and she felt her knees weaken with fright. "Why?"

"It is my way. Difficult times require strong magic."

Lys prayed quietly to other gods. It seemed to take an eternity before she found her courage. "Can you not take those from another of the tribe?"

"The sacrifice of a king's blood is the price I require," she said.

Lys had not thought about her promise these past few years. She had carried out her duties and strove to be a good wife to Iaun.

"I have made the pilgrimages into *Ande-dubnos* each year as you required of me, and have bathed in the sea of dreams."

"You swore it," the maiden said, her hand on the sword at her belt. "And know this. The dreams of your people grow weak. You must continue your duties." She waited for Lys' response.

"What will you do if I refuse?"

"I will cut them from you now," Cathubodua said, her hand tightening on her sword's pommel.

"I will keep my oath." Lys sobbed, the words tasting like ash.

The days shortened toward summer's end, the sixth since her daughters had arrived. Since Iaun had returned from his trip into the West, his ships laden with goods, a change had come over him. Although solicitous, he behaved with a reticence towards her that made Lys uneasy.

"I don't understand what is wrong with Iaun. Has he said anything to you?" Lys stood next to Gwened as they received reports of grain and wood harvests from some of the folk. Iaun had left to oversee plans for the reception of emissaries from a tribe he had visited.

Gwened clenched his jaw and turned away from her.

She put a hand on his shoulder. "Tell me, Gwened."

"Iaun is planning to send me and some of the men back to your people, Lys. He wants you to go with me this time," he answered.

"More raiders?" she asked, feeling frightened for her people.

"There is a rumor that the Romans are on the march. The men are eager to engage them. They also need to be kept busy or they start fighting amongst themselves."

"Can we take the children?"

"We can take the boys, Lys. The girls should stay here with Nolwenn," was all he would say. She had a suspicious feeling that he was not telling her everything.

The morning of their departure, Gwened took Lys' sons down to the bay to make an offering to the *ar-men-hir* before their journey, giving her just enough time to lay with her husband before she left. Little did she know it would be the last time she saw Iaun Reith.

Near the end of the long march through the forests of the Belgen, the news that Gwened had kept from her but that had circulated freely through the campfires finally reached her ears. Iaun Reith had taken a new wife, accepting an offer of alliance from one of the western tribes. The clients Iaun's new bride represented had brought much wealth to the Veneti. Lys' heart filled with dread as she struggled to accept the idea of sharing her husband with another woman.

"We are nearly there," she told Gwened as she recognized the line of seven hills visible in the distance. The base of the Berg farther west that housed the sleeping dragon was also home to her small tribe. She pointed to the wide river that made her heart soar on their descent into the valley. "Look, there is the Rhine. It is not far now."

She smiled broadly when Condrusi scouts engaged them and spurred their horses back to report their arrival. Lys and her escort rode into the central compound of her village, smaller than she remembered it, where a gathering of people waited to greet her. She let Gwened help her from her horse and knelt before the man she had not seen for over a decade. Her father had aged favorably but walked with a slight stoop. His eyes were still clear as they looked her over and his stern but kind expression told her that she was welcome.

"Lys ab Gysell," he said in greeting, affection marking his tone.

"Vater," her voice caught in her throat. All the emotion she had saved up over the journey threatened to fight its way out of her breast. She rose to face him. "I have brought you gifts. And your grandsons have come with me."

He looked her sons over, and she caught the glint of approval in his eyes. They were beautiful children. Her sons had Iaun's dark hair and, in contrast, her deep blue eyes, giving them an exotic, regal appearance. Her girls had inherited both Iaun's hair and eyes and fine features and Lys regretted not taking them with her. She already missed their faces, although they were an even sharper reminder of their father's absence. She was thankful they were there with him, safe from Cathubodua.

Lys settled quickly into the rhythm of her people again and spent time with the holy men in the forest, telling them of Veneti customs and their way of life. They questioned her about the wise women and their ritual use of herbs and plants. Her boys were taken immediately into their training. Gwened kept to himself when he was not guiding patrols, but Lys joined him often by the fire in the hut they shared with the children. She enjoyed listening to him tell her about the day's events and found she looked forward to their time together.

Gwened had returned early one afternoon to have one of his men tended for a minor injury. Lys had taken to her bed after drinking a potion of willow bark to ease one of her all too frequent headaches. He lay down next to her and whispered the words of a song used to ease frightened children to sleep. They were alone in the hut, the others being busy with the tasks of high summer.

Lys turned gratefully into his embrace. "I am glad that you're here, Gwened." She whispered close to his ear, her lips brushing his cheek. "I am also glad that you were always there for my sons."

"The twins will be fine men, Lys. Not a one of your folk can match them even now on the hunt." He pulled her close to him, with only a thin wool coverlet between them, and rubbed his hardness against her thighs.

She saw the want in his eyes. She let herself enjoy the feel of him against her and trailed her hand along the inside of his thighs. He cupped her breasts between his hands and voiced the question they had already answered with their bodies. "You would give me a gift fit for a king?"

She laughed at his teasing. "Of course, you deserve nothing less," and offered him her hips.

After they had taken their pleasure together, they lay side-by-side for a short while, listening to the buzz of insects in the summer heat.

"I don't know that I could have stood losing Iaun if it hadn't been for you," she said. "You miss Nolwenn, don't you?"

"She is a good woman, and I am sure she will not be alone in my absence," he said.

"Your brother is surely happy with his new wife."

"You are still fairer than all the women half your age, Lys ab Gysell," he said, stroking her hair. "Don't worry about Iaun. You have given him enough — three healthy, brave boys and two beautiful daughters. When you return, he will welcome you again."

"What makes you think that?"

"Iaun needs to produce something with his bride first. I have heard talk that she takes something against the monthly curse. She fears a swollen belly," he said.

Lys laughed out loud. "Then she is more a fool than I thought."

After Lys gave birth to Gwened's first child, her third daughter, she faced the prospect that she must soon cross over again into *Ande-dubnos* to fulfill the duties required by Cathubodua. She sought the help of one of the Sighted women, a shapeless mother who lived alone at the edge of the village. Lys asked her for some herbal magic to help her reach the place of shadow that her people called the *Anderwelt*. The woman moved slowly and her hands had curled up into stiff claws. But she brewed Lys a *Trank* from moonflower seeds and told her to barricade herself in her hut to ensure solitude from prying eyes.

The potion did not seem to have any effect until Lys found herself walking through a featureless landscape that seemed to hang between nothing and something. She was met by tall, slender creatures with ears that narrowed at the top. One had hair of darkest red that flowed in long ringed tresses while another had short hair of a shiny gold color that crowned his head like the sun's rays. None of them smiled at her in greeting. They conducted her along paths lit by twilight to a calm, shallow sea that stretched to the very edge of her imagination.

She bathed in the water as they sang songs of power to her, the words chosen to instruct her on how to shape the waves and bring a tide to the sea formed from the dreams of her people. She felt their words flow through her. After the working, she sensed movement, a susurration in the water, but the liquid remained unnaturally calm — just the opposite of the restless ocean along the Veneti coastlands.

Lys sat on the beach afterwards and relished the invigorating tingle as the water of dreams dried from her skin. The *Anderwelt* folk bade her farewell and wandered off, singing to each other as they dwindled into a shadowy distance. One of the very tall ones, a male with a regal face and dark eyes edged with silver, remained behind to escort her back. She had never seen this one before. He wore an elegant mantle of black shot through with silver and gold threads that fell to his feet. His black hair matched it in both length and color and was streaked with strands of white and brilliant yellow.

He told her his name was Ankou as they labored up a long dune of mute sands that darkened briefly under her passing steps. "The crossroads," he said as they were close to the top.

"Is that where you're taking me? Aren't we going back now?"

He smiled sadly. "It is where you are going."

She guessed what he didn't say. Her people's dreams had been fading; the power of this place waning each year. "Cathubodua told me our ways will disappear. What will happen then?"

His voice was gentle, but grim. "When the dreams — and the memories — fade altogether, our bond to your world will lessen. Without your people, our substance and strength over chaos diminishes."

If the fées' power was fading...Lys was afraid to voice her deepest fear, but she had to know about her daughters, if their sacrifice was the only way. "She demands my twin daughters to save my people."

"Ah, a choice, but not the only one." His eyes pierced her like a feathered arrow.

She looked down. "I love my children as I love the men whose seed quickened them in me. My daughters are not with me now, and my heart aches at their absence. I would have to bring them here, only to send them to their death." Lys held her hand over her heart.

One slender finger touched her upper arm. "Which do you think will save your people more? Sacrifice or love?"

She looked up at him and felt the hardness that edged into her words. "Neither. Strength against might will save them. Naught else."

"That is one of the reasons why you gave your promise," he said softly.

Lys stopped to catch her breath as they crested the dune but found she had no need to. "What is the choice, then?"

"To refuse the promise, you must give something in its place." He looked back over the still waters below them as he waited for her to consider.

"Another sacrifice."

He held his hands together on his breast, a gesture Lys interpreted as one of distress. "We do not serve the being with whom you made your bond. Nor are we at odds with it. It will seek to extract a lasting sacrifice. It is...vengeful."

"What should I do, then?"

"Make your choice. If you choose love, I will do what I can to lessen the repercussions of whatever it...she...decrees."

"You can do that?"

"I can but try."

Lys bore Gwened's son, her last child, in a lake of her own blood, and she lay near death for several days. The women took the baby from her to find a wet nurse. They tended her as best they could and spoke prayers to the gods over her. She recovered slowly with the help of strong meat broths and potions of bloodroot to ward off corruption. Upon learning that her newborn son was both hearty and hale, she rejoiced and chose life for herself and her children. As the celebration of the waning of the dark time approached, she walked longer and longer each day to regain her strength. Lys named her son Niece, which meant choice in the dialect of Gwened's people.

Her daughters were soon due to receive their first moonblood, and Lys knew she could wait no longer. The goddess would require her sacrifice no later than the New Year, of that she was certain. She went into the woods on her own to spend the night, purifying herself beforehand to prepare.

The dancing light came to her and drew her in.

This time the benign mother faced her. "You are known to us, Lys ab Gysell. The first part of your promise you have ably fulfilled. Now comes the time for the second. You must send for your daughters soon. Their blood belongs to me."

Lys stood erect before the goddess. "I will not sacrifice my daughters to you. But know this; I make the choice in love and not to spite you."

The young warrior sprang into view. She laughed and ended it in a terrifying cry. "Sacrifice you will, for you have given your word. Is this your final decision?"

Lys sank to her knees trembling in shame and fear. "Yes. I have chosen."

She had known something bad would happen but not that it would come so soon. Lys watched Gwened and his men leave with the rising sun to head off the vanguard of leather corseted Romans who had begun massing along the Treveri borders. She had watched as he stopped to speak to a gnarled old woman with long, stringy hair washing clothes by the river. A fat crow picked at the ground near the hag's feet. Lys had not heard the words they had spoken and none of the other men appeared to see the woman. Lys ran to warn him away from Cathubodua in her guise of Death, but it had been too late. The hag had sealed his fate.

The men who bore Gwened's body back on a bed of logs reported that the battle spirit had come upon him, and he had challenged the Roman warchief in single combat to decide their fate. Gwened's frenzy had enabled him to kill the man and hide his own fatal injury from the enemy until he had safely returned to his men. She shrieked over him as they set him down within the camp, her hands raking through the lime in his fair hair. Her sons stood near her and mourned in silence for the man who had raised them.

The veil of grief settled over her as she arranged for the party that would return Gwened's ashes to his home. It had seemed appropriate to cremate him in the Treveri style, as a large contingent of Treveri had arrived bringing gifts of weapons and gold to throw on the fire for Gwened's spirit. Offerings from the Romans had also been sent with an emissary. Lys included many valuable pieces of gold and Veneti glazed pottery to travel with Gwened to his eventual resting place.

She placed Gwened's ashes in an exquisite bronze cauldron she had received from the Treveri for that purpose and packed them with valuable iron tools and casks of wine. Songs of his deeds had already been composed for his homecoming. She instructed the men returning with Gwened's remains to tell Iaun that her daughters would remain with him and his people to maintain the alliance. Gwened's last act would not keep the thirsty wolves away for long.

Her father found her as she finished lining the crates with straw.

"You wanted to speak with the holy men about a sacrifice?"

Lys stood and laid a hand on his arm. "Yes, Vater. I need to talk to them before something else bad happens."

"They have sent an escort. They already await you." He turned away from her with a forlorn expression.

She staggered out of her session with the holy men in the deep forest, stunned but sure of her decision to tell them of Cathubodua and her oath. A priest guided her to his dwelling set into the base of the mountain. He prepared the potion she had requested and shut her in after she quaffed the *Trank*. Before long, the room darkened to a small pool of light that surrounded her as she knelt on the rough wooden floor.

Cathubodua stood before her wearing a blood red tunic under a coal black leather corset, her head held proud and hair streaming out to her sides like black birds in flight. "Why are you here?" she demanded.

"I offer myself to rid my children of their bond," Lys replied.

"I accept your offer, but will not release your children. You have sworn them to me."

"What do you mean?"

She pulled iron from her scabbard, a long and cruel looking blade that shone metallic red in the pale light. "You bound them with your oath. They must honor this. In return, my gifts remain."

"What will you do with them?"

"They must travel to *Ande-dubnos* as you have done. And perform their duties as the need arises." She laid the tip of the knife at Lys' neck and drew a tiny ribbon of blood. It dripped onto her hands as she knelt and her fingers trembled.

Lys kept herself still. "And after I am gone?"

She nodded once. "They will be called to me when their time arises to serve."

"This I cannot change. So I must accept it."

The young warrior scored a second red line on the other side of Lys' neck. Her voice became treacherously low. "I am aggrieved by the breaking of your bond to me."

"I offer my life in exchange."

She spat to the side in fury. "That is not enough."

Lys' head shot up in fear. She felt the skin on her neck tear and more blood drip down. "What more do you want?"

Cathubodua placed her sword across her bent knee as she knelt to cup Lys' chin in her hand. "Hear me well and tell them. I lay a geis upon you, Lys ab Gysell, and your ancestors from this day forward."

Lys' breath rasped sharply. "Forever? Nothing is forever."

"No. You have the right there. Nine times nine generations will sacrifice as you do now. Then I am appeased."

Nine times nine — forever in deed if not in name. "How will you extract it?"

"The women and men in your family, both Iaun's and Gwened's children, are now bound to love one another to keep the blood pure. That will be the way. All who breed true will retain the power. And the responsibility."

Lys exhaled a breath. "A merciful geis. My children will be bound to love each other. And to serve the goddess."

Her fierce smile with lips drawn back more resembled a dead man's than a living woman's. "They will love only blood of their blood and that is not all." She rose and cleaned her blade on her pants. "The women will carry their children to term. And then they will die. All those who breed true. Nine times nine it must be, in unbroken succession before the geis is lifted."

"Why?"

"Because," Cathubodua said as she rammed her sword through Lys' heart. "The breaking of a blood price needs to be paid in kind."

Lys woke before the dawn, surprised that she still drew breath but realized that such a death would have been far too easy to appease the raven queen. The door of the priest's hut had already been opened. She wandered into the village and heard the stirrings of life. A few minutes later her father approached her. His pallor as he held tight onto the hands of Gwened's children confirmed that he had learned her fate. She hugged them to her one last time before she sent them back to their hut.

"Tochter, I do not understand why you do this thing," he told her. "Do not throw away your life for nothing. It's not too late."

She laid her hands on his shoulders as she looked up to him. "Before Gwened died the hero's death, I would have agreed. But my duty is to my children and my people now. I have already doomed them to much suffering."

He shook his head. "What do you mean?"

She told him the tale of her pact with the warrior goddess all those years ago. "I was greedy and vain. I should have heeded my heart instead of my lust for power."

"Make another bargain with her." Her father's face reminded Lys of a crazed animal trying to free itself from a trap. "A father should not have to see his children cross over before him."

"And now you understand the reason for my choice." Lys smiled sadly. "She has placed a geis on the children."

He paled even further. "The children? Which ones?"

"All of my children, Vater. Her sword has two edges. The Raven has cursed them, but they will also be blessed with prosperity."

His jaws clenched as he fought back tears, and his look of hurt broke her heart. She sent him away before she prepared for her final journey.

The wind blew cold across the *Hohes Venn*. Lys faced the sunrise as she waited for the ritual to be completed and thought back on her life. She smiled at the good fortune she had been blessed with in spite of her folly. The priests tied her hands and feet together behind her back and laid the mesh of wood that would weigh her down next to her. One priest darted forward, intending to strike her with a club of stone, a ritual that honored the old gods, but the others held him back. She hobbled into the sediment-choked bog on her own.

Lys lay on her back as they attached the wood to her and tried to force back the panic that urged her to struggle. Once the wood became soaked it would hold her down in her watery grave. They pushed her into the thick muck and left her to sink into the abyss.

Eyes closed. The popping sound of earth saturated with water filled her ears. She heard someone calling her name. Lys opened her eyes. Her father stood over her with a *Trank* in his hand. She smiled at him and opened her mouth. He held her head up as she drank and when she had finished, he disappeared.

Lys relaxed her senses and let her mind escape the fen. After a time she felt nothingness come upon her. She rose and walked in search of Ankou. She found him sitting a short distance away, as if waiting for her. He stood and held out his hand as she approached.

"Come," he said. "I have prepared a place for you."

"And my children?"

Ankou bent to face her fully, his expression grave. "Those who must suffer will be guided as you have been. I will bring them."

Satisfied, she followed him into the depths of the *Anderwelt* to await the arrival of her sons and daughters, one after the other.

'The Raven's Curse' was initially inspired by several visits to Brittany and an appreciation for the unique culture that the Breton people are striving to maintain. Those experiences, in turn, sparked an intense fascination with the Continental Celts. The story idea grew out of a natural desire to flesh out the back-story for the Schattenreich fantasy series. The completed story provided an unexpected, but vital, facet to the series itself. And it was a terrific chance to write some historical fantasy. More such tales are planned.

Sharon Kae Reamer is an American seismologist working at the University of Cologne, Germany. Sharon writes speculative fiction and has recently finished her third (as yet unpublished) novel in the *Schattenreich* fantasy series (www.sharonreamer.com). In her spare time, she also works as an assistant editor for the e-zine *Allegory*. She lives with her husband, son and Ramses the cat, on the outskirts of Cologne.

Katharine Kerr

The Lass From Far Away

Eldidd, 1060

> *"You ask me if the gods truly exist. Consider this: human hands make a glass vessel, then fill it with mead. Does the bit of Rhwmani glass have power in itself? Of course not! Yet the mead will make many a strong man drunk."*
>
> ~ *The Secret Book of Cadwallon the Druid*

On a summer morning she walked out of the sea onto the beach near the town of Cannobaen. Water trickled down her pale brown face and oozed from her straight dark hair. Her thin linen shift stuck to her body, all skin and bone except for her swollen stomach. For a long time she stood, merely stood on the hot sand and looked at the cliffs with bewildered hazel eyes. With a sigh she sat down and continued studying the cliffs as if they might tell her what to do.

Some yards down the beach, black rocks jutted from the ebbing tide. With their long blue skirts tied half-way up their thighs, a woman and a half-grown lass were clambering over them to harvest the bright green seaweed, as fine and sleek as a horse's mane, that grew below the water line. The younger paused, straightened up to rest her back, and looked idly around her.

"Mam," Olwen said, "there's a castaway come out of the water."

The older woman balanced her basket of laver weed on one hip and looked where the younger pointed.

"By the gods!" Cobylla, the soapmaker's wife, said. "You're right enough. I'd not heard of any ships going down. Let's go see what we can do for the poor thing."

When they gained the dry beach they paused to untie their skirts, then slogged across the hot soft sand. Although they called out greetings, the lass never turned her head, not even when they reached her.

"Look at her!" Cobylla said. "Starved and exhausted, poor thing." She handed her basket to Olwen, then knelt in front of the lass. "Here now, lass. Let's get you to safety."

The lass raised her head and looked at her. Flies were crawling across her cheek. Cobylla reached out and flicked them away.

"From the look of her," Olwen said, "she doesn't understand a word you're saying. Here, her skin's brown. She must be from Bardek."

"You're right enough, and I'll wager she only speaks that nasty strange tongue of theirs. You've got the water bottle. Hand it over."

The bottle, made of leather boiled in wax, hung from a thong at Olwen's kirtle. She untied it, shaking it to judge how full it might be. At the sound of sloshing water the lass jerked her head around to stare, her cracked lips half-parted.

"Now she understood that sound well enough," Olwen said. "She must be near dead from thirst."

Cobylla took out the stopper and handed the bottle to the lass, whose hands shook so badly that she nearly dropped and spilled it. Cobylla grabbed it, then helped her hold it to her mouth. The lass drank in long gulps, pausing only to gasp for air, until the bottle ran dry. When she let go of the bottle, she whispered a few words. Although Olwen knew no Bardekian, she could guess that they added up to "my thanks".

"Well, now." Cobylla got up, shaking her head. "We can't leave her here." She held out a hand.

The lass hesitated, then slowly reached out and took the proffered hand. Cobylla pulled her up only to have her stagger and nearly fall. When Cobylla put an arm around her waist, the lass leaned against her.

"She's trembling, poor little thing," Cobylla said. "She'll never be able to reach the town."

"I'll run on ahead and fetch one of the men," Olwen said. "She'll be easy to carry, I wager. She's so thin."

Olwen, however, found help nearer to hand than back in Cannobaen. She crossed the beach, climbed the decrepit wooden stairway that snaked up the cliff, then at the top paused to catch her breath. A wild meadow crowned the cliffs with tall grass, stretching a good half a mile inland. A dirt road meandered through the meadow, and some yards along it Olwen saw a mule, tethered and grazing next to a big pile of canvas packs.

"The herbman!" she sang out. "Now this is a bit of luck!"

At the sound of her voice the herbman himself appeared, rising from the waist-high grass where he'd been kneeling. In one hand he held a trowel made of silvery metal and in the other, a clump of little green plants trailing muddy roots. He was a tall man with ice-blue eyes, an untidy thatch of white hair, and frog spots thick on his face and hands.

"And just why am I such a lucky sight?" he said. "Has someone been taken ill?"

"Indeed, good Nevyn, or stranger than ill," Olwen said. "My mam and me, we were a-gathering of the laver weed, and there was this castaway, come out of the water. She's half-dead, poor thing."

"Ye gods! Here, I've not heard of any shipwrecks."

"No more have I. It's a strange thing."

Nevyn tucked his trowel into the pocket of his muddy brown trousers, then walked with her to the edge of the cliff. Down on the beach, Cobylla had managed to get the lass to the foot of the stairs. When Olwen called out, Cobylla looked up and waved.

"She can't climb," Cobylla yelled up. "She's much too weak."

As if to prove the point, the Bardekian dropped to her knees on the sand with the suddenness of a sack of meal falling from a wagon.

"Here, hold this." Nevyn handed Olwen the clump of herbs.

The old man trotted down the steps with a vigor surprising in one his age. When he reached the women below, he picked the lass up as easily as if she'd indeed been that sack of meal. He said a few words to Cobylla, then carried the lass up the steps while Olwen watched, amazed. Cobylla followed more slowly, puffing and panting all the way. At the top Nevyn set the lass down in the grass; she stared up at him, seemed to be about to speak, then merely stared the more. Nevyn turned, reached down, and gave Cobylla a hand up over the edge. Cobylla put her laver basket down and began to wipe her sweaty face on the wide sleeve of her dress.

"Well, it was lucky, all right," Nevyn said to Olwen. "That I was here, I mean. You have my thanks for rescuing this poor child."

"Why?" Olwen said. "Is it that you know her or suchlike?"

"I don't. It's just that she's very near death."

"I did wonder about that." Olwen was about to ask more, but she glanced at Cobylla and found her mother waving a frantic hand behind Nevyn's back. Olwen knew that wave; it meant hold your tongue or get a good slap for disobeying. Still, she couldn't resist one more question. "She comes from far away, doesn't she?"

"Very far," Nevyn said. "Hand me back those herbs, and I'll just be taking them and her both back to the dun with me."

Olwen and Cobylla stood together and watched Nevyn saddle and fetch his mule. Although the canvas packs looked bulky, close up Olwen could see how lightly they sat on the animal's back. She held the mule's lead rope while Nevyn lifted the lass up and settled her behind the pack saddle. Olwen got her biggest surprise, though, when Nevyn spoke to the lass in the strange language: Bardekian, it had to be, because the lass answered him readily enough.

"Just telling her to hang on tight," Nevyn said to Olwen. "My thanks again, and we'll be off."

Nevyn strode away, leading the mule through the grass toward the road. The lass clung to the swaying canvas as the mule picked its way over the uneven ground.

"It's a good thing you held your tongue." Cobylla whispered. "I'd not have you prying into old Nevyn's affairs."

"What? Why not?"

"Why not, she says, and her my own daughter!" Cobylla rolled her eyes heavenward. "The old man's a sorcerer, that's why! Ask too many questions and get changed right into a frog, most like, or somewhat else nasty."

"So that tale's true, Mam? I'd heard it, but—"

"I've had it on the best authority, from Lady Lovyan's own maid. And would the noble-born be sheltering a common old herbman in their dun and treating him like a lord? Of course not! But Nevyn always takes our lady's hospitality when he's in Cannobaen, doesn't he? So, well, then, there you are!"

By this time Nevyn and his laden mule had reached the dirt road. Olwen stared, her mouth slack as a half-wit's, as they turned onto it, heading west, an ordinary old man leading an ordinary brown mule — but then, there was nothing ordinary about the lass from far away, and he had spoken to her in her own strange tongue.

"Come along," Cobylla snapped. "Let's get along home. We need to get this laver into brine before it shrivels in the heat."

Although Olwen followed her mother, she looked back every now and then until at last, Nevyn and his mule had passed beyond her sight.

Some miles west of town, Dun Cannobaen stood near the edge of the cliffs. In most ways it was a typical Deverry dun; a high stone wall enclosed a ward, cluttered with sheds and pig-sties, stables and a smithy, while in the middle rose a squat round broch tower. At the moment, a dragon pennant fluttered at the top of the broch to show that Lady Lovyan, wife to Gwerbret Tingyr of Aberwyn, was in residence. Outside the walls, however, rose a marvel: a slender tower some hundred and fifty feet tall, wound round by a flight of stone steps: the Cannobaen light. At night a lightkeeper tended a fire on top of the tower to warn ships of the dangerous shoals just off-shore.

Bardek merchant ships came close to wrecking themselves on those shoals even in good weather. In the winter, when the Cannobaen light guttered and turned faint in the driving winds and rain, a ship that left its departure too late in the year would come to grief, generally losing all hands. One summer storm had swept over Dun Cannobaen just a few days past, but fortunately the light had held steady, and no ships had foundered, not as far as Nevyn knew. The lass clinging to the pack saddle presented something of a mystery.

When Nevyn led his mule through the dun's gate, a page came running, followed by Lady Lovyan's youngest son. Lord Rhodry Maelwaedd hovered on the edge of manhood, a slender lad turned positively thin by a bad illness the winter past. Although he had the typical Eldidd coloring of raven-dark hair and cornflower blue eyes, he was unusually handsome, almost girlishly beautiful with a blush of tanned skin over his high cheekbones. He bowed to Nevyn, then stood staring at the lass.

"A castaway," Nevyn said, "or at least, she came out of the sea this morning. It looks like you've been taking the sun."

"I have," Rhodry said, "just as you ordered. Here, shall I carry that poor little lass inside for you?"

"I can carry her myself." Nevyn tossed him the leadrope of the mule. "You might stable Old Brown here for me. Just leave the packs on the pack saddle. I'll fetch them in a bit."

Rhodry may have been noble-born, but like everyone else in the dun, he did whatever Nevyn told him to do. The page hurried off to find Lady Lovyan. Nevyn lifted the Bardekian lass off the mule's back, then carried her inside to the great hall, a round chamber filling the entire ground floor of the broch. On opposite sides of the hall, a group of tables stood by a hearth, a battered and chipped cluster of plank tables and benches by the servants' and warband's hearth, a nicely polished table and chairs at the honor hearth.

At the servant's hearth a shabby lass stood stirring a simmering kettle that held stew from the smell of it. Too rich, Nevyn decided, for a patient who had starved for several days. He carried the lass over to the table of honor, set her down on a chair, then strode over to the opposite hearth.

"Is there breakfast porridge left?" he said.

"Always, my lord," the servant said.

"Fetch me a bowlful, will you? But water it down. It needs to be very thin."

When Nevyn returned to the table of honor, he found the castaway sitting in the straw on the floor.

"Here!" he said in Bardekian. "Wasn't that chair comfortable enough?"

"I can't sit there." She whispered so softly that he had to lean over to hear her.

"You were told you had to sit below any free man or woman?"

She nodded.

"What's your name, girl?"

She never answered, merely stared at the straw on the floor. Nevyn would have continued questioning her, but Lady Lovyan was coming down the winding stairway in the center of the great hall. This stairway was a piece of dwarven work, and something of a marvel in itself, a tight spiral of iron rather than the usual stone.

Although she'd grown stout over the years, Lovyan was still a handsome woman with just one thick streak of gray in her dark hair. That morning she'd dressed in blue, with a kirtle in the blue and green plaid of Aberwyn round her waist. She stood by the chair at the head of the table of honor and considered the lass, who kept her gaze firmly on the floor.

"So this is our castaway?" Lovyan said. "The poor child!"

"She is," Nevyn said. "She's utterly exhausted."

"No doubt." Lovyan paused to sit down, smoothing her dresses under her. "We had that one bad storm, but I certainly haven't heard of any shipwrecks. She comes from far away, doesn't she?"

"She does," Nevyn said. "Bardek, in fact. Fortunately I know their language. I studied physick there some years back."

"Fortunate, indeed! Do tell her she's safe here."

"I already have. She's either too drained to speak much, or she's simply not willing to tell me her name. Huh." He paused to consider the problem. "Now, if there wasn't any shipwreck, she may have simply fallen from the deck or even jumped. I do know she was a slave. There's a brand right there on the back of her neck."

Lovyan winced with a little shudder of disgust. The lass sat stone-still between them on the floor, her hands clasped in her lap and her gaze fixed on the empty air. When Nevyn opened the second sight, he could see that her pale grey aura hung shrunken around her — except in one location. Around her swollen belly flickered light of a silvery-blue.

The servant hurried over, carrying a wooden bowl. She curtsied to her ladyship, handed Nevyn the bowl, and scurried off again. Nevyn inspected the bowl — lukewarm oat porridge, liberally swirled with butter and thinned with boiled water — then knelt beside the girl.

"Can you swallow a spoonful of this?" he said in Bardekian. "It's very smooth and should go down easily, even with your mouth so cracked and sore."

When he held out a full spoonful, she turned her head away.

"Come now, surely you must be starved after being in the water for so long."

She neither moved nor spoke.

"You're with child." Nevyn brought out his best weapon. "Do you want your child to die?"

She jerked her head up.

"I won't hurt you," Nevyn went on. "No one here is going to turn you over to your master. You're escaping from slavery, aren't you?"

At that she looked up and turned toward him. When he held out the spoon again, she took the mouthful. Her lips moved as she chewed the food and swallowed it.

"No," she spoke at last. "Not escaping." She smiled, but there was something terrifying in that smile, her thin lips drawn back from strong white teeth, her eyes far too wide and unblinking. "There's no escaping now."

"Well, we'll just see about that! If they come looking for you, they'll have our ladyship's troop of soldiers to deal with."

Nevyn offered her another spoonful, which she took. When she held out her hands, he gave her the bowl. She continued eating, but slowly, carefully, pausing between each bite.

"Why won't you tell me your name?" Nevyn said during one of these pauses.

"I have no name."

"Come now, surely they must have called you something!"

"Before, I was Evy."

"Before what?"

She took another spoonful of the porridge and looked away. Nevyn waited, but she held to her silence until she'd finished the porridge. She handed him the bowl and spoon.

"Thank you." She folded her hands in her lap.

"Do you want more water?" Nevyn said.

"Please."

The page, all goggle eyes and curiosity, brought a tankard of water. She held it in both hands to drink in cautious sips.

"Now, you won't be able to eat much at one time for a few days," Nevyn said. "But I'll make sure you get plenty of food. We don't want you dying, after all."

"Oh, I'm already dead." She looked at him, then began to laugh, a high-pitched hysterical giggle.

When Nevyn grabbed her by the shoulders, she fell silent, but her eyes once again grew wide with terror. An animal in a trap, Nevyn thought. His own eyes began to ache until at last she blinked and released them both.

"Why did you say that?" Nevyn made his voice as soft and gentle as he could.

She turned her head away, then lifted the tankard again and resumed drinking. Nevyn stood up with a shrug.

"I'd be hysterical, too," Lovyan said, "if I'd been adrift at sea for days."

"So would I, most like," Nevyn said. "But I think me somewhat stranger's at work here, my lady. I've got an idea of what it might be, but I hope to every god that I'm wrong."

The dun's servants normally slept out in the stables or in front of one of the hearths in the great hall. Considering how frail Evy was, Lovyan decided that she should sleep in a little storeroom off the women's hall on the second floor of the main broch, a tiny wedge-shaped space, but it would do. A page carried up a straw mattress; one of Lovyan's serving women gave the girl an old dress of hers. Nevyn found a big earthernware pitcher and filled it full of fresh water to place beside the mattress on the floor.

"I want you to drink as much water as you can," he told Evy. "There's a chamber pot over in the curve of the wall for you to use when you need to."

The lass nodded to show she'd understood. She was sitting on the mattress, with the faded blue dress billowing around her, her legs crossed, her arms tight over her chest, as crumpled and crouched as if she expected him to suddenly turn and strike her. Nevyn glanced around the chamber, which smelled of dust and mildew, and saw a narrow window covered by an ox hide pegged to the wall. He took down the hide to let in fresh air and a sliver of sunlight.

"Thank you." Evy's voice took him by surprise. "For everything you've done for me."

"Most welcome." Nevyn left the window and knelt at the foot of the mattress. "Will you tell me how you came to be in the water?"

She considered for so long that he assumed she'd say nothing, but at last she caught her breath with a gasp and spoke. "They threw me in for a sacrifice."

"Because of the storm?"

"Yes. The waves grew so big, and the sky — oh, it looked like night, so dark and close the clouds were. The captain said the ship was doomed, but some of the sailors, they said they could turn the Veiled Lady aside if they gave her a sacrifice." Her voice dropped to a whisper. "A bone for the bitch, one of them said."

"And they chose you for the sacrifice because you were a slave."

"Yes."

"I saw where they branded you, on your back where it wouldn't spoil your face. They used you as a whore, didn't they?"

Her eyes filled with tears. "Please don't tell the archon," she whispered. "She'll throw me out."

"You mean Lady Lovyan. Don't worry. She understands what men do to the women they own, and she'd never blame you. They were going to sell you to a brothel in Abernaudd?"

"No, in Cerrmor. But the storm drove us off-course. I was so ill by then, with the ship tossing around and the waves — oh, they came right over the deck, and so cold! I thought it would be better to die than to go — to go where they were taking me."

"You'd never been in a brothel before?"

"I was, yes, in Myleton. But this one in Cerrmor — I was born there." She raised her head and looked straight at him. Her eyes flickered briefly with defiance and life. "A man killed my mother there. I didn't want to go back. So I thought, better I go to the goddess now."

"I see. Did they do some sort of ceremony?"

She nodded, looking away wide-eyed, as if she saw it all again, the careening deck of the ship, the sail flapping helplessly in the wind, the waves breaking and foaming as they ran across the fragile planks, the terrified men chanting what spells and charms they knew. Nevyn could imagine the scene all too well.

"One of the passengers said he knew how to do it. They were going to drag me up to the bow, but I walked. Do you see? I wanted to die, just then. I walked with them, and I lay down where they told me to lie."

"I understand."

"They were going to bind my hands, but then this big wave came and just swept me away. I thought I was going to sink and die, but the waves kept tossing me up into the air." She paused, trembling, and raised her hands to clasp her face. "That's when I saw her."

"The Veiled Lady?"

She nodded again. "She came walking on the water, so big her head touched the sky, and she was turning and turning like she was dancing. All her veils spun around her, and they were black."

A cloud? Nevyn wondered. A waterspout, perhaps, off at a distance? Or had the terror of the men onboard and the lass in the water evoked the image of the Bardekian death goddess?

"And that's when I saw the wood floating toward me," Evy went on. "It was old and gray, part of a broken ship. I didn't realize that till later, you see, when I had time to look at it. But she brought me the wood, so I climbed onto it. She went away then. And so the storm passed, and I drifted, and days and days went by, I think." Her voice trailed away. "Maybe only three days."

"It couldn't have been many more than that, or you'd have died of thirst." He smiled and turned his voice soothing. "But you didn't, and now you're safe."

Behind him something rustled, something moved. Nevyn looked over his shoulder and saw birds settling on the windowsill, three big ravens, their black plumage glittering with blue in the summer sun. He felt his blood run cold.

Evy cried out. "Safe? No, never that, never again!"

Nevyn got to his feet and turned to face the Three.

"You can't have the child," he said. "It wasn't dedicated to you."

The answer came to his mind without sound. We know.

Nevyn turned so cold that he shivered and swore under his breath. With a cascade of croaks and caws that sounded like laughter, the three ravens leapt from the sill and flew, still shrieking. As they climbed into the sky they seemed to merge into one huge raven, then vanished. Behind him Evy began to weep in great gulping sobs.

"She sent her birds," she stammered. "I belong to her, and she'll never let me go."

"We'll just see about that! There must be a way to break the curse. Maybe she'll accept a horse instead."

She choked back her sobs. Next to her on the floor lay her old rag of a dress, still crusted with salt in odd patches. She picked it up and began wiping her face on a sleeve.

"I'll have to think about this," Nevyn went on. "I've learned some strange lore over the years."

Evy smiled, though her eyes stayed so blank and lifeless that he knew she doubted him. Since he doubted himself, Nevyn said no more, merely left the chamber to let her sleep.

That night he consulted with other dweomermasters he knew, scrying them out for mind-speaking through the fire in his chamber, but no one knew how to break such a ritual spell. When Nevyn contacted Nesta, a dweomerwoman who lived in Cerrmor, she told him that as far as the guilds knew, no ship had gone down in the recent storm.

"If one had," Nesta said, "the guild would have heard of it, especially one bound for Cerrmor. News like that travels fast."

"So the goddess accepted the sacrifice. Or so the crew of that ship's going to believe."

"There had to be a man of some power onboard that ship," Nesta went on. "Ordinary sailors can curse and pray and beg all night in a storm, but their ship goes down despite it all."

"That's true spoken. The lass mentioned a passenger."

"Huh! I wonder what sort of man he was. Not one of us, I'll wager."

"Just so. He seems to have worked some sort of rite with power behind it, for a certainty. I was wondering if the priestesses in a Moon temple could undo it."

"I doubt if they'd want to. Once their goddess has spoken, they wouldn't dare interfere." Nesta hesitated, and he could feel her thoughts scurrying this way and that. "The goddess isn't known for letting anyone out of a bargain."

"Unfortunately, you're right. And the lass went willingly enough at the time. Hence the ravens, I suppose."

"I'd say so, truly. I doubt me if there's aught anyone can do, though it aches my heart to admit it."

It ached Nevyn's as well. He found himself remembering a Moon-sworn priestess he'd known back in the years of the civil wars that had once torn the kingdom apart. Nothing that he'd said or done back then had changed her mind and her grim wyrd one jot. Yet, he reminded himself, perhaps things would be different with this lass. He had four or five months, he reckoned, until the baby was born, to figure out a remedy.

Late into the night he consulted his books of dweomerlore but found nothing to help. He did string some beads and little packets of herbs onto leather thongs. If she believed that they'd turn aside evil, the belief would give her strength to resist the curse upon her, even though they had no dweomer power of their own. What counted now was bringing her mind back to the land of the living. In the morning, when he gave Evy the charms, she accepted them as politely as she'd accepted everything else, but from her flat little voice he could tell that she didn't believe in them.

"Once we go back to Aberwyn in the autumn," Nevyn told her, "I'll consult with the priests and priestesses there about lifting the curse."

Evy sighed and looked down at her handful of charms. "When I die," she said, "will someone take care of my baby?"

"Of course, but I'm not going to let you die."

She merely smiled. Before he left her chamber, he insisted she wear the charms. She slipped them over her head and let them dangle with all the enthusiasm of a dutiful child swallowing a bitter medicinal.

Over the next few days, Evy grew stronger, thanks to decent food and rest. At that time, a lord who supported a great many servants gained prestige. Gwerbret Tingyr had many faults, but miserliness was not one of them. Lovyan had so many servants at Dun Cannobaen, her summer residence, that none of them worked very hard. All of them took an interest in the lass so miraculously saved from the sea, particularly when her pregnancy became common knowledge. Their small kindnesses acted as further remedies, giving Evy reasons to want to live, or so Nevyn could hope.

The little town of Cannobaen had heard her tale as well.

One foggy day Nevyn came out into the ward to see Rhodry lounging against the wall by main gate and talking with Olwen, the soapmaker's daughter. Rhodry was smiling at her in a way that boded ill for the lass's virtue while she giggled and glanced at him sidelong. With a sigh Nevyn strolled over to speak with them. Rhodry straightened up and arranged a solemn expression. Olwen looked modestly at the ground.

"Come for news of little Evy?" Nevyn said.

"I have, my lord," Olwen said. "My mam was wondering how she fared, and so is half the town."

"Ah, I see. Well, she's doing very well, remarkably well, in fact, considering what she suffered. I have hopes that her baby will be healthy enough to live despite it all."

"That's splendid, my lord."

"So it is. Now run along, and tell your mother that I'll give her any news the next time I ride down to town. No need for you to walk all the way up here."

"My thanks, my lord, I'm sure." Yet Olwen looked bitterly disappointed.

Nevyn waited until she'd left, waited in fact until she'd got out of earshot, then turned on Rhodry.

"I know what you're thinking," Rhodry said with a squeak in his voice.

"Do you?" Nevyn said. "Then I suggest you remember that a common-born lass like that has little to look forward to in life but a good marriage, and if you trifle with her, it's not likely she'd ever get one."

"I do know that. I — uh — I'll take it to heart."

Rhodry made him a bob of a bow, then turned and hurried away, breaking into a trot, then disappearing around the side of the broch at an all-out run. Nevyn made a mental note to speak with Olwen's mother next time he went to Cannobaen about more than the state of Evy's health.

With the first chill of autumn, Lovyan packed up her retinue and returned to the gwerbretal dun in Aberwyn. Although Evy and most of the other servants stayed behind, Nevyn travelled with her ladyship. He wanted to ferret out information about the ritual that had bound Evy to the dark aspect of the goddess. She of the sword-pierced heart, she who sees the world with the eyes of night — at times she seemed to look out of Evy's eyes as well.

By that time Aberywn had grown large enough to shelter several holy temples. Nevyn visited them all. The priests of Bel told Nevyn that they knew nothing of such women's matters. The priest of Wmm did know of the ritual, but he assured Nevyn that its details lay hidden, even from the scholar-priests on the Holy Isle of Wmmglaedd. Nevyn could practically smell the fear oozing from the various holy men when they spoke of the Dark Goddess. The priestesses of the Moon, who most likely knew a great deal, sent him brusquely away for daring to question their goddess's doings.

"No help, no lore, naught," Nevyn said to Lovyan. "A useless lot, these priests."

"So it seems." Lovyan paused for an exasperated sigh. "I'm shocked at those sailors, I truly am. Most Bardekians are such civilized people."

"Just so. Still, terror will make men do barbaric things. No doubt they felt it was her life or theirs."

"Well, that does seem likely, but still, I can't help despising them for it."

"Me, either."

"If you want a horse for a sacrifice, I'm sure I can get Tingyr to give you one."

"My thanks, but it wouldn't do any good, even if I could find a blasted priest willing to get off his behind to work the ritual. The men on shipboard offered the Dark Goddess a human life, and despite the nasty way the Moon priestesses spoke to me, I did glean that a human life is what She'll demand."

Nevyn returned to Dun Cannobaen in a foul temper. Seeing Evy, oddly enough, only fed his bad mood, simply because she looked well and strong, a good stone heavier, with rosy cheeks and glossy hair. She should be looking forward to a long life, he thought. Those cursed cowardly priests! But she still looked on the world from some great distance away. Although she smiled from time to time, no answering spark flashed in her eyes. Whenever anyone spoke to her, she was as courteous and as reserved as some great lady making her way through a foreign court.

As the winter settled down over the dun, keeping the Cannobaen light burning became the center of everyone's life, from the chamberlain who held his authority from Lovyan herself down to the lowliest forester who brought in a mule-load of firewood. Evy worked in the kitchen, scrubbing pots and chopping turnips, doing whatever the cook asked with her unvarying politeness and complete lack of interest in the life around her. She rarely spoke, or so the cook told Nevyn, even though she was learning how to speak Deverrian remarkably fast and well.

"She told me once that she was born in Cerrmor," Nevyn said. "So she probably had a child's knowledge of the language before she was taken away. I don't know how she ended up a slave in Bardek, though some very poor people have been known to sell their daughters to slavers."

"Huh!" Cook hefted a cleaver and glared over the blade. "Just let that lot come around here!" She laid it down again. "Poor little mite! She never laughs, never weeps. Ye gods, at times I'd swear she was asleep, but she keeps right on working." She shook her head. "Mayhap it's the baby, but I've never seen a lass taken quite this way."

"She seems to want the baby, though," Nevyn said.

"True spoken. That's the one thing that brings life to her eyes, like, mentioning the baby. It kicked her a good one the other day."

"Did it now? Her time must be drawing near, then." And my time to save her, he thought, is nearly gone.

On a day when pale sun broke through the clouds and made the rain-washed stones of the dun shimmer, Evy and the cook's young daughter went outside to the ward to fill storage jars with well water. Nevyn climbed the catwalks up to the top of the dun wall where he could get a bit of fresh air and keep the two lasses in view. Anyone who saw him would have thought he was lost in thought, just from his slow walk, his hands clasped behind his back, his head bent as he paced back and forth on the wide stones, but he was studying Evy. When he opened his second sight, he could see her aura, a pale greenish gray like the tarnish on silver. It wrapped tightly around her body — except over her womb. The aura of the child within glowed a pale gold like a lantern inside a basket, strengthening its mother's own aura at that point.

After all the months of decent food, rest, and even companionship, her aura still flickered at the point of death. Yet she'd never displayed the slightest symptom of a disease. Nevyn remembered an odd bit of lore he'd picked up in Bardek. None of their learned masters of physick would have spoken about the aura, since none of them had studied dweomer. However, one master had talked to him about "the vital force". It could be drained from below by the body, Master Hanno had said, or from above, by a disturbance of the soul.

That night, after everyone in the dun but the lightkeeper had gone to bed, Nevyn retired to his chamber just above the women's hall. He lay down on his bed, crossed his arms over his chest, and summoned his body of light, a man-shaped creation of bluish-silvery astral substance, joined to his physical body by a silver cord. When he transferred his consciousness over to it, he could see with astral eyes, a far more powerful dweomer than the etheric second sight. All around him the stone walls of the dun glistened black. Outside the window the air pulsed with flecks of silver light, and the stars had grown huge and swollen, hovering over the earth.

Nevyn drifted out of the window in his chamber and sank down until he came to one of the windows of the women's hall. He could pass right through the oxhide covering and sail across the hall, where the wooden furniture and floor covering of woven rushes still gleamed with traces of the red-brown vegetable aura that their materials had extruded in life. Evy had left the door of her little chamber open. Nevyn drifted in, took up a position at the ceiling, and studied her sleeping body. What he saw shocked him so much that he nearly snapped back to his own body in the chamber upstairs.

He steadied himself in his body of light, then sank down a few feet in order to see more clearly. He could barely discern her aura and that of the child through the black astral tangle around her. Like a huge cloud of thorns, black spiky lines surrounded her and dug through the greenish glow of her aura into her flesh. With sharp tendrils they grew into or perhaps out of her etheric double, binding her round, imprisoning her in a web of darkness, sucking life and light from her aura and from, or so it seemed, her very soul. The ritual had netted its prey for the Dark Goddess, sure enough.

Nevyn left the chamber and floated back to his physical body. He glided down the silver cord, reunited consciousness and flesh, then banished the body of light. For a long while he lay still, thinking over the vision. He had seen his defeat, and it sickened him. He could never banish those black forces without harming her. If he went back to the astral to strip them away, her life-force would gush out and bleed along with them, just as pulling a barbed spear out of a warrior's side will rip out his life by making the wound ten times the worse.

At length he got up and went over to the window; he pulled back the oxhide covering and leaned onto the sill. Although the winter air bit him with cold fangs, it was a clean thing, natural and pure, unlike what he'd seen in the chamber below. He wanted to scream his frustration into the wind and fill the sky with curses. Instead he took a deep breath and calmed himself. With the physical cold of the night air came the touch of another sort of chill — an omen warning, that somehow Evy herself presaged — something. As usual, the omen flickered in shadow rather than displayed itself in plain light. Somehow, some time, perhaps soon, perhaps years away, something or someone related to her would come his way, and it would bring more evil with it.

"My curse upon whoever did this to her!" Nevyn said to the wind. "Blow him evil! May he rot in the lowest hell!"

Distantly he heard ravens, cawing in what sounded to his ears as triumph, though they rarely if ever flew during the night. With a snarl Nevyn stepped back and let the oxhide flap down over the window, shutting out the cold and their chatter both.

Not long after, on the shortest day of winter, when a storm raged around Cannobaen, the cook and the groom's wife helped Evy deliver a baby boy, as small and delicate as his mother, but healthy withal. When they brought Nevyn in to have a look the pair, he saw life in Evy's eyes for the first time as she smiled down at her newborn, whom she named Mor, meaning 'ocean'. Over the next few weeks, however, as her strength returned from the childbirth, her reserve returned with it, except when she was nursing or otherwise tending the baby.

"He's the one joy in her life," Cook told Nevyn. "My daughter's fair taken with the lad, too. She tends him when Evy's about her work."

"But otherwise—"

"Ye gods, Evy goes about as if she's half-dead, the poor mite!"

That's because she is, Nevyn thought, but aloud he merely voiced a few platitudes about time and the healing of wounds.

Yet though time passed at Dun Cannobaen, Evy grew no stronger. In late spring, about the time when Evy's son Mor was eating his first solid food, Lady Lovyan and her retinue returned to Dun Cannobaen for an extended visit, riding in late one damp afternoon. Gwerbret Tingyr would join her, she told Nevyn, to take the sea air, once he'd adjudged the spring crop of legal cases.

"He's not well, Tingyr," Lovyan said. "I'm glad he's coming here, so you can have a look at him."

"He won't listen to me," Nevyn said, "no matter what I advise him to do."

"You're right, of course, but at least I'll know what's wrong. That will be some comfort."

They were sitting at the table of honor in the great hall just before the dinner hour. A servant lass brought them a basket of fresh bread, a tankard of dark ale for Nevyn, and a silver cup of Bardek wine for Lovyan.

"Welcome back, my lady," the lass said with a curtsy.

"My thanks." Lovyan favored her with a smile, then turned in her chair to glance around the great hall. "Ah, there's Cook's daughter with a baby. His skin is so dark! Is that little Evy's child?"

"He is, my lady."

Omen cold gripped Nevyn with icy hands. "Where's Evy herself?" he said.

"Taking the lightkeeper's dinner up to him, my lord."

Taking the dinner up a hundred and fifty slippery steps at twilight — Nevyn shoved his chair back, leapt up, and ran out of the great hall. He charged across the ward, scattering dogs and servants as he ran, darted out the gates, and raced to the foot of the tower. The omen-cold made him shiver, but Evy was already coming down, swinging an empty dinner-pail in one hand, walking slowly, carefully, step by step. When he looked up at the sky, he saw three dark bird-shapes wheeling just under the pale gray clouds, but they were too distant for him to identify them as ravens. He waited, his heart knocking and raging in his chest, until at last she gained the ground and safety.

"Is somewhat wrong?" Evy said to him. "You look ill, my lord."

"Naught of the sort." Nevyn let out his breath in a long sigh. "I'd just as soon you let someone else take the lightkeeper's dinner up to him after this, however."

She cocked her head to one side and looked so sincerely puzzled that he felt a flare of hope. Perhaps she'd decided to live, after all. Perhaps he could find some way to help her.

In the morning the rain broke. The storm clouds began to clear when a strong south wind blew in, driving them off to the north. Nevyn got a bowl of porridge for his breakfast and took a seat near one of the windows of the great hall. A manservant pulled up the oxhide cover and let a shaft of sunlight fall across the table.

"Most welcome, that is," Nevyn said. "My thanks."

The servant smiled, then hurried away to speak to the chamberlain. When Nevyn glanced at the staircase, he saw Evy just coming down the tight spiral of the iron stairs. The cook's young daughter came after, carrying the baby for her, and that act of kindness doomed Evy. In a flash of fear Nevyn shoved back his chair and stood just as ravens shrieked outside the window, three long raucous cries. Startled, Evy took a quick step back and missed the stair. Without making a sound, she tumbled from the high spiral of the stairway and fell with the crack of bone against iron and a hard grunt of breath as she hit the floor.

Cook's daughter screamed. The baby began to wail and sob. Nevyn rushed over, but Evy lay dead on the stone floor, her head twisted at an impossible angle. Blood oozed through her dark hair. She had hit her head and broken her neck in one swift blow. The Goddess was merciful, Nevyn thought, such mercy as the Dark One has.

"No doubt she felt very little," Nevyn told Lovyan that night. "She must have died in an instant."

"It's still very sad," Lovyan said. "What about the child? Can we find him a wetnurse?"

"Cook says he's old enough to survive on porridge and boiled milk and the like now." That's why the ravens held off for all these months, Nevyn thought to himself. They knew they couldn't let the lad die of hunger.

"Well, a wetnurse would be better, at least to feed him once a day or so." Lovyan paused to wipe a few tears from her eyes. "If you ever find out who worked that spell over our poor castaway, I'll have Tingyr arrest and hang him."

"That would gladden my heart, indeed. But to all intents and purposes, Lovva, she came to us from the Otherlands, and now, alas, she's gone back there to stay."

Afterword

The material that I have shaped, over the years, into the *Deverry* novels has always had a life of its own. 'The Lass from Far Away' really should have been part of the revised *Daggerspell* in order to lead into the revised *Darkspell*. I did the revisions back in the late 1980s. Unfortunately, 'Lass' didn't make an appearance until 2008, a bit on the late side to fit into my plans. I make no pretence of understanding why or how these things get written, except to point out the obvious, that fiction doesn't proceed from the rational part of the mind.

Biography

Katharine Kerr spent her childhood in a Great Lakes industrial city and her adolescence in Southern California, from whence she fled to the San Francisco Bay Area just in time to join a number of the Revolutions then in progress. After fleeing those in turn, she became a professional storyteller and an amateur skeptic, who regards all True Believers with a jaundiced eye, even those who true-believe in Science. An inveterate loafer, baseball addict, and rock and roll fan, she begrudgingly spares time to write novels, including the *Deverry* series of historical fantasies or fantastical histories, depending on your point of view. She lives near San Francisco with her husband of many years and some cats.

Peter Bell

The Trinket

They burned Gederus in the yard outside the barracks. Dawn had brought the first break in rain for ten days and the men, still cold and filthy from the construction work, cast anxious glances at the black weight of cloud that threatened to stamp out and drown the struggling flames. Those closest to the pyre stole a guilty pleasure from its warmth.

All except Rufinius, who stood to attention at the head of the bonfire, his nostrils thick with the smell of pitch and roasting meat.

"This man was the best of us!" His voice cracked open the still air. "A leader of men and a soldier of Rome! Today, we honor him."

He nodded to the priests, who stepped forward and began reciting the prayers for the dead. Rufinius did not listen. Instead, he narrowed his eyes against the smoke and surveyed the army standing ready around him. A full century of men, their plate armor dull and glassy in the pale sunlight, the auxiliary soldiers and craftsmen standing in a looser huddle farther out. Surrounding them all, the fledgling town of Isca Augusta rose black and skeletal from the churned clay of the earth.

He tried to ease some circulation back into his toes and felt the pendant shift beneath his tunic. He could be rid of it in an instant, he realized. Just throw it on the fire with the other offerings and never mind what the woman might say. But even before he saw her, watching him from the crowd, he realized it was nothing more than a lazy idea. He had come too far and done too much to just throw the thing away.

She stood at the rear of the crowd, one face among hundreds, but her unwavering stare stood out like a beacon, fixing him with an intensity that made him look away.

With a slight start, he realized the priests had finished their ministrations and the men were waiting for him to continue. He cleared his throat.

"You won't get far."

It was a winter's day in Londinium, the snow still thick on the ground, but if she felt the cold at all, she did not show it. Instead, she picked her way down the temple steps, her raven hair dusted with gray, watching him with a steady, almost bored eye that nevertheless made him pull himself up, as though he were being studied.

"Rome is a long way, and the emperor's justice travels more quickly than a deserter. You'll never reach the coast."

An incriminating flash of shame took hold of him. "You're mad, old woman! I'm not going anywhere except to my bunk. Away with you!"

She laughed, and it was a sound like knives being drawn. He turned hurriedly away.

"You think you're the first?"

She followed a few steps behind him, speaking loud enough for one or two passersby to turn their heads in her direction. He quickened his pace.

"I must have seen a legion's worth of young men pay their offerings to your gods, all of them crying for their homelands." She laughed again. "Your gods aren't much use here, I'm afraid."

Her words had the bite of truth to them. He had made landfall in Britannia two days ago, one of a boatload of raw recruits sent to bolster the Second Augustan Legion before its westward march to face the Celts, and already he hated the place. It wore the stamp of the empire badly, like an ugly child playing in a beautiful woman's clothes.

The march from the coast had been a miserable affair shrouded in a freezing fog through which the bare trees, frozen marshlands and craven daylight that seemed to make up this wretched island, could just be discerned.

The natives were little better. Like the land that supported them, they were drained of color and vivacity, their ghostly complexions criss-crossed with tattoos, like swollen veins. He imagined them eating its food and drinking its water, digging the very essence of the place out of the frozen soil and consuming it, contaminating themselves until even their blood ran gray.

He began pining for the sweep and plunge of the hill country where he had spent his life working the baked russet soil in the shade of the ash trees. And by the time the gates of Londinium came into view, he had made up his mind — he had to get out.

The woman approached him, swinging her hips in a mockery of a flirtatious swagger. Her accent and dress were Celtic, although her clothes were the finest he had seen in months, and her Latin was flawless.

"You've made up your mind to leave."

"I haven't."

She began circling him closely, her bare shoulder rubbing his sleeve.

"You have. And I can help you. But I need you to do something for me in return."

Her eyes were fierce and unblinking, the faint smile still in place beneath them. They had found whatever they had been looking for in him, he realized, and she was awaiting his response.

"I don't want your help," he said, resuming his course. He would have to leave before the night watch began and they barred the gates.

"Warm clothes, food and safe passage as far as Rome," she called after him. "To the very gates of Caesar's palace, if that's what you want."

He walked on, slow and deliberate, the town holding its breath in the crisp air.

"In exchange for what?" he asked, finally turning back.

Her smile broadened. "I'll show you."

The sun was failing and the snow reflected the purple taint of the sky as they approached the edge of the woods. Firelight burned strongly from within, painting blocks of shadow across the ground and a hum of voices could be heard, broken by an incongruous series of grunts and slaps. A cheer went up. Something moved against the flames.

Following the woman, Rufinius emerged in a circular clearing lit by a trio of bonfires. A crowd of people stood in a loose ring around its fringes, watching two naked, glistening figures as they grappled in the centre.

The woman did not wait for him, but found a space from which to observe the contest. A little awkwardly, he took up a position at her shoulder.

The two fighters pulled apart and, in the second before they slammed back together, he was able to make out their features. One of them was a Celt, his face flowing with blood and tattoos, his hair spiked in the style of a warrior.

The other man was Gederus.

Despite his brief spell in the settlement, he had already acquired the faintest trace of the awe in which the other legionaries held the man.

"He's afraid of nothing," they all whispered. "Throttled a Vandal chieftain with his bare hands. Going to be a Centurion before another year's out."

It was easy to believe. He was like a bear, standing a head taller than anyone else in the legion and even now had his opponent backing in unsteady circles around the clearing. A feint, a quick step, and he seized his prey, locking the man's arms within his own. The crowd babbled excitedly, money and tokens changing hands.

"Stop him."

The woman was at his ear, watching the Celt strain against Gederus as she might a stage play or a feat of acrobatics. He recognized it as the seasoned gaze of an expert critic.

"Why? He's winning a fair fight."

"Not the Roman. The Celt. He will become desperate, take up a rock and kill your legionary."

He tried to laugh, but her tone was businesslike.

"How can you possibly know that?"

"I know battle. The nature of it drives me; its quality sustains me and — there!" She thrust a pointing finger towards Gederus. "See what he wears!"

True enough, he saw that Gederus was not entirely naked after all; something gold winked in the hollow between his pectoral muscles.

"That pendant was mine once," she said, her voice betraying the first traces of emotion. "I gave it to the man I loved, on the eve of a great war. He never returned. Now your legionary wears it for luck." She sneered. "It's nothing but a bauble to him. A trinket." And with astonishing strength she gripped Rufinius' forearm and trained her fierce eyes on his. "Steal it for me."

He tried to pull free but her fingers bit deeper.

"I have come a long way in search of this," she hissed. "If the legionary dies now, they will burn him with it, or use it to pay for the cremation. If I lose my prize, you will lose my favor."

Her words sent a cold prickle of doubt crawling through him. "You really are mad," was all he could manage.

The Celt was weakening, his hands planted on the ground as he tried to throw Gederus off. His arms trembled and gobs of saliva dropped freely from his mouth.

Rufinius looked around wildly, unable to pull free of her grasp, hoping desperately that none of the others had recognized him.

"Do this for me," she intoned, "and you will never have to beg for work from those ignorant farmers again."

He flinched. "How do you—?"

There was a gasp from the crowd and he looked up in time to see Gederus fall backwards, clutching his face. The Celt sprang up, a shard of rock raised to strike, but Rufinius was moving, suddenly free of the woman, his feet leaving the ground as he caught the man by the waist and drove him to the dirt. The stone clattered to a stop between them.

There was an instant of shocked incomprehension. Then the warrior lunged for the stone.

Neither man saw Gederus coming; there was just the flash of steel and a wet *smack* as the short sword punctured the Celt's neck, locking his body in a single, agonizing convulsion. A gush of blood escaped the man's nose and a short, sharp exclamation — almost a laugh — burst from his lips. Then, with a grinding of bone, Gederus twisted the blade and he was dead.

"Put this thing on the fire," he commanded the crowd, now watching in silence. Then, reaching out a hand, he hauled Rufinius to his feet. "Thank you, friend. You've got a sharp eye."

Rufinius could not muster a reply, but looked back to the woman, fear and questions in his eyes. The firelight poured shadows into the lines and hollows of her face and, smiling, her mouth became a toothless burrow, gouged in festering soil. She nodded, the gesture loaded with complicity, before drifting away into the wooded shadows.

Now, in the damp and sludge of Isca, he stooped and clawed up a handful of mud.

"This," he announced, raising the rank pile for the crowd to see, "is Roman soil!"

The words were met with a roar of approval.

"We do not fight to claim it from uncivilized hands. We fight to protect it from those who have no place here! Imagine building a fine house only to find, as soon as it was completed, that it was overrun with thieves and savages. What would you do?" He surveyed them. "You would take up your sword and drive them out!"

A murmur of assent from the crowd, but a wry smile from the woman.

"Gederus understood this." He pointed to the flames as they continued the hungry work of lifting skin and hair and clothes from the body. "He fought and died that we might keep this land pure. Keep it Roman." He lifted the clod still higher, thick black ribbons of liquid dirt streaming down his wrist. "Tell me, legionaries, what greater claim can we hold to the land than this? That the blood that ran in his veins now runs through this soil!"

They erupted, to a man, and he felt the glow of pride start to kindle in him.

"He fought for you," he urged them. "Will you fight for him?"

With a sound like a rainstorm, every sword was drawn and held aloft.

"Will you fight with me?"

"Yes!" they roared.

"Then we will drive our enemies out of this land and into the seas!" he cried. "And let every Celt understand that if they are not Roman, they are dead!"

The applause, the cheers, the stamping of feet and bellowing of voices rose like a solid thing, prickling the hairs on his arms and rising on clattering wings towards the clouds.

And then he saw the woman beckon him and turn away.

With a last look at Gederus, curled like a newborn in his nest of blazing branches, he stepped down and followed her. The time had come to close the deal.

Three days after the death of the Celt, the cold finally broke and they marched west. The countryside burbled and sang with the slow death of winter, the snow decaying to a brownish slush beneath their sandals.

Rufinius marched in the front rank of the column alongside Gederus, who did not seem in the least embarrassed to show his gratitude to the small, rattish yokel whose intervention had saved his life.

"Your accent," Gederus announced as they shared a skin of wine the morning after the fight. "You're from the country?"

"The Piano Grande."

"You lucky devil!" Gederus beamed. "More beautiful than all the buildings of Rome. Why on Earth did you leave?"

Rufinius dropped his gaze, embarrassed. "I grew up a vagrant, moving from farm to farm as the work demanded. Shepherding, plowing, harvesting, cutting wood...And ever since I could remember, people had been telling me how lucky I was to be part of the glory of Rome. So I finally decided to go and find some of it for myself."

"And they sent you to us, you poor bastard!"

The words had obviously been meant as a joke, but something in the pained smile he got in return caused Gederus to knit his brows together. "If you think this is bad, wait until we reach the Silures' territory. The most barren collection of rock this island has to offer, but they'll slaughter anyone who comes near it. There are some hard fights ahead."

Rufinius knew this all too well; it had been almost the sole topic of conversation since his arrival. The Silures were the most savage and hostile of the Celtic tribes, refusing all civilization, choosing instead to flee westward into the mountains and valleys. This was where the legion was bound.

"How many battles have you fought?" he asked.

"Fifty. Not including the paid fights. How about you?"

He toyed with the wine skin, feeling the first tug of jealousy. "None."

He had not forgotten his deal with the woman, but all his attempts to acquire the pendant had so far come to nothing. Gederus never removed it, not even when he slept or washed. He caught Rufinius staring at it as they relaxed in the baths, soaking in the caldarium in the few hours before the legion set out.

"A fine piece, isn't it?" he said, lifting it to the light and letting it spin slowly.

"Very nice," Rufinius conceded, perhaps a little too quickly.

What at first appeared to be just another piece of Celtic knotwork was, in fact, a twisting golden serpent, exquisitely detailed down to the scales on its back and the curve of its fangs as it devoured its own tail. A single stone, black and cold, marked its eye.

"Where did you get it?"

"A group of bandits surprised me on the road in northern Gaul. The best of them was carrying it."

"Why don't you sell it?" The question sounded awkward and loaded to his ears.

"Never sell anything you earn in a fair fight," Gederus replied firmly. "The man who beats me can take it. Nobody else."

Rufinius reflected on this as they marched. What if, a few weeks from now, some Silure peasant was wearing the thing?

He was still trying to concoct a means of stealing it two days later, when the legion left the road and struck out across country. The putrefying remains of winter made the going hard. Twice they had to abandon their route and find higher ground as they met rising flood waters and valleys blocked by mudslides.

They were fording a river, white water surging around their thighs, when the first attack came. The tree-line on the far bank shivered and burst into a horde of screaming figures, ghostly white and naked, the flash of bronze and iron in their hands.

Rufinius, already preoccupied with keeping his footing, froze, his hand at the hilt of his sword, his lungs gripped tight by fear. With a bellow of fury, the first warrior entered the water.

"That happened to me, at the start." Gederus indicated Rufinius' trembling hands as they sat with the rest of the legion on the riverbank, their clothes steaming.

Rufinius found it hard to speak. His mind was still ruled by the memory of the vibration that had travelled up the length of his arm as a man's face opened in a blossom of red meat and gristle beneath the point of his sword. The young warrior had misjudged his attack, leaving himself open and Rufinius, seeing his chance, had very nearly backed away from it. The idea of releasing something as absolute and irreversible as death on a man had terrified him. It still did. Only the threat of having his ashes scattered in this alien wasteland had prompted him to action, all notions of flight or mercy stillborn.

The few surviving Celts had soon fled, surprised by their opponents' overwhelming numbers and leaving the corpses of their kinsmen to a trio of carrion crows circling overhead.

"So what saw you through?"Gederus asked.

Rufinius shrank a little under his comrade's searching gaze.

"I don't know what you mean," he said, glancing at the length of gold chain just visible around his friend's neck. "I had training..."

Gederus waved the words away. "Every man fights for something, even if it's just his pay. What is it you fight for?"

He offered the first lie that occurred to him. "For Caesar."

"That's very noble," Gederus nodded, and he began to relax. "But it's crap."

Rufinius searched frantically for any trace of accusation in the words.

"We all took the oath when we enlisted," Gederus went on. "We all eat and sleep and shit for Caesar. But tell me, when you were knee deep in that water with your enemy at your throat, did you spare him a single thought?"

Rufinius opened his mouth to argue, considered lying, then shut it again.

"You need something of your own to stand for," said Gederus. "Only a monster fights without cause. So I'll ask you again; what'll it be?"

"I...don't know."

Gederus coughed, spat and stood up. "Well I suggest you decide before we run into any more Celts. I'd be sorry to lose you." He started towards the point where the column was reforming.

Rufinius remembered the sight of him striding calmly through the waters to meet the charge, his sword and dagger at the ready, silently marking up each of the attackers for death.

"I don't want to die here," he called after him.

Gederus paused. "That's as good a reason as any."

"And what about you? Why do you fight?"

"Honestly?" Gederus hoisted his features into a lopsided smile. "Because it's the only thing I'm good at."

As the legion moved further west, crossing the brown and turgid expanse of river that marked the fringe of the Silures' territory, the frequency and savagery of the attacks increased.

Every time the alert was sounded, Rufinius felt the same paralyzing fear that had gripped him in the water. But whenever he drew his sword, the killing became a little easier, his thoughts a little clearer, until he found something approaching calm in those frantic, deadly contests. Gederus explained the phenomenon to him as they marched.

"When you're fighting a man for your life, it shakes out everything that's not essential. You stop caring if your woman really loves you, or who owes you money, or where you're going to sleep tonight. You just want him to die so you can go on living."

Rufinius nodded, relieved that someone else had understood this first.

"And when you realize how much of yourself you've abandoned," Gederus continued, "you start to see what's left. And that's the real you."

The sensation grew in him like a weed; the need to put down and destroy the enemy before they could do the same to him. Every Celt he butchered prolonged by a fraction the separate contest he played each night against Gederus, lying awake in the hope that this time, his friend might finally be careless. But Gederus never once failed to bind the chain around his wrist, falling asleep with the pendant locked securely in his fist.

Two games; one soft and subtle, full of smiles and false conversation; the other brutal and honest, played with swords and blood and luck. He only had to win this first game once. But he could not escape the burgeoning fear that, sooner or later, somebody else would beat him at the second.

At last they reached a broad river valley at the foot of steeper hills. The battle here was long and savage and it was twelve hours before they finally drove the Silure warriors to higher ground. Before the sun set, their Centurion announced that this was where they would make their mark; a fortress, to dam up the mouth of the valley and control access to the river until reinforcements could be called for.

Within a week, the defensive wall was in place and, the very next day, it started to rain. It came in torrents, filling the air until even breathing had to be done with the face tipped downwards. The foundations of the new buildings inside the wall began to disintegrate and the river burst its banks, filling the valley with its fetid, sucking waters.

For Rufinius, this came as a tremendous relief. If they could not cross the valley, neither could the Celts and that one, deadly game could be put on hold. So it was with a cold shock that he received the news that Gederus was to be sent into enemy territory.

"The Centurions want to mount an attack as soon as the waters recede," he explained as they huddled round a meager fire. "I'm going across to scout out their defenses."

Rufinius considered for a moment, then formed the words with a slow dread. "Let me come."

The Centurions, impressed by his performance to date, offered no objection so, before dawn the next morning, both men stole out into the rain, which had lessened to a stubborn drizzle, and followed the valley to its narrowest point.

Fear gnawed at Rufinius like a fire at dry timbers but he could not bear the prospect of seeing the key to his prison carried off into those hostile peaks, never to return.

They forded the river with difficulty and made their way in silence through the dark and sodden valleys beyond. What they found there filled them both with a leaden certainty about the legion's prospects.

Every wind-blasted peak was crowned with a fortress, ready to rain down arrows on every side, while teams of warriors stalked like specters between the withered, stunted trees that clung to the slopes.

Filthy, cold and soaking wet, he and Gederus turned towards home. They were halfway there when the first cry went up.

"Have they seen us?" Rufinius asked, panicked.

A chorus of voices rose in response, arrows diving into the soil around them. Then they saw the warriors coming, wild and hard at their heels.

"Run!" spat Gederus.

Their flight was confused and directionless, and it was pure chance that finally brought them to the river's edge, the alien calls still loud in their ears.

As they struggled through the surging water, Rufinius experienced a moment of startling objectivity — the two contests had converged. The final moves must be played now, or he stood to lose everything.

Gederus reached the bank and hauled him free of the torrent. Turning to hurry onward, he realized Rufinius still held him by the arm.

"Give me the pendant."

"What?"

"Please." He held out a hand, the fingers flexing impatiently. "I need it."

Gederus pressed a protective hand to his chest. "What for?"

There was a splash as the first of the Silures entered the river.

"Just give it to me!" he shrieked.

Gederus pulled away, his countenance hardening.

"I don't know what you're playing at, but if you don't come with me now I'll cut you down and carry your corpse home."

"Then do it!" With fumbling fingers, Rufinius drew his sword. "Fight me for it."

Gederus looked him over and for an instant might even have accepted the offer, but a glance at the opposite bank was enough to convince him to shake his head and step away.

And that was when Rufinius slashed open his cheek.

The two men staggered apart, eyes wide. Rufinius felt his hands begin to shake while, with deliberate calm, Gederus drew his sword and leveled it at his friend's head.

"Do you really want to do this?"

Rufinius held his ground. "Yes. Do you?"

The big man hesitated and Rufinius made his move. Another darting slash, a twist, and he felt something wet burst along the edge of his blade. Gederus fell against him, throwing an arm around his shoulder and almost bearing them both to the ground. His mouth worked to take in air but only succeeded in producing red froth. Then he slumped to the ground and lay still.

Rufinius was still kneeling over the body when the first of the Silures reached him and, as the sediments of personality were pared away again by the purity of battle, he realized that something had changed. It almost didn't matter what they did to him now; he had played the game and won. And yet, somehow, he fought, long and hard and well, until at last he stood alone, the master of a crop of bodies lying open to the rain.

When it was done he re-sheathed his sword, fastened the pendant around his neck and began the long task of dragging his friend's corpse back to the fortress.

She was waiting for him in the lumber yard, the great stacks of moldering timber forming a narrow alleyway that screened them from the activity of the rest of the fortress. She was younger than he remembered, her features stronger, more handsome. There was something of the blush of motherhood about her.

"You have it?" she asked.

He held it up for her to see.

"You are an exceptional young man," she said, cupping it in her hands as she might a small bird. "You have earned everything I promised you."

Rufinius looked around, uncomfortable. He could make out the axe wounds in the rough flesh of the timber, home to countless things that burrowed and teemed.

"I don't want it," he said at last. He had been expecting the woman to show surprise or anger, but she did neither. She just watched him.

"I thought I was fighting to escape, but in the end I was just fighting. I wanted to beat them, to win myself a prize." He shrugged. "Well, there it is."

The woman was smiling, but it had none of the callousness of her former manner. "And what drives you to battle now the prize is won?"

"Honestly?" And he smiled himself. "It's the only thing I'm good at." He took a step back, towards the space and noise. "Enjoy the pendant."

She laughed then and swept towards him, pressing it back into his unresisting hands. "I got the prize I came for," she whispered, her lips at his cheek, her breath hot and stinging. "What need have I of trinkets?"

She forced her lips against his for an instant and was gone, the taste of earth and blood all that remained.

Rufinius stood there for a while, turning the pendant over and over, the single black eye winking at him. Then he slipped it round his neck and started back to the barracks, where the Centurions would be waiting. The flood waters would recede soon. There were battles ahead.

I'm not usually a character-led writer.

That's not to say I don't appreciate how vital a strong, multi-faceted character is to good story, but it's usually that first, tantalizing plot thread that fires my imagination.

'The Trinket' came to me back-to-front, when a particular sentence in the submission guidelines leaped out and grabbed me: "All stories must be set in the world of the Celts". And there he was — a grim-faced Roman legionary, knee-deep in Welsh mud while the freezing rain drummed a relentless tattoo on his helmet.

A bit specific, you might think, and hardly Celtic. But I grew up a pilum's throw from Caerleon — founded by the Second Augustan Legion about seventy-five years after the birth of Christ — which still manages to feel as much Roman as it does Welsh. It was a Wild West town; the sharp edge of the empire, where civilization was imposed upon the wilderness that lay just beyond Caesar's reach. It is a good place for a story to unfold and an excellent place for the Phantom Queen to do business.

My vague reservations about transplanting her from Ireland to Wales soon evaporated once the writing was underway. She didn't seem to mind the journey — she was having fun. And, very soon, so was I.

Peter Bell was born and brought up in Newport, South Wales; a handful of miles from the remains of Isca, where much of "The Trinket" is set. He left to study French and Spanish, living in the ancient Moorish city of Granada and operating roller coasters at Disneyland Paris before settling in Cardiff with his wife, Anna.

A keen writer since childhood, Peter is a member of the British Fantasy Society and is currently working on his first novel. 'The Trinket' is his second published short story.

Michael Bailey

The Dying Gaul

Oh! let that eye, which, wild as the Gazelle's
Now brightly bold or beautifully shy,
Wins as it wanders, dazzles where it dwells,
Glance o'er this page, nor to my verse deny
That smile for which my breast might vainly sigh
Could I to thee be ever more than friend:
This much, dear maid, accord; nor question why
To one so young my strain I would commend,
But bid me with my wreath one matchless lily blend.

Such is thy name with this my verse entwined;
And long as kinder eyes a look shall cast
On Harold's page, Ianthe's here enshrined
Shall thus be first beheld, forgotten last:
My days once number'd, should this homage past
Attract thy fairy fingers near the lyre
Of him who hail'd thee loveliest, as thou wast,
Such is the most my memory may desire;
Though more than Hope can claim, could Friendship less require?

~ Childe Harold's Pilgrimage
(To Ianthe)

On woolen sheets we lie, vulnerable and as white and bare as the stars against the black marble sky, placed by the hands of love gods in a triangle of three.

Ianthe: I cannot have her; she belongs to another in marriage.

Her wondrous beauty — she is on her back — stares upside-down at a set of rotten eyes that capture and hold her own as she is penetrated, moaning her fake moans, the tears welling on her cheeks from both pleasure and pain, while her quavering body creaks the bed underneath. A head is mounted high on the wall, held by an iron stake: a fallen barbarian whom her husband Cadmon had slain with much contempt — a worthy foe. The pegged part of this dead man watches as Cadmon exits the luscious gap between her legs. He tosses her aside like spoiled meat and I, just a boy, reach for the silk flesh below her navel, but my wrist is taken and held at my back as he flips me around and pilfers me next, the fingers of my other hand only capable of caressing her thigh before they are guided away. Ianthe takes herself in one hand and her breast in the other. She cries out to the man on the wall and the sound is angels with clipped wings falling from heaven.

She is twice my age and I have known her half my life. Harold, my sweet, she calls me. She is my love, but I cannot have her; I can only be had for now, she tells me when we are alone. I am not yet of age, but I see the way she looks at me when the three of us are together or even when we are not. Her smile holds a secret. Her body smells of lust. Her touch is desirous, but cautious. We can never be together without Cadmon, she says, for I am not yet a man.

Someday I will join the battle and become a greater warrior than Cadmon could ever be. Someday he will die in melee and I will take his place inside my love. I will take her from the back, from the front, from the side, and she will cry out, but only because it pleases her and because it is me and not her joyless husband. There will be no pain as her body swallows my seed to bear a child. She will whisper my name: Harold. Together, we will melt.

For he through Sin's long labyrinth had run,
Nor made atonement when he did amiss,
Had sigh'd to many though he loved but one,
And that loved one, alas! could n'er be his.
Ah, happy she! to 'scape from him whose kiss
Had been pollution unto aught so chaste;
Who soon had left her charms for vulgar bliss,
And spoil'd her goodly lands to gild his waste,
Nor calm domestic peace had ever deign'd to taste.

And now Childe Harold was sore sick at heart,
And from his fellow bacchanals would flee;
'Tis said, at times the sullen tear would start,
But Pride congeal'd the drop within his eye:
Apart he stalk'd in joyless reverie,
And from his native land resolved to go,
And visit scorching climes beyond the sea;
With pleasure drugg'd, he almost long'd for woe,
And e'en for change of scene would seek the shades below.

~ *Childe Harold's Pilgrimage*
(from Canto the First)

I spy her through a silken shade. Ianthe dresses with patience and dignity, the white fabric draping over her shoulders and down like an ocean wave sprayed against the upper shore of her bosom. Her long brown hair is in braids, and it falls between the valleys of her back.

Her bare feet on the floor bend against the cold, her toes dimple. Gold rings jangle from her ankles as she shifts balance and places more jewelry on the soft lobes of her ears. She looks back and sees my stare. I blush and so does she. A smile forms from the edge of her carved mouth as she turns back to her husband.

I see the red spider webs stretching between the yellow of Cadmon's eyes as I part the shade that separates us. I had heard his stupefied drinking the night before as I lay in bed thinking of nothing but Ianthe and that sweet caress of her thigh. They had argued through the night.

Cadmon does not see me just yet. He sees the crescent smile on her face.

He brings the backside of his hand across her mouth and the smile is gone as quickly as it had formed. He stands a full foot taller and towers over her, his face flushed. He wears only a torc around his neck. His giant triangle of a chest reveals a pair of sweaty breasts larger than those of my love, strewn with crisscrossed battle scars. Bulging abdominal muscles mock his flaccid manhood; it hangs below them like the husk of a shriveled reptile. He stands before her like a giant with a wrinkled date wedged between his legs.

I desire nothing more than to see his head nailed above the bed someday, as Ianthe takes me in as her own. To see her struck fills my heart with a wrath that burns and rises within my throat. There is nothing I can do but swallow it back down, for Cadmon is three times my size and he would take my life. He could easily crush my throat with a single hand.

A single tear falls from her check. One falls from my own.

Ianthe holds her head and sobs as Cadmon leaves her. He takes his sword from against the wall and walks naked out into the cool morning air. He must train for battle. The tip of the sword scrapes across the floor.

As I part the silken shade further, I wait eagerly for the sound to disappear, meaning Cadmon's absence. I quietly rush to her aid. She is bent in half, clutching her face. I pull a delicate hand away from her swollen jaw. Her lip is split and leaking red. She doesn't want me to see her cry.

Her hand pulls back, but mine is stronger. I tell her I love her, but she pushes me away. She tells me to leave, that we can never be together for it would mean the death of us both, but I stay at her side. She shakes as I wipe the blood from her mouth and lift her head so that she looks directly at me. I kiss the wound, my eyes never leaving hers. I taste her blood on my lips.

Ianthe kisses me back and touches my tongue with her own. She quakes, as do I. Her sputtering breath is warm and smells like ripened peaches. She takes my palm from her cheek and this time she is stronger. She flattens my hand under her own and guides it down the soft skin of her neck, her chest, and underneath the fabric of her gown. The curve of her left breast leads to a mound of blissful heaven. The god at its peak trembles between my fingers. Her other hand finds a forbidden part of me.

Cold steel and sick warmth ends our connection. Cadmon separates me from Ianthe with his sword. As he pushes me back, the edge digs into my flesh. His blade at my neck, I only come to his chest. His eyes bulge, as do the dark veins on his brow. He breathes fast and raspy and I taste the hot drink on his breath. He looks down at me, ready to add my head to his collection.

My head is not worth your efforts, I tell him, but he doesn't listen. He has taken many lives and many heads, all worthy opponents. I am nothing to him but a tighter hole of pleasure.

Ianthe cries out.

Cadmon turns.

Spare his life, she pleads.

Cadmon twists back to me, ready to slice the blade through my neck.

I close my eyes, ready to die, my last thoughts on Ianthe and our encounter, her soft skin against mine, her eyes to mine, her lips to mine. Her breast under my fingertips. I imagine for a moment my head nailed above their bed — our bed — watching her beauty forever.

Cadmon leans into me.

Banish him! She shouts and I open my eyes in horror.

Kill me, I say, unable to grasp the thought of exile.

He pulls the blade away.

Tears run the course of my cheeks as I look to Ianthe. She stares at the ground before moving her hands to her gown. She loosens the straps and lets the fabric fall from her shoulders to the floor, leaving us in her nakedness. The sight of her saddens me more. In all of her goddess beauty, it is the swelling purple of her cheek that draws my attention. I look to Cadmon's sword, but I would try at my own life before attempting to take his.

Again he raises the blade. For an instant, I feel there is hope. But instead of dismembering my head, he uses the handle to strike me down.

The sun, the soil, but not the slave, the
same;
Unchanged in all except its foreign
lord–
Preserves alike its bounds and
boundless fame
The Battle-field, where Persia's victim
horde
First bow'd beneath the brunt of
Hellas' sword,
As on the morn to distant Glory dear
When Marathon became a magic
word;
Which utter'd, to the hearer's eye
appear
The camp, the host, the fight, the
conqueror's career,

The flying Mede, his shaftless broken
bow;
The fiery Greek, his red pursuing
spear;
Mountains above, Earth's, Ocean's
plain below;
Death in the front, Destruction in the
rear!
Such was the scene – what now
remaineth here?
What sacred trophy marks the
hallow'd ground,
Recording Freedom's smile and Asia's
tear?

The rifled urn, the violated mound,
The dust thy courser's hoof, rude stranger! Spurns around.

~ *Childe Harold's Pilgrimage (from Canto the Second*

A ship awaits my departure, but I look back to it with baneful eye. It is there to lead me to foreign lands, away from what most I desire. The hilltop provides an awful view of the flat blue sea to my back, the ship nothing more than a brown crumb dropped onto the water. At my front is a battle. Perhaps Cadmon will die this time, which would null my expulsion from this land. I could lay with Ianthe and we would not have to worry about hiding our love. As I sit clutching my knees to my chest, I hold a pile of rain-soaked soil and wonder how much blood has spilt on this land I have called home for the thirteen years of my life. I remember running up these hills as a child, and rolling down them on my sides. I remember the laughter, and it pains me to bring it all back, but I must, for it now amounts to nothing more than fallen memories as it passes through my fingertips.

A gray cloud looms over the battlefield, casting everything underneath in heavy shadow. The wind whirls cold.A crow lands near my feet and tilts its head to look to me with a beady black eye. I toss some dirt at it and the bird flutters.

Watch, it says as it dances. It shakes the earth off its wings and turns its neck toward the battle. It looks back to me and caws. Watch.

Watch what? I ask, and I know then it is Morrigan.

The crow doesn't answer. It only looks at me with a crooked head and what I assume are distrustful black eyes.

The two sides of war below grow eager as they wait for the horn. From my seat they are nothing but riled ants merged together, angered and ready to attack the opposing threat.

Listen, says the crow, as if it were she starting the battle.

For a moment, there is nothing but silence. Both sides below take a shared breath. I listen as a distant horn croons death. And then a thunderous roar erupts from the crowd and I wonder if it is only thunder from the clouds reigning over them. Soon these separate armies merge as one, as shield and sword create a cacophony of music from a symphony comprised of metallic and wooden instruments.

The harmony of life taking death, says Morrigan. The crow dances once again, wings fluttering. The music is for her.

Drums pound. Cymbals crash.

The crowd below dances with her. Most fall.

If only he would die, I tell the crow.

Morrigan says, I guard your death, but nothing more.

As the sun moves directly overhead, it passes through a hole in the clouds, removing the battlefield from shade. It reveals a field of red as her music dies down.

Only the soft moan of fallen men remains. One side has won, but only a handful basks in the glory, if it can be called such a thing. Those clinging to life are either left for dead, or pierced one final time with a blade by the victor.

Morrigan flies to the ended battle, cawing, urging me to follow.

She leads me to the dead.

I walk through a maze of fallen barbarians, naked and covered in the life that once filled their hearts. They stare at me with hollow eyes. A hand missing its two smallest fingers grabs my leg before falling limp at my feet. I step over a twitching man, a blade pierced through his throat. He chortles blood and finally stills. Morrigan tells me to retrieve a blade. I choose a dagger and pull it from someone's back. I pass once glorious men, now missing appendages. Those that cling to life, I ease to death, for that is what she tells me to do. I approach two men clutched together tightly in their nudity, arms wrapped around one another and moving as if making love, and I realize it is simply one man fallen over another; the end of a spear poking through one to his lover, binding the two in an eternal embrace. I cut each of their throats.

I cannot save them all, I tell her.

Our journey ends at a large granite stone, and it is Cadmon leaning against its base. One hand braces his body upright; the other rests on his thigh. He is alone, and naked except for the crimson torc around his neck, exactly as I remember him from earlier that morning. He looks to the ground. At first he appears untouched, only fatigued from war.

Morrigan perches atop the rock. She urges me closer.

Cadmon looks to me with shame and I notice his heavy panting and dripping torc. Blood surrounds his body and he seems to float buoyantly within it like the ship at sea set to take me away.

He has lost his manhood on the ground next to him. Someone has cut it off, and it is to that flaccid member and the attached flaps of skin clinging to it that holds his gaze. He bleeds from a hole between his legs; it pulses out of him.

The black crow on the rock laughs as his body slowly drains.

I wait for him to die before carving off his head with my dagger.

I see before me the Gladiator lie:
He leans upon his hand – his manly brow
Consents to death, but conquers agony,
And his droop'd head sinks gradually low –
And through his side the last drops, ebbing slow
From the red gash, fall heavy, one by one,
Like the first of a thunder-shower; and now
The arena swims around him – he is gone,
Ere ceased the inhuman shout which hail'd the wretch who won.

He heard it, but he heeded not – his eyes
Were with his heart, and that was far away;
He reck'd not of the life he lost nor prize,
But where his rude hut by the Danube lay,
There where his young barbarians all at play,
There was their Dacian mother – he, their sire,
Butcher'd to make a Roman holiday–
All this rush'd with his blood – Shall he expire
And unavenged? Arise! ye Goths, and glut your ire!

~ *Childe Harold's Pilgrimage*
(from Canto the Fourth)

I carry Cadmon's head with pride. It hangs at my side — now all but drained — as I think of Ianthe and how it has come to pass that we can be together as I had once dreamed. Cadmon watches the ship at sea as his head swings back and forth in pendulum. The vessel sails away without me aboard and his dead eyes cannot look away.

Those I pass glance strangely, for they recognize Cadmon and his sad fate. Is it respect, curiosity, fear? It doesn't matter. I swing his severed head by a wad of matted brown hair as one would swing a basket of fruits.

It is my gift to Ianthe.

And she waits for me.

Watch, says the voice of the crow. I look around, but the black bird is nowhere to be found. The phantom word is only in my head; it sends cold water down my spine as I walk toward my love.

I see her through the silken shade. On woolen sheets she lies naked, vulnerable and as white and bare again as the early evening stars forming in the sky. She is the essence of beauty, and the outline and curves of her slender body remind me that our love will no longer be a triangle of three. We can now be two as we form into one. She will take me inside. She will moan and call out my name. Harold, she will whisper into my ear. Ianthe, I will mutter in a broken breath. Her back will arc skyward with pleasure. We will melt like the wax from two candles placed close together. Tears will run down our cheeks from the bliss.

Ianthe: I can finally have her; she belongs to no one now. She is mine. I am hers. I raise the head as I enter the room.

But the smile on her face holds a secret, and her eyes cannot see what I offer.

The handle of a dagger protrudes from the soft flesh beneath her navel. Dead hands grip the hilt. She has taken her life.

I replace the head staked to the wall with that of Cadmon's. He looks upon us as I weep over Ianthe and slide the blade from her stomach. I toss it aside as easily as Cadmon had tossed Ianthe the night before. I kiss her cold lips. She kisses back. I confess my love and this time, fear doesn't make her push me away.

Cadmon watches with cloudy eyes.

'The Dying Gaul' is an experimental piece of fiction on my part. It is a love story, of sorts, and I tend to stay away from love stories as a general rule. Love is an emotion. It's easy to write about and it's been done to death. If I'm going to write a love story, someone is going to get maimed a few pages into it.

Romance novels could be to blame: some chiseled warrior man-handling some large-busted woman on the cover...they're all the same, with titles like *Eternal Flame of the Heart*.

This tale is also a period piece, and I normally avoid writing about the past. 'The Dying Gaul' is also a tragedy; and horror cannot be horror without tragedy to some degree. Someone has to get hurt; someone has to die; something bad has to happen to a character the reader has fallen in love with, or it's not truly tragedy.

Prior to discovering the call for submissions for *The Phantom Queen Awakes*, I knew absolutely nothing about Celtic mythology. Blame the U.S. educational system. I do. *Childe Harold's Pilgrimage* popped up during my extensive research for this project, and I was instantly drawn into its words. If you haven't read the narrative poem by George Gordon (Lord Byron), I suggest dumping the title into an Internet search engine and finding a copy.

Also stumbled upon during my Celtic self-enlightenment was a marble sculpture called The Dying Gaul (hence the title of my story), a Hellenistic work from the late third century BC, sculptor unknown. The work reveals a naked man wearing only a torc, kneeling over his shield as he fights against death; the look on his face is a complex mix of emotion. This was the character I wanted to portray with Cadmon, and I have Lord Byron to thank:

He leans upon his hand – his manly brow
Consents to death, but conquers agony,
And his drooped head sinks gradually low–
And through his side the last drops, ebbing slow
From the red gash, fall heavy, one by one...

Michael Bailey is the author of the nonlinear novel, *Palindrome Hannah,* a finalist for the 2006 Independent Publisher Awards for horror fiction. He is currently revising his overly-complex follow-up novel, *Phoenix Rose,* and has started a third, titled, *Psychotropic Dragon*.

A collection of short stories and poetry, *Scales and Petals,* is also in the works. In writing this bio — in third-person, no less — he has also come to realize that all of his novels start with the letter P, which is disconcerting because only one of them sounds like it. While he doesn't write a great deal of short fiction, some of his darker tales have appeared in various literary journals, comics, print magazines and anthologies in the United States, Australia, the United Kingdom, Sweden and as far away as South Africa (from a Californian's point of view). His short story, 'Defenestrate', previously appeared in the glorious *In Bad Dreams* anthology, published by Eneit Press.

James Lecky

The Children of Badb Catha

"They're savages," Optio Olcinius said. "Worse than the bloody Iceni." He snorted and spat a wad of phlegm onto the wet ground and wiped his mouth with the back of his hand. "It's no way for a Roman to die."

"It's no way for any man to die," Larcius Servius said. "Cut them down, Olcinius."

Optio Olcinius Decimus nodded curtly and spat again, seeming to try and get the abattoir stench of the grove from his mouth. He was a big, gray bear of a man, a veteran of the campaigns in Caledonia and Germania and no stranger to violence, but even he balked at the prospect of touching those ruined, wretched figures.

There were eight of them, hanging like broken playthings from the lower branches of the grove's oak trees. They had been soldiers once, before the Gaels had taken them, and now they were meat for the crows.

How long did they take to die? Larcius wondered, as he watched his men take the bodies down and wrap them in blankets. Did they scream and cry out to the gods while the flesh was stripped from their bones or did they face death like a good legionnaire should, stoic and defiant to the last?

"What now, Centurion?" Olcinius asked when the corpses had been tended to.

"Now we do our duty," Larcius said.

Olcinius grinned wolfishly. "Some good, old-fashioned Roman vengeance, eh, Centurion?"

"Roman justice, Optio Olcinius." Larcius corrected. "Civilized men do not indulge in vengeance." He kicked his horse into a trot while behind him, the centuria formed together with practiced efficiency.

Roman justice or Roman vengeance? They were the same thing, Larcius decided, or at the very least, they had the same outcome. He had seen it in Gaul, Britannia and Caledonia. And now it had come to Hibernia, the newest, farthest outpost of the Empire.

The decades since Gnaeus Julius Agricola and his legions had crossed the sea that the Gaels called Muir Meann had been years of steel and iron, blood and fire. Agricola himself had boasted that he could subdue the whole island with a single legion. He had been wrong.

True, he had smashed and scattered the tribes with ruthless efficiency, slaughtered their druids and desecrated the shrines of their gods, but the Gaels had refused to admit defeat and it had become a war of attrition, hit and run, atrocity and reprisal. More blood, more steel. More death.

That morning, as the centuria had set out from Campus Roborum on the banks of the Modarnus River, Larcius had known what they would find. The local tribes — the Vennicnii and the Erdin — had been restless and belligerent for months now, raiding across the river from Dungallum for cattle and slaves until even Quintus Cassius, the sedentary and slow-witted commander of the Roborum garrison, realized something had to be done.

But with typical caution, he had sent his troops out in small patrols of no more than ten men.

"When they see the might of Rome, the Gaels will flee back into the hills," Quintus had announced. "No need for a legion when a contubernium or two will do the same job. We'll put the fear of Mars into them, eh?"

It had been inevitable that Roman lives would be lost, and equally as inevitable that Larcius would have to clean up the mess.

The contubernium under Decanus Catulinnius had been missing for over a week before word of their slaughter reached Roborum, and another two days passed while Quintus wailed and moaned and offered up sacrifices to his household gods in repentance.

Finally, he called Larcius to his villa.

"They have to be taught a lesson," he said. "If word of this gets to Eblana or, Pluto forbid, Rome itself, our careers will be ruined. Take a centuria into Dungallum and show these barbarian bastards what it means to take Roman lives."

"They will be punished, Tribune Cassius, you have my word on it."

Quintus waved a soft, podgy hand to dismiss him. "Do it by whatever means you deem necessary, Larcius." he said. "Rome demands blood from those who kill her children. You know your duty."

"Quite so, Tribune."

"One other thing, Larcius," Quintus said as the centurion turned to leave. "These Gaels make poor slaves — I don't see the need to bring any back with you. Remember the words of Cicero: 'In time of war the law falls silent'."

Larcius knew what the Tribune meant, just as he knew that any disaster or scandal would fall on his own head. A fool he may have been, but Quintus Cassius knew how to cover his tracks. As commander in the field, Larcius would hold sole responsibility for any decision.

"Do not concern yourself, Tribune Cassius. If Rome demands blood, then blood she will have."

By late afternoon, the centuria had reached the Rapa hills, guided by Conall O'Ceirin, an Erdin collaborator whose love for Roman silver far outweighed his tribal loyalties.

"A mile, maybe a mile and a half to the next Vennicnii settlement, centurion," Conall told him. "There'll be plenty of work for your swords there." The scout was a small, dark man with braided hair: the broad axe and iron sword he carried were those of his people, but his clothing — the short tunic and red battle cloak — were readily accepted gifts from Rome.

"These Vennicnii," Larcius asked, "they are the ones who killed Catulinnius and his men?"

Conall shrugged. "Would it matter?"

Larcius did not answer.

But no, he thought, it would not matter. An example needs to be made. Guilty or not, Roman justice makes no distinction and laws fall silent during a time of war.

It was growing dark by the time they reached the village and the autumn chill had begun to work its way into Larcius' bones. The gods must hate this country, he decided, and who can blame them? Too wild, too savage, and too full of hatred.

"Orders, centurion?" Olcinius asked.

"Surround the village and burn it to the ground," he said. "Kill everything that moves."

"Women and children?"

"I said everything," he snapped. Then his tone changed slightly. "But keep one of them alive — someone will need to tell the tale." There was a sour taste in his mouth as he spoke. He took no pleasure in this bloody work, but no matter what, he was first and last a soldier of Rome and it was his duty to protect her. In that, if nothing else, he could take pride.

The Gaels came to meet them when the centurion attacked. A score of warriors charged from their roundhouses, howling harsh battle cries. They were tall, fierce men who swung their swords and spears as if they were no more than toys, but their savagery was no match for Roman discipline and Roman steel. They charged and they died.

And when the warriors were dead, the real massacre began.

It took them over two hours and when it was done, the night was full of blood and flame. They piled the bodies in the centre of the village and put them to torch. Soon, the crisp night air was filled with the foul stench of burning flesh.

Larcius stood on the outskirts of the village, head bowed, sword in hand. His tunic was drenched with gore and his ears rung with screams.

Somewhere out in the darkness his men hunted down the few women and children who had managed to flee from the slaughter. He heard an infant crying, the sound thin and pathetic then abruptly cut off.

He wiped his sword clean on the edge of his cloak and sheathed it.

"Centurion."

Larcius turned and saw Olcinius, Conall and two legionnaires coming towards him. Between them the two soldiers held an old woman. She struggled feebly in their grip, cursing fluently.

"Let her go," Larcius ordered.

The woman swayed and almost fell as they released her.

"I am Gaius Larcius Servius, do you know of me, old mother?" Larcius asked. Of course she would, his reputation as a soldier preceded him, even into the wilds of Dungallum.

She nodded, her gray hair falling across her eyes. "I know you for the murderer you are, Gaius Larcius, just as I knew you would come here. But do you know me?"

And it seemed to him for a moment that he had seen her face before — in the dead of a dozen campaigns.

"Who are you?"

She brushed the hair from her eyes and stood erect. The hair was dark as a crow's wing: her face was pale and young, the lips a carmine slash in her alabaster features.

"I am Badb," she said.

She was old again in a heartbeat, but older than any living human being could be, as though death itself had refused to claim her. The fetid perfume of old blood clung to her hair and tattered clothes.

"I am Macha."

Her eyes were black, fathomless — inhuman. Her hands ended in long, gnarled claws and when she spoke her voice was a cruel, staccato croak: "I am the Morrigu."

Before he realized it, his sword was in his hand, rising free of the scabbard with a soft and familiar swish of steel. She stumbled forward to meet it on taloned feet and they came together in a deadly lover's embrace, her hands upon his shoulders and his *gladius* stuck deep into her abdomen.

"I know your soul, Gaius Larcius," she hissed. "I know your fears and your misery and I will make it a weapon to destroy all that you hold dear. As you have slaughtered my people, so I will slaughter yours."

Larcius gave a startled yell and pushed her away. She toppled backwards onto the muddy earth and when she struck the ground she was an elderly woman once more, her rheumy eyes unseeing and her thin hands held up in supplication.

"You saw her, Olcinius," Larcius said. "You saw what she became, didn't you?"

"I saw an old woman, Centurion," the Optio said. "Nothing more."

With effort, Larcius gained control of his shaking hands and put away his sword. When he spoke again, his voice was measured and even, as befitted a Roman officer.

"Throw her on the fire with the others," he said, then turned away, walking into the darkness.

"I know what you saw, Centurion," Conall said.

The Erdin scout found Larcius by the edge of a small stream not far from the burning village, meticulously washing the blood from his hands.

"It was nothing," Larcius told him. "A trick of the light or a passing fever of the brain, nothing more."

Conall grimaced slightly. "Oh, it was more than that, Centurion Servius, it was the Morrigu."

"You heard her speak? You heard her name herself?"

Conall shook his head. "Her words were for you alone, but I recognized her all right."

"What was she?"

"The goddess of life and death — Venus, Juno, Mars and Pluto all rolled into one."

"It's of no consequence, she's dead now."

"Even you can't kill a goddess that easily, Centurion." Conall squatted beside Larcius and stared into his face. "What did she say to you?"

"Nothing you need concern yourself with." Larcius stood and stared at the water, lost in his thoughts.

The wind rose, bringing the smell of burning wood and flesh, and with it came the harsh squawk of crows. Dawn was hours away, the carrion birds should not have been stirring yet, but their cries echoed over the hills as they called to one another.

"What did she say to you, Centurion?" Conall asked again, and this time there was fear and urgency in his voice. "What did Badb Catha say?"

The cry of birds grew louder and closer until the night was filled with their screeching and the beating of their wings. The sky was thick with them, so many that they blotted out the stars.

Larcius ran back to the village, Conall following in his wake. What they saw there was like a vision of the underworld. Amid the burning huts and roundhouses, in the greasy light of the human pyre, swarms of birds pecked, scratched and bit at the legionnaires while the men scurried about, desperately trying to protect their eyes and faces. The shrieks of men mingling with the harsh cries of birds were like the cacophonous music of Pan himself.

"Form ranks, damn you, form ranks!" Larcius bellowed, trying to instill order in his panicked troops. A viciously pointed beak struck him, tearing a long strip of flesh from his cheek. He flailed and grabbed the bird, breaking its neck with a satisfying snap. Another flew at his eyes and he cut it in half with one swift slash of his *gladius*.

All around him, his men were roaring and dying, torn apart in a storm of wings. He saw a legionnaire fall, weighed down by a murderous flock of sleek, black bodies, his face a bloody mask. Another walked blindly into the burning wreck of a roundhouse, his eyes dangling against his cheeks like two obscene baubles. The high, hysterical scream of a horse cut through the night as Larcius' mare died in the onslaught.

Then, as rapidly as they had come, the birds dispersed and the stars could be seen again, sharp pinpricks of light against the dark blanket of the sky.

Larcius found Olcinius in the middle of the burning village. The Optio's face was marked with long, deep scratches and one eye was swollen shut and bloodied.

"In the name of Orcus, what's happening, Centurion?"

Larcius shook his head. "I don't know."

By dawn the fires had burned out, leaving nothing but smoldering ashes. Even the pyre had dwindled to a pool of congealed fat decorated with charred flesh and protruding bone. Its thick stink lay over everything. Nearly half of the centuria had perished in the crows' furious onslaught and the few of those who remained bore the rapidly festering marks of claw and beak as if the very touch of the birds carried corruption with it.

Larcius Servius walked through the dead and wounded in a daze. How could this have happened, how could his proud centuria have been so badly mauled by mere birds? The gash on his cheek throbbed with every heartbeat, his skin was coated with cold, greasy sweat, his vision swam and a fierce nausea threatened to overwhelm him.

He forced the sickness down and gulped in great breaths of foul air, waiting for his vision and mind to clear.

The birds had not attacked again — instead, they filled the trees surrounding the village, sitting silently on branches as if waiting for a sign — but they had trapped the centuria as effectively as a ring of steel.

He found Conall O'Ceirin near the outskirts of the ruined village, sitting on a small mound of earth and staring at the trees. His cloak was wrapped tightly around him and his face and hands were covered with a myriad of deep scratches.

"What are they?" Larcius asked, nodding towards the dark flock that stared intently back at them.

"The vengeance of the Morrigu," Conall said. "The children of Badb Catha,"

"You used that name before," Larcius said. "Last night, before the attack. What does it mean?"

"It's an old name for the goddess, Centurion — the Battle Crow — fitting, don't you think?"

"Your gods have a curious sense of humor, Conall O'Ceirin."

"Don't they all?" He turned his head to look at Larcius. The centurion appeared older than his forty years, his features drawn and haggard like the face of a man who has seen too much in too short a time.

From the branches of a great oak at the edge of the village one bird, larger than the rest, rose gracelessly into the slate-gray sky. It wheeled around the village three times then hovered directly above Larcius, screeching at him. And it seemed to him that there was mockery in the sound.

It's taunting me, he thought, the bastard is taunting me.

"Bring that thing down," he barked to an archer.

"Don't waste your arrows, Centurion," Conall said, "They won't do any good against the Battle Crow."

Filled with sudden rage and frustration, Gaius Larcius Servius threw his head back and screamed at the sky: "What do you want with me?"

And the voice that replied and whispered in his head was a strained croak, the words forced from a throat that had never been meant for speech. "I want your stain removed from this land, Roman. I want you and everything you stand for wiped from the memory of men." The bird swooped closer. He could make out every feather, every knot and gnarl of its claws, every line of its beak and, most of all, the glittering, malevolent intelligence in its obsidian eyes.

"Where is your pride now, Gaius Larcius Servius? Where is your honor? Will they keep you warm when you lie in the green earth of Inis Ealga?"

The crow screeched with demonic fury and drove towards his head, claws extended, beak open wide. He flung his cloak in front of his face and the claws tore through the red material, their fury barely suppressed.

"When darkness falls," the cruel voice told him, "when darkness falls you will be mine." And then the bird whirled away into the sky. He watched as it returned to its perch on the oak's branches and began to preen itself, the movements languid and insolent.

"Olcinius!" The Optio was by his side almost immediately.

"Yes, Centurion Servius?" The Optio's wounded face was covered with a blood soaked bandage and his skin was pale.

"Have the men prepare torches. We're breaking out of here. We'll see how well these damned birds like fire."

"Yes, Centurion." He hesitated for a moment. "What in the name of Juno's tits is happening, Larcius?"

It was Conall who answered. "The magic of the old gods, Optio Olcinius. The Morrigu feasts on blood and death, and Rome has brought those in plenty since she came to Hibernia."

"Why here? Why now?" Olcinius asked. He was a practical man, unused to any problem that could not be solved at the point of a sword and, perhaps for the first time in his life, he knew the cold caress of fear. They could see it in his scarred face and hear it in the barely suppressed tremble in his voice.

"The village was under her protection," Conall said. "The people we killed were her children."

"How can you know this?" Larcius said.

The Gael laughed, the sound was small and bitter. "I am a traitor to my people, Centurion, but I know their ways and the ways of their gods — my gods — before I turned from them and took your silver."

"I fear no gods but my own." Larcius said, his voice defiant. "And if the Morrigu feasts on blood and death then we will feed her till she bursts."

By noon the centuria was ready to move.

But as Larcius watched his men gather themselves together, he realized that his troops were a pale shadow of the proud force that had left Campus Roborum, as if the sinister attack in the night had not merely wounded their bodies, but had scarred their souls as well.

The legionaries swayed where they stood, but kept on their feet through iron resolve. An unnatural, fetid stink rose from their wounds and the fierce light of growing desperation burned in their faces. Each man held a *gladius* in his right hand and a burning brand in his left. Behind them, their pilum and shields had been neatly stacked — such equipment would only hinder them now.

Larcius stood before them, hands on hips and head thrown back arrogantly, though it was an arrogance he no longer felt.

"Soldiers of Rome," he barked. "There is your enemy!" He drew his sword and pointed it towards the trees and the birds that perched there. "Not men, but animals — and what animal does not fear fire and steel?"

But even as he spoke he heard the voice of the Morrigu echo through his mind. "Come to me, Gaius Larcius Servius. I will quench your torches, blunt your blades, and my vengeance will be terrible."

There is no longer a place for you in this world, bitch, he thought, and he knew that she could hear him, go back to the hell that spawned you. He picked up a torch and signaled the centuria to advance.

As the soldiers passed the village perimeter the flock rose to meet them, their squawks and squeals filling the air. As one, the birds banked and swooped toward the Romans, screeching their battle cries. And at their head was the creature Conall had called Badb Catha.

The black wave broke upon a shore of fire and steel.

Larcius swung his sword in a tight arc, cleaving through fragile flesh and brittle bone with each stroke. As he fought, he thrust out with the torch and the creatures shrieked at the touch of the flames. But for every crow he killed another took its place, then another, and another, and another...

His men were dying, torn to pieces by beak and claw: the birds were above them, below them, behind them, between them. To his right he saw Olcinius fall under a great swarm, his sword rising and falling even as they ripped the flesh from his bones. To his left, Conall O'Ceirin swung his axe two-handed, its long reach bringing down scores of crows as they flew towards him.

Then, abruptly, Larcius was free of the butchery, slipping and sliding on the blood-soaked earth. Conall was by his side, grabbing his arm to steady him.

"Run, Centurion, run!"

Larcius pushed him away. "I will not leave my men."

"Your men are dead, Larcius. Look!"

The slaughter was all but complete. A legionnaire stumbled blindly with birds clinging to his head and limbs, pecking at his flesh. The man sank to the ground as a final, wordless scream was torn from his ruined throat. The rest of the centuria lay where they had fallen, their bodies now perches for the crows.

Badb Catha sat at the centre of the carnage. Her form was human, but her features shifted constantly between youth and age, beauty and hideousness, animal and woman.

She looked directly at Larcius and smiled.

"Join us, Gaius Larcius Servius," she said. "Your men are waiting for their commander."

As she spoke, the flock took to the air with a great beating of their wings, the sound as loud as thunder in the quiet aftermath of battle.

And then, as Larcius and Conall watched, the legionnaires began to move, rising to their feet and forming ranks. Behind them, the dead soldiers in the village rose and joined them until the entire centuria faced their commander once more.

No blood flowed from their wounds, but their flesh was gray, corrupt, their eyes gleaming with unholy fury and a gangrenous stench surrounded them.

As one, they drew their swords and advanced upon the horror-struck Centurion and the Erdin turncoat. And Badb Catha was at their head.

They marched. The centuria marched through the Rapa Hills towards Campus Roborum. Above them a silent black cloud flew, keeping pace with their tireless steps.

Larcius was at the head of his men, a crow perched upon his shoulder. From time to time the bird would nuzzle his cheek, running its beak along the suppurating wound that ran from ear to jaw.

Its voice echoed through his skull.

"I will give you work for your swords, Gaius Larcius Servius, and I will give you legions to command. March then, Centurion! On to Roborum, to Eblana and, in time, to Rome itself."

Afterword

Despite the fact that it is the land of my birth and the place where I continue to make my home, I have written very few stories set in Ireland. With 'The Children of Badb Catha', I sought to redress this balance a little.

Irish mythology has fascinated me ever since my ten-year-old self picked up a copy of Rosemary Sutcliff's *The High Deeds of Finn McCool*. But that fascination has rarely found its way onto the page since better writers than I have told and re-told the stories of Irish heroes: from the warriors of the *Tuatha Dé Danann*, to Fionn mac Cumhaill and Cu Chulainn.

But stories have a way of forcing themselves into the air regardless and with the announcement of *The Phantom Queen Awakes* I was finally able to find a narrative lynchpin — that of the Morrigan herself — that allowed me to write a tale that brought my obsessions and cultural heritage together.

As with so many of the tales I write, 'The Children of Badb Catha' had a difficult birth, and I am greatly indebted to Amanda Pillar for correcting the historical inaccuracies that loomed large in the original draft and for her and Mark S. Deniz's honing of the story into a leaner and more focused narrative.

The Roman Ireland presented here is, of course, pure speculation, since Agricola's 'single legion, with a moderate band of auxiliaries' never crossed the North Channel.

But what if they had?

James Lecky is a writer based in Derry, N. Ireland. His previous fiction has appeared both in print and online in a number of publications including *Beneath Ceaseless Skies, Heroic Fantasy Quarterly, Sorcerous Signals, Aphelion, Mystic Signals* and *Emerald Eye: The Best Irish Imaginative Fiction*.

L.J. Hayward

The Plain of Pillars

He came to her on Samhain, the night between life and death, between summer and winter, and watched her bathe. She stood, unashamed of her nakedness, feet apart, and drew the river across her skin in slow strokes. Her bones chilled the water, bringing the first touches of winter to the world. Where the water dripped from her rust-red hair, it fell as ice back to Unshin.

"You could doom us all to a cold death if you wished." He lay on the bank.

Morrigan cast a glance over his broad, rounded body and some of the cold inside her melted. "I would never wish such a thing."

Dagda returned her look with appreciation. Then he sighed. "But sometimes, you do."

She turned and looked across the river at Ireland — pure and honest and in danger. If the danger came only from the advancing Fomorians, there would be no division in her heart.

"Yes," she whispered. "Sometimes I do."

She left the water and went to his side. He draped her red cloak around her shoulders and drew her to the ground.

"So cold," he murmured, his hands warm as they touched her arms and breasts.

Morrigan pushed his hands aside. "No, Dagda. Not this time."

"No?" He sat back. "You have never refused me before."

Her throat tightened at the hurt and confusion in his voice, and the words she desperately wanted to speak caught fast to her tongue and stayed inside. He was such an uncomplicated thing, all action and intemperance, ruled by his desires. How could she make him understand that the world was moving beyond the simple passage between winter and summer, death and rebirth? He saw only the present. His gaze never strayed beyond the next meal, the next woman, the next fight. And right now, she was merely two of those things to him. He would not listen.

But she had to try.

"Dagda, I have seen the future."

"I have seen it as well. It is full of Fomorians, tearing up our land, stealing what is rightfully ours and enslaving our people." He gestured to the river, the droplets of ice she had left behind drifting on the current. "This is a dark time for the *Tuatha Dé Danann*. They need us to bring them through it."

"But what if we fail? What if we should not even try?"

"If anyone can, we can. And why should we not try? You cannot tell me that what the Fomorians have done has not angered you. This is our land. You hate Bres as much as I do."

Morrigan got to her feet, holding her cloak tight. The breeze caught the material and lifted it like wings. She had the sudden desire to fly, to go far away, let the wind take her to a place where she was not this person, not this woman.

"There is more than Bres out there, Dagda," she said, instead of fleeing. "There are greater dangers than an invading army."

"Do you mean the giant Bres brings with him? Balor of the Evil Eye? We will defeat him as we have defeated all others."

"I do not mean Balor. He is an enemy we can see and fight. He is the least of the dangers I have seen."

Dagda stood, took one of her arms in his strong hold and turned her to face him. "Then what else is there? Morrigan, you must tell me. If we have more than one enemy approaching, we must know so that we can prepare. Why did you not tell Lug about this earlier?"

"This is not an enemy we can see clearly, nor fight with steel and muscle. The greater enemy I foresee is the future, Dagda. I have seen what this world will become and I am horrified. What if our actions now lead us to that future? What if it leads us to something even worse? Perhaps it would be best if the Fomorians are allowed free reign of this land. Perhaps I should coat the world in winter and leave it there."

He was quiet for a long time, holding her arm so she could not escape. She was grateful for the tether because the desire to run spiked. Beneath her cloak, her skin itched with the need to move, to change and be free. She had to stay, she had to convince him. He was simple but good and she would hate to leave him behind.

"Morrigan." Dagda said her name with barely enough breath to give it sound. "My sweet winter." His arms went around her and gathered her close to his warmth. "I do not pretend to know how you see what you see, and I do not doubt what you see. You see so far and your sight has been a boon to the *Tuatha Dé Danann,* but I fear you are also blind. There are many things you fail to see."

She struggled to free herself but he held tight.

Dagda continued, "Many think I am stupid and I know I am not as talented as Lug, nor as clever as Nuada. I do not see things as you see them, but I do see you. I see the queen of the battlefield, the mother of the land and a woman lost in the dark. As each summer comes to an end, I see the despair grow in you. This is what you do not see."

His voice was deep and soft. Morrigan leaned against him and tried to wrap herself in that voice.

"This darkness that comes upon you is not eternal. Let me show you."

And because she wanted him to be right, she let him.

He lowered her to the ground and made love to her. When they lay satiated in each other's arms, Morrigan felt some of the bleakness inside burn away.

The first of his needs fulfilled, it was no surprise when Dagda moved to the second.

"Have you learned of the Fomorian movements?"

Morrigan left his side and wrapped herself in her cloak. "I have. They will make land at Mag Ceidne."

Dagda stood, pulling on his clothes. "Then we shall meet them at Mag Tuired."

"The Plain of Pillars," Morrigan whispered to the night.

"It will once again know battle and once again, our victory."

She smiled at him, sad but tolerant. "You trust to the past too much."

"And you do not. That is why you fear the future. Lug wishes to know how you will help our efforts."

It was in her to deny her aid, but the warmth of his embrace suffused her still and quickened her blood. The desire to fly returned, but now it was to fly toward something, not away from it.

"Indech mac De Domnann," she said. "The Fomorian king. I will go to Scetne and destroy him. Come battle, he will already be doomed."

Dagda's teeth flashed in the dark. "My sweet winter."

"Where do the *Tuatha Dé Danann* mass?" Bres demanded.

"Mag Aurfolaig," Balor of the Evil Eye replied. His voice growled from behind the iron lid required to keep the power of his eye from casting death wherever he looked.

Indech mac De Domnann spread his feet and crossed his arms. "I believe they mean to meet us at Mag Tuired. It is a site that will work in their favor. Already, they have experienced a great victory there."

Balor turned to Indech. "Had the *Fir Bolg* the power I possess, they would not have been defeated."

"You rely too much on your power," Indech said. "Your greatest strength is your greatest weakness. If anything will win us this battle, it is the strength of my Fomorians and the steel they wield."

"And you underestimate the might of the *Tuatha Dé Danann* champions," Balor said. "Your men are little more than fodder. A means to tire the enemy only."

Hands curled into fists, Indech took a step toward the giant man.

"Now, now, my lords," Bres said, coming between them. "Our enemy awaits us at Mag Tuired, not in here. I did not bring you here—"

"No," Indech snapped. "You did *not* bring us here. We brought you. This is your mess we are here to fix, Bres. You have no chance without us. Do not forget that."

Indech spun on his heel with a grunt of anger. He left the tent, left Balor and Bres to argue over the folly that was the coming battle. Balor could do as he wished but Indech knew the true fighting would be between his army and that of the *Tuatha Dé Danann*. They would meet sword for sword, spear for spear and when the Fomorians triumphed, it would be Indech who forced tribute from the defeated.

A raven cawed. The carrion bird huddled on a branch of a tree close to Bres' tent. It meet Indech's gaze with a single, ice blue eye.

What had been the wild tale Bres told about ravens? No, not all ravens. Just one. The Morrigan. A fearless, cold, battle-hard woman who could turn herself into a raven. One of Bres' feared champions of Ireland. She did not fight alongside the other legendary champions. Instead, she flew above the battlefield, watching with her far-seeing gaze, speaking prophecies that forged the hearts of this land's warriors into potent weapons.

In the tree, the raven turned its head and peered at him from the other eye. A shiver rolled down Indech's spine.

It was just a bird. A filthy, scrawny scavenger drawn by the smell of cooking meat.

Bres' stories of mighty champions had inflamed Balor's battle lust. The giant's need to destroy was as much reason why they were here as Bres' pleading. Without Balor's support, Bres would never have convinced the Lords of Fomor to send their army. Indech had come with them only to ensure victory. Balor was too arrogant and Bres — a half-breed tainted with *Tuatha Dé Danann* blood — was gullible enough to believe the stories about these so-called champions.

The Dagda. A man of such impressive girth that he could eat as much as an army in one meal, whose battle club was so large it required a wagon to move it. Idiocy. And Nuadu, the *Tuatha Dé Danann* high king; the man who toppled Bres from the throne by honor of a silver hand that moved as one of flesh: whose sword could not be escaped once it was drawn. Ridiculous.

And then there was this boy called Lug, with the skills of all men and a spear as unconquerable as Nuadu's sword. Bres feared him most of all. The *Tuatha Dé Danann* had entrusted the coming battle to this boy's command. Madness. Indech's Fomorians would crush him without fail.

The Plain of Pillars would no longer ring with *Tuatha Dé Danann* victory, but instead with that of Fomor.

"My Lord!" an approaching warrior called.

"What news?"

"A *Tuatha Dé Danann* man has come asking for a truce. He claims to be the champion Dagda."

"The Dagda?"

The raven bowed its head once and once only. Something squirmed in Indech's stomach. He took a dagger from his belt and threw it at the bird. The creature fluttered out of the weapon's path. Settling back to its perch, the raven resumed its silent, cold stare.

"My Lord?" The warrior stepped up, sword ready.

Hands clenched, Indech said, "Do you not think a sword is excessive against a dumb bird?"

The warrior sheathed his weapon. "I thought only of the stories of the Morrigan. Do you think the raven unnatural?"

"I do not. The only thing unnatural about it is this absurd idea of magical champions. Bring me this man."

The Dagda both did and did not live up to the stories. He was certainly large and the club by his side impressive. Still, neither sight supported the exaggerations wholly. But there was an air of magnificence about him. He held his head high yet did not look down on anyone. His bulk was great but he moved with ease. The guard of Fomor warriors walked with weapons bared but relaxed.

"Indech mac De Domnann. King of Fomor." The Dagda bowed his head once and once only.

Indech resisted the urge to look behind him at the raven. "And you are the Dagda of which we have heard so many stories."

"I will have to take your word for that, since I have not heard these stories."

Indech circled the champion. "Then I think we shall have to explore the reality. Bring me the cook!"

Over the next hours, bowl after bowl of porridge was placed before the Dagda. He ate them all and asked for more. With each ladleful of food consumed, the Fomorian warriors laughed with — and at — the Dagda, and Indech's apprehension grew as the *Tuatha Dé Danann* champion's stomach grew. The man's appetite was prodigious, equaled only by his capacity. When at last the cook came to Indech to proclaim that no more porridge existed, the Dagda released an earth-rumbling belch and toppled over, snoring before he hit the ground. At first the warriors continued to laugh, but slowly the joyous noise faded as they began to realize what had happened. Each man turned to Indech, asking him to refute the scene before them.

Unable to satisfy them, Indech roared, "Take this man from my camp! I do not want to see him again."

One of the warriors drew his sword. "My lord, why not just kill him?"

"He came under a truce, you fool. Put up your sword and remove him from my sight."

Indech stalked away. In the tree by Bres' tent, the raven still watched him.

"Do not think this means I believe the stories," he snarled at the bird. "It means nothing. Do you hear me? Nothing."

"Father? Are you well?"

His daughter, Fionn. Sweet and gentle, yet cursed with a sharp wit and love of satire. She had been known to ridicule any man who did not give her what she wished. As such, Indech had not been able to forbid her journeying with the army.

"I am well." His tone was sharper than he intended. "You should be in your tent. The camp is no place for you."

Fionn tilted her head. "But, Father, I heard the Dagda was in the camp. I wished to meet him and find out if the stories are true."

"Aye, the fabled Dagda was in camp. At least it was a *Tuatha Dé Danann* calling himself such. But he is gone now. The next any Fomorian will see of him is on the battlefield, where his fat stomach and thick head will avail him little. Now return to your tent."

Gray eyes flashing, Fionn nodded and retreated.

On its branch, the raven rustled its feathers, the sound of cloth brushing steel.

This time, Indech used a stone and he did not miss. It hit the branch square and cracked it. The bird lifted up in surprise as the branch broke away. Wings snapping furiously, it squawked at him and darted into the night sky.

"Curse you," Indech wanted to scream, but it came as a whisper. "I shall prove you false in battle."

Morrigan soared away from Indech both satisfied and angered. His courage was tested, the fault lines that would break under pressure had been laid. Her plan had moved along faster than she had hoped, thanks to Dagda's arrival. His display had bolstered her subtle influence over Indech. While she appreciated Dagda's efforts, she resented them as well. Why had he come? What had he thought to gain in going into the enemy camp?

As if drawn by her questions, he appeared. The Fomorian warriors had dragged Dagda's slumbering body from the camp and left him in a ditch. But he was not alone.

Circling closer, Morrigan recognized the girl; the young, pretty thing that had come to Indech, calling him 'father' and wanting to know about Dagda. Fionn kicked him awake, then stood over him, insulting his fat body, deriding his poor mind. Dagda laughed and did nothing to defend himself.

Poor, simple Dagda. Morrigan wanted to swoop down, to claw out the girl's eyes and tear the meat from her skinny bones.

Wing dipped, ready for the plunge, Morrigan saw Dagda move. He stood and took the girl upon his back. Her arms wound around his shoulders and her legs around his waist. His hands slid over her bared thighs.

Knowing the potency in his touch, Morrigan pulled up. She circled and watched.

Below, Dagda did not get far. The girl wrestled him to the ground and they fell together, arms and legs entangled.

Cold stabbed through Morrigan. She cried out her anger, screamed out the betrayal. He did not hear her, consumed as he was in the Fomorian girl.

Fleeing, Morrigan tried to leave the pain behind with Dagda and Fionn. This girl was not the only one he had betrayed her with — she was simply the latest. It was not in Dagda to remain faithful, just as it was not in him to limit his other appetites. He would eat until he slept and fight until he dropped.

Returning to Unshin, Morrigan settled to the ground in human form and walked amongst the *Tuatha Dé Danann* host until she found Lug. He sat with his foster fathers and druids and devised the battle that lay ahead.

"I would speak with you," she said, continuing past and back into the night.

Young and unworthy though he looked, Lug was formidable. He followed her without question but did not submit to her anger.

"You have word of Indech."

"The Fomor king is defeated. He is yet to understand it fully, though."

"I thank you, Morrigan."

Red cloak drawn tight, she said, "I want to know why you sent Dagda to the Fomor camp. He told you what I would do and yet you send him after me."

Lug's face betrayed no hint of anger at being questioned. "I did not send him after you. He is there to spy for us. That is all."

"Wrong. He is there to eat his fill of their porridge and bed their daughters. You know him well enough to know that."

"Yes. I do know him well enough. That is why I sent him. You must trust me, Morrigan. I know what it is I do. And you must trust Dagda as well."

"I want to trust you. But there is so much about this world that we do not understand. How do you know that this battle will advance the way you believe it will?"

Lug smiled. "Morrigan, who has the power of prophecy, asks me this."

The desire to fly away returned, a sharp dagger in her guts turning and twisting.

"I see into the distance of time, yes, but I cannot see how we get there."

"Then allow me to be the one to put our feet on the right path. You may see the destination, but I see the journey. Let me show you the way."

He meant to comfort her with his words, but they merely strengthened the need to hide from the inevitable battle and the undeniable future. If only she could make them see what she saw. If only they would believe it.

"I thank you, again, for what you have done, Morrigan," Lug said. "But I must ask more of you."

Swallowing her fear, she faced him, shoulders back. "I have stood fast this far and I shall continue to do so. I will pursue what I have begun and I will kill for you."

The young leader of the *Tuatha Dé Danann* nodded his thanks and left her. There were many more he needed to see before battle was joined.

Morrigan returned to the river, to where Dagda had met her, where he had tied her to himself and therefore to Lug. She did not go amongst the host again, could not bear to watch the laying of Lug's path toward the future she had seen. Yet she heard of Dagda's return and of how he had managed to secure Fionn's help against her father and the Fomor. There was much rejoicing and Dagda was hailed as the greatest champion.

Trust me, Lug had said and so it seemed she should. He had sent Dagda to the Fomor, knowing the champion's weakness and had profited by it.

Perhaps this meant that Lug could see the path, and perhaps it meant the path he saw led them not to the horrors she had seen, but away from them.

Her spirit warmed once more, Morrigan leapt into the air on the first day of battle between the *Tuatha Dé Danann* and Fomor. The fury was great on both sides. It stripped the warriors of titles and prestige until there were no kings or lords, just ferocious and proud men. Morrigan wheeled above it all, watching moments of tremendous courage and moments of wrenching shame.

Warriors screamed in righteous anger. Swords and shields clashed, bodies thundered together. Quivers rattled and spears and javelins hummed on their deadly flights.

Men, beautiful in their towering battle-madness, fell beneath enemy blades, betrayed by blood-wet ground and their own weariness. As they hacked at each other, hands and feet almost met. Spear-shafts as red as the hands that held them gored deep. Warriors fell to their knees and their heads were swept from their shoulders. Rivers of blood cut gorges in the soil.

And Morrigan witnessed it all.

Inspired by Lug's confidence, she rose on air heated by spilled blood, lifted to dizzy heights where she could rejoice in the carnage. This was the right path. Defeat the Fomor, retain the land that was destined for the *Tuatha Dé Danann*; deny the future she saw each time she closed her eyes.

As the days of battle wore on, Indech noticed something very strange. His warriors fought bravely and savagely. Their accounting on the field of blood was beyond impressive. Day after long, weary day, they cleaved and hacked their way through the *Tuatha Dé Danann*. Warriors on both sides fell and were trampled beneath their friends and enemies alike. The sod turned to blood-red mud and caught the downed men firmly. The Fomor counted the dead in hundreds.

Yet while Indech's army dwindled, that of the *Tuatha Dé Danann* did not. Each morning the host that formed up on the far side of the field at Mag Tuired never grew smaller. Each night the dead *Tuatha Dé Danann* were taken from the field and somehow restored.

Bres babbled tales of the healer Dian Cecht and his powers. Indech demanded that someone be sent into the enemy camp to discover the hidden ranks that were replacing the dead. Ruadan, son of Bres, went and returned with talk of a magical well that healed the dead. He also spoke of a smith, Goibniu, who crafted new swords and spear-points with incredible speed to replace those lost during battle. Ruadan was sent back with intent to kill Goibniu. He returned, unsuccessful, to die at his father's feet, pierced through by one of Goibniu's spears.

Leaving behind the dead youth and his keening mother, Indech vowed that the *Tuatha Dé Danann* would know defeat on the morrow. It was past the time this madness ended for good.

"Father." Fionn came to his side. "Tell me, have you seen the lone raven that flies above the field of battle?"

Hands curled into fists, Indech looked to the sky and searched for the bird even though the day's fighting was long over.

"You have seen it," Fionn said. "Do you think it is the Morrigan?"

"Tales," he snapped. "Lies told to try to frighten us. You do not believe them, surely?"

"I have been watching the bird these last days. Whenever a *Tuatha Dé Danann* line wavers and looks about to break, the bird is there, swooping low and calling out in her carrion voice. And the men listen to her and they gain strength again. Their line grows firm and they repel your warriors once more." Fionn tossed her long hair. "I think it is the Morrigan. I think their battle goddess watches over them."

Indech's eye twitched as he tried to suppress his anger. "I think you are a silly girl to believe such things."

Lips thinned to mere white lines, his daughter said, "Then perhaps this silly girl should leave." She turned and walked away.

Watching her go, seeing the confident sway in her hips, the arrogant tilt of her head, many things became clear to Indech.

Since the Dagda had come to their camp and Fionn had disappeared for several hours afterward, strange things had been happening. Accidents that saw two or three warriors injured: a well that turned bad and killed a score of men. Horses going wild and throwing their riders. And at each one, Fionn a silent witness.

Indech caught her just outside her tent. With a firm hand on her arm, he steered her inside.

"Father! What is the meaning of this?"

"You must think me terribly stupid, Daughter. Did you believe I would not know what you were doing? You've been killing your own people. Why do you work to subvert our cause?"

Fierce gray eyes narrowed. "What cause? We are here only because Bres was too pathetic to keep his throne. Fomor has no need of Ireland nor tribute from its people. This is folly, Father. Our people are dying for nothing! Hundreds have died in your battle and yet you question me about a score of men. The *Tuatha Dé Danann* belong here, we do not. Their gods and goddess fight alongside them and we are alone. Does that not mean we are wrong and they are right?"

Indech resisted the urge to smack her mouth. "Gods and goddess? I have seen nothing of the sort."

"You are not blind, Father. You have seen. You only wish to ignore it because you fear it. The Dagda is as strong as a hundred Fomorian warriors. Nuada is far cannier than you or Bres could ever hope to be. Their leader, Lug, is a champion of champions. Their high king has deferred to him in this battle. And the Morrigan. She is a goddess of war. A phantom queen who steals the might and blood of her enemies so swiftly, those whom she kills do not even realize they are dead for days to come. You are dead, Father, and have been since the raven cast her gaze upon you."

Fionn's laugh was scornful and it stirred Indech's fury as little else had. His resistance broke and he hit her. Fionn tumbled to the ground, mouth gaping in shock, eyes wide. Blood dripped from her split lip.

"You will never speak to me again," Indech snarled. "From this day, you will be as dead to me as you think I am. If you try to leave this tent, you will be killed."

Indech left before he could do anything worse. He ordered ten warriors to watch her tent and had them swear to strike his daughter down should she try to leave.

With a few harsh commands, he gathered Bres and Balor in his tent.

"This situation is preposterous. Our enemy is laughing at us. Balor, you must take to the field and end this thing."

Balor rumbled something that might have been amusement. "I thought we needed no more than your warriors to win this war, Indech."

"That was without the benefit of Bres' *honest* assessment of the *Tuatha Dé Danann*." Indech cast a baleful look on Bres as he circled the deposed king.

"I told you the truth," Bres snarled.

"No. You told me ridiculous stories of champions that had never been defeated, of strange magical feats by druids, and spears and swords with fantastical properties."

"And is this not what you have found?" Balor crossed his arms, his tone betraying the smug expression the lid concealed.

Hands curled into fists, Indech said, "What I have found is that the *Tuatha Dé Danann* have a mysterious means of refreshing their force each night. There must be caches of hidden warriors and weapons that we have not discovered. Had Bres not filled his own head with lies of—"

"They are not lies, you fool!" Bres shouted. "You heard Ruadan's testimony of what he saw while in their camp. It was your refusal to see what is directly before your eyes that killed my son."

The words, so close to those Fionn had spoken to him, made Indech's blood seethe.

"And your gullibility has seen thousands of my warriors killed. I say we end this on the morrow. I say we do not give them the time to replenish their ranks again. Balor claims that he can sweep their army from the field with one look from his eye. I say we let him try."

The great iron lid turned to Indech. "You do not believe in the skills of the *Tuatha Dé Danann* but you are willing to trust the *power* of my eye?"

Indech forced himself to speak calmly. "Aye. Perhaps it is time to fight fire with fire."

And while Balor of the Evil Eye took to the field, a giant in black armor with a glowing eye, sure to draw the might of the *Tuatha Dé Danann,* Indech would strike the distracted enemy and finish this madness once and for all.

"This will be the final day of battle," Morrigan said.

Lug asked, "You have foreseen this?"

"No. Today is the day Indech mac De Domnann finally realizes that he is dead."

"Aye," Dagda rumbled. "The man will not stand by the end of the day."

"And what of Balor?" Lug looked between them.

Morrigan shook her head. "His life I have not touched. Balor of the Evil Eye is your fate, Lug."

The young leader of the *Tuatha Dé Danann* squared his shoulders. "He is my origin and my fate. I will meet him today." He smiled. "Though I would like my greatest champions by my side when I do so."

Dagda pounded his fist to his heart. "It will be so."

With a single nod, Morrigan pledged the same.

Drawing his sword and thrusting it high, Lug turned to the massed warriors of Ireland. "Today we are victorious! Today we reclaim what is fated to be ours!"

The great host cheered and Morrigan leapt to the sky, carried high by the fervor of Lug's warriors. They were glorious in their passion. She wheeled overhead, drinking in the heady rush of their ferocity. Today would be a day of heroic battle and devastating defeat. Yet it would not be the *Tuatha Dé Danann* who retreated from the field.

Beneath her, the Plain of Pillars was a treacherous tangle of ploughed earth, drying blood-mud and the littered remains of Fomor dead. So different to what she had flown above mere days ago. A lush, green plain slowly giving way to the touch of frost. Winter was coming, a time of death and cold, but always, ever always, summer would return and death would give way to blossoming potential and sweet life. Yet all she saw then was now in ruins.

Was this what the world was to become? Something beautiful and precious made ugly by the wars of men and gods? Were they all destined to drown in blood? Would every plain become a battlefield sowed with the hearts of the young, only to be harvested in hate?

Morrigan cried out her pain and the armies below roared back. Glittering with deadly light, swords and spears rose in challenge and once more, the *Tuatha Dé Danann* and the Fomor clashed.

Lug was a shimmering beacon amongst the men of Ireland. Released from his promise to not take to the field, the greatest of champions fought at the head of his warriors at last. They rallied to him, they battled more valiantly, they died to protect him and they lived to give him everything they could. The front line of the *Tuatha Dé Danann* swept aside the Fomor and drove a spear-point into their enemy's heart.

Then, from the back of the Fomor, came a massive black shape.

Morrigan flung herself down for a closer look.

Balor.

The giant waded through his own warriors with no regard for who he knocked over, who he stood on in his drive toward the front. The heat of his concealed eye reached up to Morrigan, caught her in a crushing grip. She battled free and climbed back to dizzying heights. From here she saw his destination.

Wings beating hard, she raced him back to Lug.

"Balor of the Evil Eye," she shrieked down to him and Dagda. "He means to meet you now."

Dagda laughed and swung his huge club. Lug grew grim and determined. He sent his faithful warriors back, determined to keep them safe from Balor's power.

"Come, my sweet winter," Dagda called. "We will destroy this enemy together."

His words burned away the despair of what she had seen from on high.

Something caught the corner of her sharp, raven eye.

Flaring her wings, Morrigan twisted and faced the disturbance.

The echo of Dadga's battle lust burst into flame in her chest.

"Indech!" she screamed and flew for him as an arrow fired from a bow.

Diverted by the appearance of the fabled Balor, the *Tuatha Dé Danann* host had left its flank exposed. A small, fast group of Fomor had splintered away and now raced for this new vulnerability. At their head, Indech mac De Domnann.

Morrigan dived down over the heads of the distracted *Tuatha Dé Danann,* crying out for their attention. They looked up at her and cheered, and swung around to see where she flew. Made aware, filled with her need for blood, they saw their enemy and as one, charged.

Shifting into her human form, she touched ground in front of her magnificent warriors and stood tall before the Fomor king.

Indech, eyes wide, jaw dropping, skidded to a clumsy halt. From behind, his warriors swarmed forward. They parted around him as river waters around a rock. The furious charge of the *Tuatha Dé Danann* similarly swept around Morrigan, their passage flaring her red cloak around her body. The clash of battle was deafening and yet, Morrigan did not flinch. She had no sword or spear but did not fear the long blade gleaming in Indech's hand. For it appeared he forgot he held it. The enemy king was struck dumb and she felt the disbelief, the doubt, the anger, the zeal for victory, drain from him as the blood was drained from his warriors.

Morrigan smiled. In his eyes, she saw him know the truth. He was dead.

"No!" Indech roared the denial and spun. He fought his way free of the battle and fled back toward the Fomor host.

"Be victorious, my warriors!" Morrigan sang to the fighting men and lifted once more from the ground. There was another promise yet to keep.

Back to Lug and Dagda she went, as fast as she could. Again, she landed and resumed the shape of a woman.

Drawing her red cloak tight, she took her place beside Dagda, just behind Lug. Around them, the opposing armies had backed away. This single combat would define the future for all.

Beyond Lug was Balor of the Evil Eye. He towered over his men, his lidded face tilted down toward the young champion. He carried a monstrous sword but it was not his greatest weapon.

In contrast, Lug had passed off his spear and sword. He stood before the giant, small and defenseless.

"Balor!" Lug called so all men on the field could hear him. "Your host is defeated. Ireland belongs to the *Tuatha Dé Danann* and they do not pay tribute to anyone! Retreat or die."

The *Tuatha Dé Danann* warriors bellowed their agreement, chorusing to a cacophony of swords smacked against shields.

Over the din, Morrigan could just hear Balor laughing. And beneath the amusement, she heard something else.

Through the Fomor host came Indech, screaming. No one but those close to him could make out his words, and they began to push away from each other, trying to flee the Plain of Pillars.

"Too late," Morrigan whispered and Dagda nodded, his grin wide and gleeful.

"Who is this boy before me?" Balor rumbled as the noise lessened. "I would like to see this talkative fellow who converses with me."

And the great lid began to rise on his ill-gotten eye.

"Stop!" Indech stumbled from the front line of Fomor. "It is all true..." His voice died away as the red light of Balor's eye shone forth over the *Tuatha Dé Danann*.

Heat cut across Morrigan in a cruel sweep. It blasted the air from around her and scorched her skin. Cries rose from the closest warriors. There was a loud clatter of weapons dropping from burnt hands.

Lug was a mere blur in the suddenly red world. He stood tall, his clothes and hair smoking. The leader of the *Tuatha Dé Danann* reached to his belt, bare of weapons of steel, and pulled forth a simple sling — a child's toy, a means of hunting small game for a meal. Already loaded, he swung the sling expertly and loosed the stone right into the evil eye.

Balor roared and staggered. His gaze swept up to the sky, the lid falling back to fully reveal the killing power of his eye. Morrigan, gasping for cool air, was thankful she was not on the wing. The giant spun violently, a useless attempt to regain his balance. The red swath of his eye fell upon his own ranks. Those closest to him vanished instantly. Those behind, turned to ash.

Panic rose in the Fomor as their greatest weapon cut through them. They turned and fled, slashing and stabbing at their fellows in a desperate attempt to outrun Balor's dying act.

Indech, utterly lost, stared as Balor crashed to his knees. He did not even move when, with a final groan, the giant toppled over. The very crown of his head struck Indech in the chest. A great gush of blood spurted over the king's slack lips. He collapsed under the weight of Balor's head and was pushed into the blood-mud.

Lug, his deadly sling still in hand, went forward to look down on his fallen enemies. Morrigan and Dagda followed.

"Declare," Indech gasped. "Who...who is the...man?"

"A man who does not fear you," Lug said.

Tears streaming from his eyes, Indech found Morrigan and lifted a hand to her, pleading.

"You are dead, King Indech mac De Domnann," she told him.

Stepping away from Indech, Morrigan turned to the men of Ireland. She flung her arms to the sky, her cloak billowing out like wings.

"Kings of Ireland," she cried so all would hear. "Arise to the battle!"

They answered with a battle cry louder and more beautiful than anything she had ever heard before. Weapons rose into the air and the *Tuatha Dé Danann* charged once more into battle, to drive the last of the Fomor from their precious green isle.

It was at an end. The Fomor were defeated, sent back to sea forever. Bres was captured and spared — though his continued life came at great personal cost. The former king was no more, instead forced to plough the grain fields and milk cows.

The Plain of Pillars, with a turning of the seasons, returned to its splendor. Rich green, nodding grass-flowers, darting rodents and, overhead, hunting birds.

Morrigan soared over the battlefield, recalling the carnage and blood-mud and rotting corpses. All was peace now. The plain was returned to them, the glory of their land their own once more. Yet as the world moved on, Morrigan could still feel the tug of the past, the killing and the loss would never leave this place. It would reach forward into the future from the past and shape the destiny of men and gods.

Despair filled her breast as she fled the Plain of Pillars and sang out at long last the prophecy she had feared to tell Dagda when he came to her on Samhain...

"I shall not see a world
Which will be dear to me:
Summer without blossoms,
Cattle will be without milk,
Women without modesty,
Men without valor.
Conquests without a king ...
Woods without mast.
Sea without produce...
False judgments of old men.
False precedents of lawyers,
Every man a betrayer.
Every son a reaver.
The son will go to the bed of his father,
The father will go to the bed of his son.
Each his brother's brother-in-law.
He will not seek any woman outside
his house...
An evil time,
Son will deceive his father,
Daughter will deceive ..."

~ Translated from the 'Cath Maige Tuired' by Elizabeth A. Gray.

Afterword

Back when I was discovering fantasy as a genre, some of the first books I came across (and loved) were Katharine Kerr's *Deverry* series and Kenneth C Flint's *Sidhe* series. Needless to say, these books inspired a fascination with all things related to Celtic mythology and it paved the way for an interest in ancient history in high school. All that led to a university degree and a subsequent working life in science. Logical, really.

When the call for submissions for this anthology came out, I was thrown right back into those days of Kerr and Flint devotion and the decision to submit was made for me. The tripartite nature of Morrigan intrigued me, so I set about reading everything I could about her, searching for that spark of *something* to inspire the unfathomable creativity of the back-brain. Nothing jumped out at me. Then I found a translation of the *Cath Maige Tuired,* the tale around which Flint set some of his *Sidhe* stories. Still, little in the tale stood out to me. Morrigan's part was vague and confusing. Then I reached the end and found her prophesy. The opening lines—

I shall not see a world
Which will be dear to me

—caught my attention like a sprung bear-trap. This woman had just fought tooth and nail to save a world she believes will turn into something she could hate. I was immediately struck by the disparity between the two images of Morrigan in the tale — the cucumber-cool creature who went to King Indech and took from him "the blood of his heart and the kidneys of his valor" and the heartbroken woman who saw a future world she could not love. What would make a person swing between these opposing natures?

The only answer I could find was love. Love of a man. Love of country. Love of life. The Morrigan loves Dagda, so she listens to his council, takes his comfort and lets him talk her into doing things she otherwise wouldn't do. She loves her country, so she fights for it and sacrifices the lives of her people for it. She loves life, so she despairs over the losses, and grieves that perhaps those losses were in vain.

Morrigan isn't just a goddess of war, fertility and prophecy. She's a woman with doubts, fears, passion and hormones — as well as a kick-ass ability to turn into a bird. Awesome.

'The Plain of Pillars' is a war story. It's about greedy kings and larger-than-life heroes. It's about honor and betrayal. But mostly, it's just about a woman doing anything she can to protect the things she loves.

L.J. Hayward lives in southeast Queensland. Well, she works there and sometimes makes an attempt at this thing called 'life'. She's had stories published with Eneit Press, Aurealis and Morrigan Books and is still working toward that editor-eye-catching novel. Like Robert A. Heinlein, she feels that writing isn't something to be ashamed of, but she does do it in private and washes her hands thoroughly afterward. You can read her idle prattle at Plot Happens (l-j-hayward.livejournal.com).

Linda Donahue

The Silver Branch

The hound bayed mournfully, refusing to approach the river. Aodhan petted it, wondering what had gotten into the beast. Then he saw the washerwoman.

A wretched crone hunched across the ford, frothy water rushing around a lump of stone beside her. Furiously, she washed a goblet — Aodhan's goblet, the amber pattern embedded in the silver a unique design. His daughter Bav had made the cup.

Aodhan waded halfway across, shouting, "Who dares steal my cup? Do you not know of me?"

The hag raised her head. "You are Aodhan, chieftain of your tuath."

He moved closer. Her tattered robes fell about her bended knees and stretched long on the ground. Nearer now, he saw that the stone wasn't stone but a man's body dressed in dark leather, half on the shore, half in the stream. The corpse had worn his beard trimmed short and neat. What showed of his flesh bore a sickly pallor.

Recognizing his own clothing on the corpse, Aodhan staggered backwards, nearly slipping in the stream. Though he knew the answer, he asked, "Who are you?"

"I am she who sleeps on Mount Knocknarea deep in the Cairn of Maeve."

"The Phantom Queen," Aodhan whispered. The Morrigan. His steps faltering, he retreated to where his hound waited. "How do I die?"

"By poison."

"Who would do me such harm?" he asked.

"Your death comes at the hand of one you trust."

A poor death for a warrior chieftain. Death at a coward's hands. Aodhan returned home, his heart burdened — not so much by the knowledge of his death, but that someone would want to murder him.

He crossed the narrow bridge to the crannog, a fortress built upon an island of rocks. For the night he ensconced himself in his chambers, seeing no one, not even his wife or daughter. When he greeted the sun the next day, he wondered if he had bested the Morrigan, if fate had been averted.

Nonetheless, for a fortnight he refused to drink from his goblet and refused any food or beverage he did not prepare himself. Thus he survived until summer's end.

On the first night of Samhain, his tuath always feasted, celebrating the harvest and a wealth of trade. Among Ireland's many clans, none were as skilled at working with silver as Aodhan's people.

"You do not seem to enjoy the music," Dagda said, seated beside him. "And you haven't touched your mutton."

Aodhan took his wife's hand. "I feel too thankful to be alive to eat." He smiled, his words a half-truth. The image of his poisoned corpse still haunted his dreams.

"If you won't eat, shall we dance?" she asked.

Aodhan escorted his wife amidst happy revelers. Not a one cast him an evil eye. No one appeared devious. But that was how a murderer must be, if he wasn't to be caught.

So while he danced, he kept an eye on the table, remembering all who paused near his plate.

"I believe our daughter fancies that young man," Dagda said. "She's danced with him three times now."

Aodhan nodded in the young man's direction. "He'd make a fine alliance."

Then his gaze fell upon a woman, tall and slender, not of this tuath or of neighboring clans. Long blonde hair fell to her hips. She glided like mist between the revelers. Her red gown clung to her, seeming to drip down her body and puddle over her feet.

As the woman moved towards the door, Aodhan kissed his wife and promised to return...hoping he could keep that promise.

He followed the Morrigan. Seeing her head for the river, he paused. A gift might appease her.

Aodhan ran to his chambers and took his best creation, a silver branch with filigree leaves and flowers. He ran after the Morrigan's shadow, hearing the throaty caw of crows and wolf howls rising on the misty air. Her animals called to her.

Yet the Morrigan wasn't by the ford as expected.

A lone white heifer plodded towards a sidhe, a passage grave, this one an ancient mound as old as the land. Atop the rise stood a dolmen, a portal tomb. The moon shone upon the dolmen's massive capstone, making it brighter than the silver in Aodhan's hand.

Singing, like none Aodhan had ever heard, came from the portal.

"I know you're here," he shouted.

The heifer reared onto its hind legs. As it straightened, it became the Morrigan wearing a white cloak. The hem of her gown trailed across the land like a bloody streak. She strolled beneath the capstone, neither shunning nor acknowledging Aodhan's presence.

Aodhan quickened his pace. He paused but a breath at the portal entrance before entering the Otherworld.

There, the sun shone at midday.

The Morrigan, her hair as golden as honey, strolled towards a stout keep surrounded by a gleaming brass fence. A moat, shimmering like glass, surrounded her fortress. And a brass net hung from a frame.

"Have you another prophesy for my death?" Aodhan shouted.

The Morrigan turned her head, her neck long, pale and graceful. She swept out her arms, spreading her white mantle, its beauty so great it would shame a swan. A silver brooch, decorated with twisted gold knotwork, held her cloak.

Aodhan offered her the silver branch. "A gift," he said, his voice softer, his tone less abrupt. "I have not yet died of poison. Might this old warrior have a better death waiting?"

"You die by poison," she said. "But not today."

Joy lifted his heart, temporarily. Would he live only as long as he was careful? That, too, was undignified for a tuath chieftain.

The Morrigan took the branch. "The craftsmanship is superb. Come inside. I have enjoyed the hospitality of your celebration. Allow me now to return the gesture."

She lifted her hem. Silver sandals graced her feet.

Aodhan followed her across the narrow bridge to her keep. Inside the Great Hall, she placed the silver branch in a vase.

When she served him food and wine, Aodhan harbored the fear that perhaps hers would be the hand that murdered him. Yet no food had tasted better and no wine sweeter.

Sitting before a hearty fire, Aodhan said, "I do not wish to die of poison."

"I do not write the fates of men."

"But you can change them."

The Morrigan remained silent, neither confirming nor refuting Aodhan's words.

"Who would murder me?" Aodhan asked. "I have no enemies."

The Morrigan extended a hand. "Serve me for a day and I shall reward you."

Grateful, Aodhan agreed.

For the remainder of this day, into the night and until midday again, Aodhan served the Morrigan. He fetched water. He polished the brass fence and mended the brass net. He repaired the clasp on her cloak-brooch. He did all that the Morrigan bid.

At midday, she approached with the same silver branch he had given her. As she waved the branch, he heard a musical tinkling. Now, instead of three silver flowers, the branch contained eighteen crystal blooms.

"You have seventeen true enemies, Warrior Chieftain Aodhan," she said. "Whenever you wish the death of an enemy, speak his name and crush a bloom. Sometime before night descends on the day, your enemy shall fall."

Aodhan dropped to his knees, clutching the precious gift. "May I ask why there are eighteen blooms if I only have seventeen enemies?"

"One of those blooms holds power over your own life. When you crush that bloom, your life is forfeit."

"Which one is mine?"

"Only I shall know that."

Then I must choose carefully, lest I crush my own bloom by mistake. Naturally, the Morrigan wouldn't give him such a powerful gift without any risk involved.

The branch in hand, Aodhan returned the way he'd come.

When he strode into the village, everyone stared as if at a ghost. Some fell to their knees weeping. A young man who looked much like a boy named Keir ran across the bridge to Aodhan's crannog. Dagda returned with the youth, weeping.

Dagda flung her arms around Aodhan's neck, tears streaming down her face.

"What is the matter?" Aodhan asked, wondering if perhaps he had died during the feast, only to be resurrected.

She stroked Aodhan's face. "You haven't aged a day."

Before Aodhan could laugh at that, he looked into Dagda's beautiful blue eyes and saw the lines time had carved into her face. And standing behind her, he noted the boy Keir had indeed grown into a man.

"How long?" Aodhan asked.

"Nigh on three years, my husband."

"Come, Aodhan. You must meet your son-in-law and grandson."

"My what?"

"Our Bav is married. In your absence, her husband Fiallan has led the tuath. Now that you are back, he will — must — step aside."

Aodhan nodded, knowing he was in no condition to challenge a young man. But if he must, he would; he would rather die fighting to reclaim what was his than die by poison.

Yet Bav had married well, the young man she'd been so enamored of at the harvest festivity...which seemed to have happened only yesterday. Fiallan welcomed Aodhan with a respectful bow, his words and manner showing eagerness to relinquish his power to the elder Aodhan. And Aodhan's grandson was a handsome baby with Bav's red locks.

That evening Aodhan sat alone with the silver branch. He hoped to never meet one of his enemies, to never crush a bloom and risk killing himself. But he would do so to protect his family.

The tuath celebrated Aodhan's return with a feast.

Aodhan sat at the table's head. Once the sun set and the invisible fée could stop their tasks to listen, the tuath gathered for Aodhan to tell of his journey, his immram into the Otherworld. So all could gather close to hear, Aodhan sat on the floor near the fire.

"She lives on a green island, her home the Crystal Keep. On a brass net hangs musical blades that, when shaken, produce such sweet notes as to lull a man instantly to sleep. From the moat, whose water is as clear as glass, she refills the Cauldron of Creation." During Aodhan's stay, he had fetched many a pail to refill the cauldron as the world continually drew from it life waters to feed the world's trees.

"In the cauldron's depths, the Morrigan sees the world, its past, present and future."

In it, she had the power to add ingredients or dish out the soup, thereby altering the way in which she collected on a man's fate.

"Is the island beautiful?" the arch-druid asked.

"There is only beauty," said Aodhan.

At Aodhan's answer, the druids nodded sagely, as if they, too, had visited the Otherworld, their nods supposedly confirming the truth of Aodhan's tale.

"No death or decay," Aodhan continued. "Every tree grows perfectly, without a misshapen bough. On leaving her service, I gazed deep into the forest outside her keep. As the light penetrated that lush canopy of crisscrossing limbs, I knew what beauty had inspired our own artisans, for the tree limbs made perfect patterns of knotwork."

Throughout the night, logs were added to the fire so Aodhan could continue his tale. The mead bowl passed from lip to lip, oftentimes with a toast. When Aodhan's throat tired, he waved for musicians to strike up a merry tune.

As Aodhan returned to his chair, he spied Pert near the table. The man, a grower of herbs, turned abruptly. He stood before Aodhan's goblet, the one the washerwoman had been cleaning in the river.

A cold chill traced Aodhan's neck. His hairs prickled as they had only ever done on the battlefield. Then, as now, they warned of an enemy nearby.

"Pert. Why so distant? Did you not enjoy my tale?" Aodhan laughed as if joking with an old friend...with someone who had been an old friend.

Old friends made the most devious enemies. That Pert would kill Aodhan by poison stung deeply and was more bitter than bad mead.

Pert laughed back, his timbre strained. "I needed to stretch my legs."

"And now I need to cool my throat." Aodhan grabbed the goblet and pretended to drink.

Wily Pert didn't watch to see if Aodhan drew a mouthful.

For the remainder of the night, Aodhan watched Pert nurse his korma. Often Pert watched back. Then, as most of the tuath departed for their own beds, Aodhan slipped away to his chambers.

He removed the bundled silver branch, its blooms protected by a wool blanket. Staring at the eighteen flowers, wondering which was his, and thinking only that his odds were good, Aodhan wrapped a hand around one. Break a bloom and an enemy dies.

He felt the crystal against his palm. It didn't feel like he held his own life. But how would that feel?

Gently, he squeezed the bloom, tighter and tighter, yet not quite with enough force to shatter it. Softly, he said, "Pert," then crushed the flower.

Tiny crystal shards speckled Aodhan's palm like snowflakes.

He felt no different. Did Pert?

Aodhan wandered back to the gathering. Only a few lingered, conversing. He spied Pert, staggering towards a tree, no doubt to relieve himself.

A wolf's eerie howl threaded the night. A shadow passed before the moon, though not a cloud darkened the starry sky. All conversations ceased. Even Aodhan held his breath, noting the crackle of power in the air. As he thought on it, he realized he'd felt that same faint sensation thrice before — by the ford, at the Samhain feast and on the Morrigan's isle.

A shade swelled over the treetops and engulfed Pert. A flash of canine fangs, a snarled growl, and a single scream punctured the silence. When the shadow retreated, Pert was gone, nothing but scuff marks left to show he had ever been there.

Someone cried, "A wolf took him!"

Aodhan didn't move. The Morrigan had come for Pert, not him. And her promise had been swiftly carried out.

Another familiar sensation thrummed through Aodhan, one he hadn't felt since his last battle. That sense of victory and great power flowed through his veins, making his heart beat stronger. He had survived and an enemy had fallen in defeat.

Several men gathered with clubs and axes, ready to hunt the wolf. Aodhan led them, knowing they would never catch it.

They did, however, find Pert, his body shredded and gnawed.

In spring, spears usually fall as plentiful as rain.

Aodhan's chariot carried him to the battlefield's edge. Fiallan stood by his side. The Tuath de Turi had never been good neighbors or bad, only self-serving. Fiallan knew them better, his former clan having been troubled often by Turi and his men. Among Turi's ranks were many who would rather steal than barter, rather kill than harvest. Turi's kinsmen had left Aodhan and his people alone because the Tuath de Aodhan was strong.

Now Fiallan's enemies were Aodhan's, which, no doubt, accounted for many of the seventeen blooms...sixteen now that Pert was gone.

Turi stood among his men, as big as a bear for which he was named. He ran downhill, his battle cry like a growl.

The ground unfit for a chariot, Aodhan led the charge on foot. They would fight in the vale between hills.

Turi's sword met Aodhan's. On all sides, men battled with sword, spear or wood axe.

Turi, younger and stronger, fought hard.

Aodhan's muscles strained. Sweat ran into his face. If he was to die, at least it would be a hero's death — a fit ending for a warrior.

"When you die," Turi grunted between swings, "I'll have your land, Aodhan, and your woman."

"No thief," Aodhan wheezed, "will steal...what my kinsmen...have built."

Turi's sword slipped along Aodhan's blade, striking the hilt. The blow vibrated through Aodhan's hand, making the bones ache as they did when frost covered the ground. Aodhan's grip weakened. He struggled to shove Turi's blade, and Turi, backward.

Turi threw his weight into another blow and his sword cut deep into Aodhan's arm.

Aodhan's sword fell from his grip. Pain drove him onto one knee. With his other hand, he grabbed his dagger.

As Turi drew back, Aodhan stabbed him. Aodhan's aim not as true as it had once been, the dagger cut deep into Turi's side. Though grievous, the wound wasn't fatal.

Turi staggered, his hand pressing against the gush of blood. Bloodlust flared in his eyes as he raised his sword, his arm quivering.

Keir stepped into the swing, blocking it with his spear. He was no match for Turi, even in Turi's weakened state, and would die learning that lesson. Yet Aodhan's fingers felt too cold to grab a sword. He retreated from the field, climbing uphill to his chariot. Carefully, he unwrapped the silver branch.

"I'd hoped not to need you," he said, stroking a silver filigree leaf. He looked hard at the crystal flowers before selecting one. With his good hand wrapped around a bloom, he said, "Turi."

He crushed the flower then collapsed to his knees, feeling his strength drain. He breathed in ragged breaths while gently probing his wound. The flesh was badly torn, the muscle too, but time would mend him. If not, he would die a better death than by poison.

Below, metal clanged and good men died honorably.

And with each passing breath, Aodhan felt surer of his survival. He wrapped the silver branch securely in wool then grabbed the chariot and pulled himself to his feet. Just as he wished the Morrigan would appear and drag Turi from the field, a flock of crows circled overhead.

One crow, larger than the rest, cawed, its cry as loud as the clash of metal on the battlefield.

The Morrigan swooped downward with a hundred crows streaming behind her like a black veil. With her mighty beak, the Morrigan struck Turi's head, the force splitting his skull.

Turi keeled over. Beside him lay the mortally wounded Keir.

The Morrigan landed on Turi's chest. Perhaps he still breathed...Aodhan couldn't tell from atop the rise. Again the Morrigan struck Turi with her beak, this time stabbing his chest. When her bloody beak withdrew, it held Turi's heart. She threw it in the air, caught it and gobbled it down.

The flock of crows, a mass of flapping black wings and mournful caws, swarmed Turi's corpse.

Turi's kinsmen fled, the battle over.

Aodhan gave the crows a grateful nod to acknowledge their power before passing out.

When he came to, he lay in his chambers, Dagda bandaging his wounds. Bav and Fiallan stood at the foot of the bed. Not even a scratch marred Fiallan's freckled skin.

Aodhan smiled at his daughter; she'd married a good warrior.

"We should hunt them down," Fiallan said. "They will choose a new ruler, a new champion. They will seek revenge."

"They will fear us," said Aodhan. "The crows will convince them our druids have greater power than theirs, that we have the gods' protection."

Fiallan bowed his head. "With respect, I disagree. I believe they will seek to garner the gods' favor, then test it. We must prove our strength has no mercy, for they will show us none."

"I'll not entertain thoughts of a lengthy war...not just now."

"Will you when they attack our village?"

"If and when, yes." Aodhan raised his hand then winced. "You will see I am right. Our village hasn't so many enemies." Only fifteen left. Not nearly enough to be an army.

Lying in bed recovering gave Aodhan time to consider many things. Often he held the silver branch and ran his fingers lightly over the fragile crystals.

Twice he'd used the Morrigan's gift and twice been lucky. Or perhaps charmed.

Through the coming year, Aodhan crushed four more blooms. Four more times, enemies fell.

A dishonest trader drowned when crossing the ford. A foreigner from across the sea who sought to steal Aodhan's secrets of silver smithing fell overboard. Horrific reports claimed an eel, another of the Morrigan's form, had slithered around the man, choking him, dragging him under the briny waves. A horned cow gorged a thief. A raven plucked out a jealous man's eyes so that he stumbled off a cliff.

Over the year that followed that, Aodhan crushed ten more blooms, ten more enemies gone, as he led his people to power through conquest.

Only two blooms remained. One last enemy and himself.

Aodhan ran his hand over the silver branch. The filigree leaves had worn in places. A few had bent. A couple had broken off. Like autumn to the trees.

"You've served me well," Aodhan whispered. The branch had kept him safe, preserved his tuath. Simply holding it filled him with power.

The Morrigan might foresee a death, but with the branch, Aodhan could cause it. The broken crystal shards cut deeper and surer than any sword. He could kill his enemy from afar...although he much preferred to witness his enemy's end. He'd garnered little satisfaction from those who had died far away.

Across the green isle, surely all had heard of the great Chieftain Aodhan, impervious to treachery and attack. If his last enemy possessed any wisdom, he would never show his face, never make his name known.

On the night of the summer solstice, before the bonfire, Erim threw his spear at Aodhan's feet. The man stood tall and lean like his weapon, his hair as red as the blood that stained its tip. Erim set his clan torque beside the spear.

"I'll not fight for you anymore," Erim said. "Haven't we spilt enough blood? Haven't we lost enough lives? All so you can lay claim to more land than we can hold?"

Aodhan exhaled slowly. "I'd never thought you a coward."

Erim didn't pick up his spear as Aodhan had hoped.

"If I'm a coward," said Erim, "you are a glutton for wealth you can't possibly control."

"How can I be greedy when I'm building a stronger tuath? Would you deny us our rightful place as lords?"

"I believe, chieftain, that you desire to be more than a lord, more than a king. You seek to become a god."

"Perhaps we are the next gods. Even the gods were once of the land."

"And driven under it," Erim said.

"You speak sacrilege." At Aodhan's words, the gathering of druids nodded. Aodhan grabbed the spear. "Take back your weapon, take your place among my men."

"And now we are men...not gods?" Erim laughed harshly. "Do you not fear the gods will take note of your lust for power?"

"If they take note, they will bless us. The gods admire strength, not weakness." Aodhan felt the first prickles of a cold shiver. Why didn't Erim understand this simple principle? Could Aodhan's last enemy be within his own clan?

Aodhan recalled Pert, thinking, the first and last.

"Has some seer bespoke the future to you, Chieftain Aodhan?" Erim demanded. "How can you know you haven't invited the gods' wrath?"

"I am the Chieftain, I know."

"Suppose you are mistaken? Suppose their wrath is so great it befalls not just you, not just our tuath, but the whole of the isle?"

Muttered agreement arose among the kinsmen.

The cold prickles became sharper, stabbing pains, needling Aodhan's gut. His instincts had never served him wrong. A strange joy at knowing he would soon deal with his last enemy and sadness that his enemy had once been a friend and honorable warrior, swept through Aodhan. But he had no choice.

He couldn't let Erim sway his warriors with cowardly talk.

"Erim, however misguided, speaks from his heart," said Aodhan. "Although the gods watch over fools, they defend the righteous. We shall put his fears to the test, put my beliefs to the test. Whichever man the gods favor shall no longer be questioned."

Aodhan left the clearing.

In solitude, he unwrapped the silver branch.

"I'd hoped to never need you again." Even as he spoke the words he felt the lie on his tongue. To let one enemy live was unpardonable.

He stared at the two blooms — one Erim's; one his. Indeed, the gods would choose the champion. The Morrigan would.

Without thinking further, Aodhan wrapped his hand around a bloom. As his fingers squeezed, he said, "Erim."

As before, Aodhan felt no different.

He stared at the branch. "If the gods are willing, this man's life shall be forfeit by my hand. Meaning no disrespect to the Morrigan, I'd rather exact my own justice."

Aodhan grabbed a dagger with an antler handle and returned to the bonfire. Erim was half Aodhan's age. To defeat him before all assembled would squash any doubts. And if Erim was victorious, at least Aodhan would die fighting.

Aodhan stabbed the dagger into the heart of a stump. His blood pumped so hard he could taste it on his tongue.

"One last fight," said Aodhan. "Defeat me, and the tuath is yours."

Erim plucked the knife free. Smoothly, he spun, slashing at Aodhan.

Aodhan jumped clear then stooped quickly, grabbing up a branch intended for the bonfire. He shoved the forked end into Erim's gut. Erim grunted but held onto the blade. They circled, the branch between them; Erim slashed while Aodhan pushed.

Erim shoved down hard on the branch then climbed atop it, knocking it from Aodhan's hold. Aodhan reached for Erim's legs.

But Erim cut downward, slicing into Aodhan's forearm. Blood soaked Aodhan's sleeve; the pain would hit later, if he survived. The silver branch and the crushed flower flashed though Aodhan's mind.

At least I'll die fighting. Whether he or the Morrigan had changed his fate didn't matter. Not in the end.

Blood dripped to the floor.

Erim stood hunched, approaching like a wolf stalking prey. He slashed twice more, once striking Aodhan's thigh.

Aodhan jumped back, wincing, feeling the second, deeper cut.

Rushing forward, Erim slipped in the blood. He fell onto the dagger, driving the blade into his stomach. Blood spread across the floor in a thick pool.

"The gods have chosen," the arch-druid murmured.

Aodhan knelt beside Erim and took back his dagger, taking back his tuath.

Erim had sought to end the fighting betwixt clans. With Aodhan's last enemy dead, the need to fight was no more. A bitter irony, one Erim might have appreciated.

Still, Erim's death saddened Aodhan more than any other.

As the blood seeped from beneath Erim, it spread like a raven's wings. Aodhan grimaced. The Morrigan's sign. Even in his last battle, she held sway.

As the days passed, Aodhan felt more and more empty. Life lacked zest; it lost all zeal. It felt complete, at an end. Except that his death was foretold to come by poison, Aodhan might have welcomed an end to his lifeless existence.

"The harvest feast will cheer you," Dagda said.

Aodhan sighed at his wife. Food lacked taste anymore.

Samhain. The days slipped by so easily; Aodhan had forgotten the time of year. Would the Morrigan again roam among his kindred? Hope that she would stirred life within his breast.

If nothing else, he wanted to thank her.

During the feast, he couldn't concentrate on conversation. Perhaps the words drifting past his ears wove some tale or coherent strand. Yet Aodhan only heard random sounds.

Then Cathaoir, a man half Aodhan's age, jammed a knife in the table. "You've grown long in the tooth, old man, and your ways are as long and as crooked. It's time to step aside."

Aodhan stared in disbelief. He had no enemies left. All but one bloom had been crushed. Yet a new enemy had arisen.

A gift from the Morrigan?

Or a trick?

Perhaps there had been eighteen enemies all along and the Morrigan had only said that one bloom was tied to Aodhan's own life to temper his use of her gift. She would have realized that when the last true enemy showed his face, Aodhan would recognize him.

Or perhaps, having used the branch wisely, the Morrigan offered Aodhan a chance to die fighting. Even so, to live was always the preferable choice. But only if he lived as chieftain.

Aodhan inclined his head, saying sadly, "I accept your challenge. But I would rather not have your blood on my fine shirt."

In his chambers, Aodhan changed his shirt then sat in the corner cradling the silver branch. He stared at the last bloom. If he was wrong, and the bloom was his, crushing it ensured his doom. But if he was right...

He crushed the bloom and felt no different.

Already tables had been pulled clear. The dagger lay on the floor.

Aodhan faced the challenger. Cathaoir's eyes flashed like iron, cold and even-tempered. Although Aodhan's gaze locked on his enemy, a glimpse of red snared his attention for just a moment. The Morrigan watched, a hood drawn around her delicate face.

In that distracted instant, Cathaoir lunged for the knife.

Aodhan, a breath behind him, threw himself onto Cathaoir. Heavier and stronger, Cathaoir rolled, knocking Aodhan on his back.

Aodhan latched onto his enemy's wrists, his grip tighter than death. The dagger swung, grazing Aodhan's forearm. Still, the shallow cut stung deeply.

A good fight lasted, raising a glistening sheen of sweat. But a good victory was swift. Seeking victory, Aodhan swung his foot, hooking Cathaoir's leg. He bent his knee sharply and twisted, wrenching his opponent's knee.

Cathaoir cursed.

With a harder twist, Aodhan knocked Cathaoir onto his side, onto the dagger. The blade punched between ribs and Cathaoir's last breath bubbled out with his blood.

Sitting on the floor, Aodhan labored to breathe. He barely heard the cheers. Though he searched the crowd for red, his bleary sight couldn't find the Morrigan.

"Here, father." Bav handed Aodhan a goblet of stout, heady korma.

Fiallan hauled Aodhan to his feet. "Most impressive, Chieftain Aodhan."

Aodhan drank deeply then nodded to his son-in-law, though in his heart, he disagreed. Now, truly, his life was done. The branch was bare. There could be no more glorious fights.

Though he should feel joy in his heart, Aodhan only felt tired. Leaving his kinsmen to celebrate the harvest, Aodhan retired for the evening.

That night, he couldn't sleep for thinking of his glimpse of the Morrigan. He thought to steal away to the sidhe, the dolmen where he had once passed to the Otherworld.

But as he tried to move, cramps knotted his gut. He curled into a ball, his bowels twisting as sharp pains sliced through him. Sweat soaked his bed linens. Though his stomach roiled, nothing came up.

Aodhan shivered and convulsed for what seemed hours. Sometime during his suffering, Dagda woke and screamed.

Bav and Fiallan came running.

While Dagda bathed Aodhan's forehead with cool water, Aodhan remembered the washerwoman at the ford. He felt the Morrigan's fingers and not those of his wife bathing his dying body. And he felt the Morrigan's hand reach inside him, pulling out his soul as if plucking a root free of the soil.

Aodhan stood by the bed, watching his grieving family.

Dagda wept bitterly. Then Fiallan picked up Aodhan's torque and put it around his own neck.

"It is time," the Morrigan said.

Her words transported them. Aodhan's spirit walked the Morrigan's isle where stood her Crystal Keep.

"Though I would've preferred a more noble death, I am eternally grateful for your gift. Few men can die knowing they have killed all their enemies."

"But you only killed seven," she said.

He stopped. "I crushed all the blooms."

The Morrigan curled a hand, bidding him to follow. She led him inside the Crystal Keep to a windowless chamber. A hundred skulls, each glowing from a candle within, rested on shelves and filled small niches. In the center sat a cauldron with three legs, no fire beneath it.

The Morrigan stirred its waters with a ladle. Light of all colors radiated from the liquid. In the radiance, Aodhan saw verdant hills and stormy seas.

The Morrigan dipped the ladle and drew water from one verdant hill. "Each bloom claimed a man's life as I promised. Yet you only brought about the death of seven of your true enemies. Ten you killed could have become allies, and with you, would have united Ireland for all time."

In the ladle Aodhan saw ten faces, nine of whom he did not know. But one was his daughter, Bav's.

I've always been fascinated by stories dealing with bargains with death or the devil or some such force. The Morrigan is an interesting, multi-faceted goddess, and so I thought it would be fun to work a story with a warrior making a deal with her. I wanted to do a bargain story in which the conditions were met without trickery.

Linda Donahue, an Air Force brat, spent much of her childhood traveling. Having earned a pilot's certification and a SCUBA certification, she has been, at one time or another, a threat by land, air or sea. For eighteen years, she taught computer science, mathematics and aviation. Now when not writing, she teaches tai chi, belly dancing and writes non-fiction articles.

You can find Linda's twenty-plus stories in various anthologies from Yard Dog Press, Fantasist Enterprises, From the Asylum Books, Elder Signs Press, Permuted Press, Ricasso Press and Kerlak Publishing.

Linda also co-authored a story with Mike Resnick for Martin Greenberg's *Future Americas,* available from DAW Books. Linda's stories also appear in MZB's *Sword & Sorceress 23* from Norilana Books and in Esther Freisner's anthology, *Strip Mauled,* published by Baen Books.

Her work is soon to appear in Esther Freisner's upcoming anthology, *Fangs for the Mammaries* and you can read her first published novel, *Jaguar Moon,* available from

Yard Dog Press. In early 2010, she will feature in *The 4 Redheads in Apocalypse,* a collaborative novel.

In non-fiction writing, Linda published an article in the 2007 Rabbits USA Annual. She and her husband live in Texas where they keep rabbits, sugar gliders and a cat.

www.LindaLDonahue.com.

Martyn Taylor

The Good and Faithful Servant

Corbelathan was a brute of a man, tall, broad shouldered with flowing red hair and moustache, and an insatiable hunger for women. When there were no women around, sheep were in peril if he was in his cups, which was shortly after sunset most days.

"What's the point of being a prince if I cannot enjoy myself?" he would roar, laughing, sometimes laughing until he fell over. And we, his father's carls, laughed with him, carrying on as though we wanted nothing more than to be at Corbelathan's beck and call forever. Perhaps some of us did. For my part, my knife wanted to slake its thirst in his blood.

We were travelling to Cu Cumundi's to celebrate the wedding of Broarli to the eldest daughter of Lughoalan. Tuathan should have attended to pay his own respects to his brother kings, but, for the first and last time in his life, The Fox stumbled and threw Tuathan so that he, too, broke his leg. At his age, Tuathan could not travel. His brother kings would understand that he sent his son and heir in his place, with a suitable retinue including me as his envoy.

"I trust you," was all Tuathan said, making me flush to my ears with pride. To be trusted by Tuathan was as much as any man could ask in this life, even me.

We made slow progress, largely because the prince had the application of a gnat and, being the king's eldest son, expected his whims to be indulged by one and all, with the possible exception of Tuathan himself. His foibles had been factored into the plans, and on the night before we arrived at the wedding, I was confident we should arrive with my king's honor untarnished.

We came to a poor farmstead a little while before night, just a few miles to go but too many to do before darkness. Corbelathan had complained about the prospect of sleeping under the stars for at least the last hour and when he caught sight of the farm, he put heels to his horse, hallooing the house.

He was greeted by a young woman and a boy of about twelve years of age. He would be a handsome man when he grew. She was already beautiful.

"We would have hospitality of you," bellowed Corbelathan, dismounting almost before he came to a halt. Only the gods knew how he did not fall flat on his face.

"Be welcome to such hospitality as we can offer, my lord," said the woman, her voice as beautiful as her face. "My husband attends his lord, Cu Cumundi."

"Exactly what we do tomorrow." Corbelathan smiled, falling in beside her as she led the way into the farm house, leaving us to make sure his horse was readied for the night. While we were about that, the boy showed us where we could sleep in the barn, strewing fresh straw for our beds, saying not a word, eyeing our warrior's accoutrements with the veiled but eager interest of any boy who dreams of fame and glory, and was there ever a boy who did not?

The smells of hot food came to our noses as we finished, making our mouths water as we headed for the house.

"Leave me alone, you pig!" she screamed as we entered, removing Corbelathan's hands from her breast. "I am a married woman."

"Your husband isn't here," he leered, stumbling unsteadily after her, "and I am, ready, willing and eager to satisfy your needs." He managed to get his arms around her again, but she slipped away from him with ease, stopping in the doorway and tossing her raven's wing, glossy black hair at him as he propped himself up against the table.

Suddenly she was pushed aside by the youth, standing there with fury in his eyes and a sword in his hands.

"Is this how you repay our hospitality?" he demanded, his voice quavering but defiant, facing down five grizzled warriors and a prince.

"What about hospitality indeed?" Corbelathan wondered, hauling himself upright and affecting as much dignity as he could. "I am a prince. I can have any woman I choose!"

The boy shook his head. "You are not my prince, and you will not have my sister."

Corbelathan's head was almost brushing the thatch, and he looked from each one of us to the next, his gaze resting last on me. He winked at me, and I knew exactly what was about to happen.

"We are all friends here," he said, approaching the boy, whose sword wavered before the Prince's smile, which he had of his father — and Tuathan could charm the birds from the trees, as befitted a king. "I am truly sorry. Here's my hand on it."

I saw the tip of the boy's sword dip as he clumsily switched the blade to his left hand, which was scarcely strong enough to hold it. He reached out with his right towards Corbelathan's hand extended in peace and friendship. I saw Corbelathan clap the youth on the shoulder with his left hand, driving the hidden knife into his throat with his right, before ripping it out. The lad's blood spouted as first bewilderment filled his eyes, and then death drove him to his knees and onto his face, where he lay in a spreading black pool of his own blood. The woman fell to her knees beside him, silent, reaching out and caressing the boy's face.

"The pup put a blade to me!" fumed Corbelathan, bending down to clean his knife on the boy's shirt. "Well, let that be a lesson to him."

"Not one he'll ever forget," laughed Cormissen.

"Wine, bring me wine," crowed the butcher. "War is thirsty work."

"Is that what you call it, war?" said the woman, on her feet now, the blade in her hand, holding it a lot more easily than had the boy. The tip was little more than a hand's span from the prince's throat. A glance was enough to assure me the blade had not seen a whetstone in too long. She might bruise him with it, but she would not cut him. "Let's see how you perform against someone with a steady hand."

"Spirit," slurred Corbelathan. "I like that in a woman."

The scene held still for a moment before fury turned her face into something ugly and she drew the sword back, ready to thrust it through his throat and the spine behind it.

Before she could strike, though, Padrhaig stepped up and wrenched the blade from her grip with his bare hand, so keen was the edge on it. Dairmud moved behind and grasped her arms. Corbelathan stepped close and tore at the neck of her dress.

What did I do then to preserve my lord's honor, the master of his ceremonies, the keeper and upholder of his laws? What did I do in the face of this gross violation of every law of hospitality known to man? I left them to it, striding out into the chill, fresh darkness. I was a warrior, and had never been anything but a loyal man to my king. I had killed for him more times than I could remember and I dared say I would kill for him again if the time came. I would die for him. I had prided myself on being a man of honor but all I could taste was shame. There had only been one man of honor in that room, and he was now dead. My sword brothers would have their way with her and I could not prevent it, not if I wished to live out the night. Come morning, Corbelathan would have forgotten I had not joined in his debauch, but I would not.

My lord Tuathan had been betrayed by his eldest son, to whom I owed only slightly less fealty than I owed his father. I lay in the darkness, the sweetness of the straw beguiling my nostrils, praying to all the gods that I would be allowed to sleep. Whenever drowsiness crept upon me, though, I put the blade of my knife to my thumb. Pain is good for keeping a man awake when he must plan how he is going to get his king's son safe home again when the idiot had defiled the hospitality of Cu Cumundi.

The corpses lay in their dried blood when I went to rouse Corbelathan. He lay sprawled on his back, mouth open, dribbling, his blood smeared, still turgidly enlarged member hanging out of his trews. A voice told me to geld him where he lay. Instead, I went outside to the water butt and brought in a cup that I splashed in Cormissen's face, putting my knife to his throat as he spluttered awake.

"Wake him," I hissed into his sour face. "We should have been gone from here before now."

"Gods, my head..." he moaned. I handed him the cup and he swallowed down the remaining drops. Rubbing at his eyes, he sat up, and then he saw the two corpses. "Gods..." he murmured.

"We'll need more than the gods to help us if we are not out of this land when Cu Cumundi discovers this mayhem."

I went outside then, unable to stomach any more of that charnel house or my friends' casual acceptance of it. I didn't spew my guts in the farmyard, but that was not through lack of desire. Conflict boiled inside me, mixing with bile and hunger, reconciling itself to the need to ride away from this place as quickly as I could, as far as I could, to forget I had ever been there.

Instead of which, I stood waiting, murmuring endearments to Rowan, knowing this would be my last embassy for Tuathan. I should have prevented Corbelathan's stupidity. I could no longer do the job Tuathan had entrusted to me. The time had come to learn how to be a farmer, a husband and a better father before it was too late.

Corbelathan regarded me with the contempt he felt for everyone. There was only one man alive he feared, and sometimes I believed he was stupid enough not to be afraid of his father anymore.

"Don't be such an old woman," he croaked, "who would attack a prince?"

If he truly believed being Tuathan's eldest son and appointed heir was sufficient to excuse him the consequences of his appetite, there were no words I could use to convince him otherwise.

"Her husband?" I wondered aloud. "Her father and brothers? Her husband's lord whose hospitality has been so defiled?"

"You saw her," he whined, like a boy who still believed he could talk his way out of a thrashing. "How could any reasonable man with hot blood inside him be expected to spurn the opportunity to have such a woman?" I could see him warming to the notion, his bloodshot eyes sparkling and the tone of his voice firming into the conviction that his absurd notion was simple fact. "I could have fathered heroes on her!" he said, regardless that his record of fathering on either side of the blanket was of weak bodies and weaker minds. "Heroes!"

I said nothing. No-one could ever say anything to get through his thick skull. I considered asking him how he would respond to someone coming to his father's kingdom and abusing Tuathan's hospitality so, but he wouldn't have understood. That was why I was there. I had guile for two, diplomacy and tact, more than enough imagination for us all. I imagined the hoof beats of Cu Cumundi's carls on the turf of the other side of the hill. I heard their rage, even though I knew they were still asleep in their beds.

I climbed into the saddle, the damp of the morning making my joints ache, the weight of what had been done making my head ache.

"We must be gone. I suggest you occupy yourself on the journey home with devising some excuse to give to your father."

His roar of laughter was obviously heartfelt. "Why should I?" he bellowed. "That's the sort of thing you've been brought along to do! You'll make so much better a fist of it than I ever could. I do not have your deviousness." With that, he smacked Rowan on the rump, the crack of it sounding even through the poor animal's whinny and my cry of alarm as I was almost thrown. I wavered, flinging my arm about as though I really was in danger of being unhorsed even though my knees were tight to his flanks and my right hand gripped the reins like a drowning man's. For a while I considered indulging my desire, simply galloping away and leaving my brothers in arms to the sharp-edged fate that awaited them. Eventually though, I reined in Rowan and she came to a panting halt near where a ford took the path across the rushing stream.

A woman knelt at the downstream side of the ford, washing clothes. Something about the redness of her hair in the morning sunlight caught my attention.

"You are about your work early today," I said by way of an introduction.

With elaborate slowness, she sat up and turned slowly towards me. I gasped. She was the most beautiful thing I had ever seen, that glorious hair, complexion as white as milk but radiant, green eyes that looked straight through me, lips that made me dream of winter nights where the only warmth to be found away from the fire was in the arms of a woman.

Then I recognized the clothes she was washing, and I could have been no colder had I been encased in ice.

"Is there anything of mine there?" I wheezed, certain there could not be, because I had neither undressed nor unpacked my bags since arriving at that doomed farmstead, but wondering all the same.

My stomach fell as fast as my gorge rose as I recognized the five shirts she laid out, plain except for the embroidery at the throat and wrists, the entwined snakes that proclaimed their wearers' allegiance. That was how I knew there was nothing of mine in her wash. I never wasted my coin on fripperies to impress others — there was no-one I wished to stir. I had lived long enough to have had the vanity knocked out of me, and needed no badges to remind me of my worth. I was Tuathan's man. That was all I, or anyone else, needed to know.

She looked at me and smiled. I felt fear that was more hot and intense than anything I had ever experienced before. How else should I feel when a goddess focused on me?

She got to her feet and walked towards me. If I was asked to swear for my life whether her bare feet touched the dewy ground I could not answer. She lightly caressed Rowan's nuzzle, and I felt all the tension melt out of the animal in less time than it took to blink. I found myself staring into a face, into eyes that went beyond anything a man might call beautiful, such was their sweetness, their awful power, their dreadful, cold ineffability. Her hand moved to mine, feeling like the hand of an ordinary woman, soft and warm and pliant.

"This is not your day," she said in a voice like the rush of wind over a heather moor in high summer, just before the fire came.

What could any man say to the Morrigan when she told him the clothes she washed belonged to his comrades?

Then she was gone, in a flutter of wings, the sound of which was overlaid by the pounding hooves of the five horses riding towards me.

"Why are you waiting?" called Corbelathan. "I thought you said we should hurry."

The five of them kicked across the ford, splashing, laughing as their heads cleared of the miasma their excesses had caused. If they saw the clothes of theirs the Morrigan had left on the ground, they gave no sign. I rode on after them, my heart so heavy I was surprised Rowan had the strength to carry me.

They found us less than half a mile from the cairn marking the boundary between the lands. We rode hard all morning, not spelling the horses, until Padhraig's stumbled and broke its leg. Corbelathan, to give him his due, dismissed Padhraig's plea to leave him behind. Corbelathan was enough of a prince to lift the man behind him on his own horse. Our progress after that was considerably slower, although we neither saw nor heard any sign of pursuit behind us all day. We emerged from the trees at the base of the gentle, grassy rise towards the cairn, grinning at each other. We had made it.

Which was exactly when twenty horsemen appeared at the crest of the rise, halting there, leaning forward over their horses' ears, staring down at us with hard eyes. The afternoon sun shone on the white and ochre clay daubed on their faces and torsos, their hair twisted into stiffened spikes. We did not need to see their freshly sharpened blades to understand there could only be one outcome to this confrontation.

One of the horsemen kicked on down the hill, approaching us at a walk. As I moved Rowan towards him, I recognized him as Dar Elias, Cu Cumundi's right hand. By reputation he was wily as a fox, and as dangerous. As he rode, he stroked the head of a pigeon he held to his chest.

"Your fame precedes you," he said after reining in and ostentatiously not dismounting before Corbelathan, as courtesy demanded. "Or should I say, your infamy." With that, he lifted the bird to his lips, whispered to it and then tossed it into the air, where it quickly flew back the way we had come. It was rumored that Cu Cumundi could converse with the creatures of his kingdom as easily as with its men.

"Give me the murderer and the rest of you can go on your way," Dar Elias said, his voice deep and rolling with contempt. His only reply was the hiss of swords. Mine was not the last to appear.

Dar Elias looked from each of us to the next in line, and then nodded. "I should have expected no less from you." He lifted his left hand, and the rest of his war band came trotting down the slope towards us. As they approached we all dismounted and pushed our horses to the rear. There were men, somewhere, who fought on horseback, but none of them were here.

The heaviness that had oppressed me since the morning lifted, leaving me feeling light on my feet and clear sighted. The prospect of imminent, violent death concentrates a man's mind on what makes life worth living; the colors and scents of the country; the gruff, wary voices of his brothers-in-arms; the memories of past times, of glory and tenderness, of terror and elation.

I had known from the moment I gave my fealty to Tuathan that I should likely die for him. I had the scars to demonstrate how often I had put myself in harm's way to protect his body and his honor. It had been a good life, and while I should have preferred it to go on until I slipped away in my sleep, a toothless old man who bored the tribe spitless with his incessant tales of the older, better days, I was content for it to end here, today. To be sure, I would have preferred a better reason than protecting a sot and a rapist and a murderer, but Corbelathan was my king's son, and my honor required me to give my life just as readily for him. My blood might belong to another man's sword, but my honor would always be my own and nobody was ever going to take it away from me.

While Dar Elias' band dismounted, we grasped each other's arms and wished ourselves the fortunes of war, which would be a swift cut to the front from another man of honor, which Cu Cumundi's men were. They were another tribe, differently accented, wearing their hair differently, with different patterns drawn in clay on their torsos than we would have drawn, but they were our brothers just the same. There was no enmity in this battle, no hatred, just resolution.

Dar Elias stepped forward again, thrusting his sword point into the earth between his feet. The gesture was not lost on us, as the rest of his men followed his lead.

"I give you one last chance," he said, striking the pose of a leader of men, chest puffed out like that pigeon he had just sent home, chin high, clear eye fixed on Corbelathan. "Give up the despoiler of our hospitality to my lord's mercy and the rest of you may return to your homes without a stain on your honor."

If there was a darker or more pungent stain than the knowledge I had walked in the other direction while my lord's son was taken, I could not imagine it. I could not bear that burden. Its weight would drive me, living, into the earth.

We roared back at him. "Tuathan!" we bellowed and shook our swords in his face, promising him his blood would stain this sweet grass red in a moment or so. He smiled took his sword from the ground and raised it to his lips in salute. His men did the same as they lined up in front of us, making a curved line that would loop and surround us soon enough. There would be no testing of champions today, no stories to be embellished before the fire on long winter nights. This was to be butchery, and we were the cattle.

Any man who gives you a blow by blow description of a battle he has fought is a liar. From that moment when your opponent first raises his weapon in your face to the time you stand, gazing around yourself at the dead and dying, astonished you have survived, battle is a blur of confusion and terror. It is not a man who strikes at you, but an enemy, at once both less and more than a man. He has no face or name. He is only his desire to kill you.

Swords came at us from all sides, and we struck back as the world shrank to a tiny space, fenced in by the clash of swords, the screams of men. My sword sliced into the shoulder of the man in front of me, scarlet blood spouting onto his clay patterns. I think I saw Padhraig take a cut above his eyes and another to his throat. Then I felt the fiercest pain I had ever felt, on the back of my legs, and I collapsed into a heap, the battle continuing above me, anger erupting through my agony. Some son of a whore had hamstrung me! I groped for my sword where I had dropped it, ready to ward off the killing blow, and suddenly there was only silence, broken only by the distant singing of birds.

So this was what death was like. I smiled. In a while I would hear the song of the approaching heroes.

Then I realized I was still in pain from the cuts to my legs, but from no other wound, as I was lifted and carried to one side where my leggings were cut off. Skilled hands began to dress the wound.

"Morrigan told you today was not your day to die," Dar Elias said, squatting beside me on the grass.

"How could you know about that?" I whispered, my teeth grinding together to keep from whimpering at the very much lesser pain of my cuts being stitched.

Dar Elias looked over to where the corpses lay. I counted seven, hardly a good accounting for ourselves, but I suppose there could have been more I could not see.

"Have no fear for your sword brothers. We shall do them all the honors we shall give our own men."

"Why have you spared me?"

"Your duty is not yet done, old man," he said as I was lifted up and set astride Rowan. When they tied my feet together with a length of twine strung beneath Rowan's belly, I ground my teeth together trying not to scream. I think I whined instead, an even less dignified and less manly sound. I had been cut before and I had never hurt so fiercely. To divert myself, I wondered how they could have known which horse was mine — the one that could be guaranteed to bear me home with the minimum of guidance from me, not thinking that, of course, they had seen me ride to the battlefield upon her.

Then I saw a figure on horseback by the cairn, gazing calmly down at the scene beneath him, and the sight made me forget my own misery entirely.

It was Cu Cumundi himself.

Dar Elias led Rowan up the hill by her bridle. I could feel the king's eyes on me every step of the way, and the chill that went through me froze the pains in my legs. I bowed as best I could when Dar Elias halted beside him. "My lord," I said, affecting my best diplomatic manner.

The king was tall, elderly, with gray hair tied back from a face weathered and scarred by the passing of the years of his life. Despite the warmth of the day, he had a wolf skin cloak tied at the throat with a golden brooch. His blue eyes were those of a much younger man.

"She was his wife," he said, nodding towards Dar Elias.

I bowed my head, wondering again why I was still alive and whether it would be better to be dead.

"And you had no part in it," he went on. I looked up, about to protest he could not possibly know that, but kept silence as he shook his head to deny me. "Ask not how a king knows what happens in his kingdom."

How could I have been so stupid as to imagine anything else? Of course he had watched us. He could have prevented Corbelathan's idiocy at any time. That he had not done so bespoke schemes of which I knew nothing. Did he intend to provoke a war between us?

As if he had heard my thoughts, he shook his head. "Be on your way. Let us all go about the business of mourning."

He urged his horse past me then, clapping his hand on my shoulder as he passed in what might have been a gesture of friendship had it not been so vigorous it was like to have knocked me to the ground had I not been tied to my horse. Dar Elias stepped nimbly out of his lord's way. His men stood as he approached, greeting him at once respectfully and familiarly, as a man might greet his wife's father, their reverence for the man obvious.

A flutter of wings by the row of corpses caught my attention, white wings, and when I looked directly at the bird I expected to see a dove. Instead, I saw a large crow on Corbelathan's chest, a white crow. Cu Cumundi and his men moved aside as, for a moment, the bird turned in my direction. I felt it look directly into my eyes, and through them, out of the back of my skull and beyond. A question formed itself in the very farthest reaches of my mind — since when did crows have green eyes? Once, twice the beak darted forward. Each time the head came up there was something white and bloody in her beak that she quickly tossed into the air and swallowed. Once done with the prince, she fluttered onto the chest of my sword brother next in line and executed her office on him, and then the next, and the next and then the last. All of us watched her pluck out the eyes of each of my sword brothers, before she hesitated to move to our dead enemies. She stared up at Cu Cumundi, who shook his head a little, bowing it at the same time. She went on staring up at him for what felt like a man's lifetime, before she quickly dipped her head and then took to the air.

We all waited and watched her as she flew twice around the battlefield and then disappeared into the wood. None of us needed to ask who she was, especially not me.

Dar Elias turned to regard me with an such an intensity that I had to look away, unable to loosen my tongue from the bone dry roof of my mouth to answer his accusation, to say that going blind into the next life was a just and fitting punishment for rapists and murderers. Dar Elias had promised me my dead comrades would be treated with all due honor when the only honor they deserved was to be tossed into a communal pit, me laid atop them still breathing, and all of us covered over in lime.

As Cu Cumundi rode slowly away into the trees I saw two of his men heft Corbelathan over his horse, tying his wrists and ankles together beneath him. Then one of them led the horse up the hill and put its halter into my free hand before turning without a word to rejoin his brothers in their funerary preparations. Eventually I found my voice, or it found me.

"I am sorry," I told Dar Elias. What else could I say? Even an ambassador understands that when all else fails, he can always speak the truth. I was sorry. I was sorry for my failure. I was sorry that there was bad blood between his king and mine that had not existed before my failure. I was sorry that men had died because of my failure. That they were warriors and had expected — even wanted — to die in the service of their lord, did not make the waste of their lives any the less. I was sorry for the death of his wife and her brother. The only death for which I felt no sorrow was of the man whose selfishness had caused all the others.

"She was a whore," he said, flatly, and shrugged. "I had put her aside. Why else do you think she lived in such squalor?" There was a silence between us before he shook his head. He reached up for my hand, and I gave it to him. Dignity commands dignity in a man. We both knew that if we ever saw each other again, only one of us would walk away, but if that day was ever going to dawn, only the

Morrigan knew, and she was not about to tell us mere men until it was too late for us to avoid our fate, however mightily we tried.

Rowan walked through the night and into the next day, not that I could have dismounted even if I had desired it. We arrived in the mid-morning. Men ran out of the compound to greet us, slowing to an uncertain halt when they saw who lay over the other horse. Only when they saw I, too, was tied to Rowan did someone take the initiative, and we were both cut down. I was given a drink of water but not the opportunity to wash the dust of my journey from me before I was taken through Tuathan's hall and into his private orchard. They put me down on a stool beside Tuathan and left me there.

"Tell me everything, old friend," he commanded. Tuathan's gaze could convince a man he knew exactly what was inside his head, that lying was futile. In the tree above him, a gray headed crow glared at me. My hand moved immediately to ward off evil, but the crow only squawked and settled down, still gazing at me. Eventually, I looked away and began to speak...

"...and that is the truth of it," I said, looking him in the eye, searching there for some response to the news I had brought, although I knew it was a futile search. Tuathan would tell the gods what he felt when he was good and ready, and then only if he believed his feelings were any business of theirs.

"So, my eldest son is dead," he said, eventually, as he might have observed that a cattle pen had been broken down during the night.

I found myself only able to nod, dreading the conflagration of his temper.

He got to his feet, came to me and lifted me to mine, slipping his right arm around me. Despite his age, he was still a strong man.

"Am I not a fortunate man, my old friend, in having another son?" he asked as he walked me towards the door that led into the hall, the one that opened as we approached and from which Denathain stepped through. Denathain was the king's younger son, as tall and vigorous as his brother, but a man who considered his words before he spoke, a man who believed his rank conferred upon him duties more than privileges, a man who had chosen his woman with care and for love.

"I was at the southern crossing," he said, hurrying towards us. "I came as soon as I heard!" Sweat dripped from his face, as it should from a man who had just ridden hard. He stopped still when he saw me. "You have been hurt!" he cried, rushing to take some of my weight.

We had been close, Denathain and I, when he was young, closer than I was to my own sons. I knew him well, and the look he exchanged with his father was far more eloquent than any words. It all but stopped my heart. I had thought myself a man of experience, of the world, versed in the wiles and hard choices of kings, but this understanding froze the blood inside me.

Tuathan had plotted Corbelathan's death. Denathain had been party to his scheme.

"See to the arrangements," Tuathan commanded his son as they helped me through the doorway, handing me on to two of his household, commanding them to see me taken care of, fed and refreshed.

"Do you have any advice for me, my trusted counselor?" Tuathan called after me. My bearers stopped, and I looked over my shoulder towards my king.

"Do not invite Cu Cumundi to the funeral," I told him.

His gaze held mine for a long while until he laughed. The man laughed, laughed when he should have wept! Then he was gone, striding away from me, giving orders to anyone and everyone he passed. As I was helped past the fire I coughed, then coughed again and again until I hawked up a mouthful of phlegm that sizzled and skittered on the hot stones until it was gone.

I turned to my helpers. "My mouth was suddenly full of dust and ashes," I told them, "nothing but dust and ashes."

Now, I was empty even of them.

I discovered *The Phantom Queen Awakes* anthology through a mutual friend, had a look at the mythology and was presented with a character and a story that would allow me to say something I wanted to say — just to let you know, I am not a royalist — while allowing me to explore and play with the theme of the anthology.

Unlike Professor Tolkien, I think that these islands have a wealth of mythology, mythology that reflects our damp, cold and dangerous lands, and the obdurate, pragmatic people who live(d) here. The Morrigan and her associated mythologies have been hidden beneath later accretions, thanks in no small part to the professor, and they deserve some respectful archeology.

Martyn has been writing SF/F stories with varying success for a long time now. He has been published, but mostly in magazines long since buried. He was published in games, when they had words. He has struggled up the foothills of Auntie Beeb with radio plays, only to be knocked back down because Auntie isn't really interested in SF/F. He has been paid for writing TV drama documentaries, although they were never made.

After the Worldcon in Glasgow, he decided to get serious, and has several shorts going through the publication process, as well as the novels that his long suffering agent is presenting. His abiding interest is in what happens just beyond our peripheral vision, the fantasy that he chooses to regard as left-handed realism.

T.A. Moore

The White Heifer of Fearchair

Ulick mac Fearchair was well-known to his neighbors as a prideful man, though to a stranger he seemed to possess little that might make a man arrogant. His coffers were rarely full and his daughter languished unwed for lack of a dowry; he was no great warrior, being lame and weak of chest since childhood, and his daughter was a plain woman of no especial talent or bloodline. Nor was his hospitality storied. Ulick resented every copper that went to feed his family and a stranger at his table would dine on the moldy heels of bread that would have otherwise gone to the pigs.

No, Ulick mac Fearchair prided himself on only two things in this world.

The first was Fynnerois, his fine white cow; not only was she white from ear to tail, she was gentle as a new lamb and never calved a single bull-calf when she could calve two. Ulick doted on her as another man might his own child. Nor did he grant the gods a word of praise for his good fortune, either. Instead, he claimed all the credit for the tender care he gave his Fynnerois: the fine hay he fed in winter and the high, rich fields he led her to in summer.

The second thing that Ulick prided himself on was that he was no man's fool. In his cups, he would boast that no man had ever taken advantage of him or walked away from a bargain the richer for it. He weighted the bottom of his oat bags with stones to make them seem fuller than they were and he made beggars pay for a glass of water.

His nephew, Ennan, an orphaned lad who lived on Ulick's scant generosity, was a different sort altogether. He was a tall, fair youth with bright hair and a shining brow who accepted his uncle's abuse and the hard labor that was his lot with a willing heart. Everyone liked Ennan, all but his uncle. Petty-minded and sour-natured, Ulick judged others by his own ways, and saw slyness were others saw charm and cunning where others saw a generous spirit.

There was rarely a kind word in his mouth for Ennan, certainly not on the morning of the cattle market. A cuff from the back of Ulick's hand roused Ennan from his bed of hay in the barn and the day began.

"Work harder," Ulick chided him as they led the stare-coated cows down to the lake.

"Work faster," Ulick ordered him as they rubbed grease into dry coats and cracked hooves.

Fynnerois watched it all from her byre of sweet hay with big, dark eyes, occasionally twitching a white ear. She would never be so rudely treated.

Once the cows were ready Bebin, Ulick's daughter, came from the house with their lunches bound in cloth. Ulick snatched both, Ennan would be lucky to see a crumb, and slapped a switch against a cow's greasy flank to get them moving.

The Altnawannog cattle market was held outside of town, by the river. A fenced off field was crowded with cows, sheep and pigs, steam rising from their backs into the cold air. Crates of chickens and ducks were stacked by the fence, packed in so tightly they couldn't move. One corner of the field was set aside for slaughter — cows and sheep going quietly to their deaths while pigs squealed and fought the knife, and the blood added to the knee-deep mire of shit and piss that fouled the field. Drovers yelled and whistled, snapping their switches, and dogs barked as they darted between the stamping legs of the cows. Farmers stood back, out of the mire, and haggled with each other enthusiastically.

Ulick went to join them, uncaring, even proud of the cool welcome he saw as a tribute to his trading skills, and Ennan drove the cows to their spot. He was greeted warmly by all, but few came to look at the animals. After a lifetime of Ulick's trickery, all knew the beasts were not worth driving home for slaughter. The lack of interest would go hard on Ennan when they got home.

The sun was high and Ennan's mouth was parched when the woman walked into the market. All heads turned to watch her pass.

It was not that she was beautiful; her face was too bony and her body too lean to be called that, but her hair was a mass of wiry copper and her brows were two licks of flame over her quick, black eyes. She wore a glossy green silk tunic that was stiff with gold and red embroidery. A warrior's heavy wool cloak was folded over her broad shoulders and pinned at the breast with a twisted golden feather.

She stole Ennan's breath, but he did not desire to possess her. No one but a hero or a king would have the temerity to lay claim to this woman. She was surely one of the fair folk, though what interest one of her kin had here was a mystery. Best it remain so, too. No good had ever come from the likes of them interfering in the deeds of mortal men.

One pale hand gathered up her cloak, looping it twice over her arm, and she strode across the filthy market. The mud that clotted on her shoes and clung to the hem of her tunic gave her no pause; she did not seem to notice it. Cows moved aside to let her pass and mac Connal's bull, although it had gored one dog already this day, bowed his head to her. On occasion she would pause and touch one of the beasts with a long-fingered hand but she didn't linger long.

Not 'til she reached Ulick's cows. Something hard flickered over her face when her eyes fell on the sweating, miserable beasts. She made her way through them, touching a nose here and a protruding hip-bone there. It made Ennan feel ashamed and he bent his head, staring at his muddy feet.

"You are mac Fearchair? Who boasts he owns the fairest cow in all Ireland?"

Her voice was like a hard-rung bell. Ennan darted a quick look at her face.

"No," he said. "My uncle is mac Fearchair. He's coming now."

Ulick's passage through the crowded market was a great deal less graceful than the woman's. He shoved between the cows, slapping at their dung splashed sides, and scrambled over the lower slung bodies of pigs. The drovers watched him sidelong and hid smiles under their hands when he slipped and nearly fell.

"Lady," he said, shooting Ennan a suspicious look. "How may I serve you?"

The woman blinked slowly and gave Ulick a once over from head to toe. Her gaze was as dispassionate as any of the buyers looking at livestock.

"It is said you claim your cow is as grand as any owned by the fair folk themselves," she said.

A chill kissed the back of Ennan's spine and he pled silently for his uncle to stay silent, but Ulick's pride on Fynnerois was too strong. He lifted his bearded chin.

"Aye," he said. "My Fynnerois is a queen amongst cattle. There's none to match her."

The woman's eyes glittered with some wicked humor.

"I would see her," she said, "this wondrous beast of yours."

Ulick sucked his teeth and gestured at his cows.

"I fear that my Fynnerois is not for sale. I would rather put my daughter out in the field to be haggled over. Or send my nephew here to the butcher." He said it with a chuckle but any who knew Ulick would know the truth in his words. He waved again at his cows. "These are her get though. They share her bloodlines and her spirit. One of these fine beauties will add grace to your bloodstock and fill your pails with the richest milk in Ulster. Why, it's butter already as it leaves the teat."

The woman's smile was sharp as a knife. "Or even cheese," she said.

Ulick squinted one eye and his smile slipped for a moment before recovering. Uncertain of how to interpret her words, he chose to chuckle as if it was a witticism. He reached out and grabbed a cow by the ear, pulling it around.

Where Fynnerois was white, this beast was yellow, and where her eyes were dark, its were milky brown.

"The youngest heifer of Fynnerois," Ulick said. "Other than her mother, no finer cow can be found in all of Ulster."

"Set a blind man to search and little will be found," the woman said. An upraised hand silenced Ulick when he went to protest. "I asked to see your cow, not to buy her. Oblige me in this and you will prosper."

What went unsaid made Ennan shudder, but Ulick did not seem to sense the threat; he was rubbing his hands together unhappily. His eyes flickered greedily from the woman's finery to his listless cows. Two sources of profit, but which to pick?

"I'll watch your cows if you want, mac Fearchair," one of the other farmers said. He nodded to the woman respectfully, a gesture that nearly verged on a bow. She returned the salute and smiled.

Ulick curled his lip and spat on the ground.

"I wager you would, mac Cormac," he said. "Aye, and watch my coins into your strongbox as well, no doubt."

"Uncle," Ennan said urgently. "The Lady has said we will prosper. We should listen to her."

Ulick scowled obdurately.

"Words will not fill my coffers."

The woman drew a pouch from under her cloak and held it up. The way it swung from her fingers suggested the weight of coin within.

"If Fynnerois pleases me," she said, "this will be yours."

Ulick licked his lips and stared at the pouch. Then he turned and, slapping Ennan and the cows both, drove them out of the market and back onto the road. mac Cormac caught Ennan's arm on the way past. He was an older man — with white hair and scars from battles fought before age forced him to retire — and well-respected.

"Speak soft to that one," he said. "Your Uncle is a fool; show her you are not to be tarred with the same brush. I've known her well, over the years."

A fine, red horse waited by the side of the road for the woman but she chose to walk instead, her long stride setting a pace that left Ulick puffing and dripping with sweat. The cows did not seem to suffer any weariness and nor did Ennan, each floating stride he took seeming to carry him a yard or more. So must heroes feel, he thought.

The fine, red horse trotted beside them.

Back at the farm Ulick sent Bebin to fetch mead and Ennan to put the cows back into the field. Meanwhile, he fetched Fynnerois from her byre to show her off to the strange woman. The dainty cow pranced like a blood mare and tossed her fine-horned head. Her hide shone like ivory in the sunlight and her feet were obsidian.

The woman held out her hand; Fynnerois came to her like a calf to its mother.

"She will do," the woman said. "Give her to me for three nights and when I return her she will be in calf to the finest bull in Ireland. The bull-calf she throws from this covering will be mine."

Ulick laughed coarsely.

"Will it?" he said. "And why would I let you do this? What benefit is there for me?"

Bebin brought the mead from the house. She blanched when she saw the red woman waiting in her yard, the freckles standing out on her plain face and the cups slipping from her numb hands. Ennan caught them before they fell, so that only a few drops of mead spilled.

"She is no mortal woman," Bebin whispered to him raggedly. "What does she wish of us?"

"Fynnerois," Ennan muttered.

Bebin closed her bog-green eyes and mouthed a prayer to Danu. "We are going to die."

She took the cups back and hurried over to Ulick and the woman, essaying a clumsy curtsey in her thick skirts.

"Father," she said. "I am sure we can trust the Lady."

"You were sure you could trust that last beggar, Imbolc, not to steal from us," Ulick snapped. "We are short one haunch of lamb and a jug of ale for your surety. Now hold your tongue and let your betters speak."

Bebin bit her lip and backed away, twisting her hands in her old apron. Ennan caught her by the shoulders and squeezed gently.

"Don't be concerned, Bebin," he said. "It will be fine. Go inside."

She shook her head, brown braid whisking over her back, and fled. Ennan wiped his hands on his smock and walked across the field. The woman's patience was clearly slipping. She tossed her head, tight copper coils escaping her pins, and turned her back on Ulick.

"I will find another cow," she said.

"Not one as fine as my Fynnerois," Ulick said. "Why look at her! Even the Morrigan's heifers could not challenge her beauty."

The woman turned around, her eyes narrow under flame-lick brows. Her thin lips pursed and then smoothed into a smile.

"A pouch of gold," she said. "My horse left as surety."

Ulick hesitated, his mistrust tormenting him, and Ennan did not think the woman would tolerate her honor being questioned again. He took a shaky breath and dared to speak for his uncle.

"Done and done, Lady," he said.

Those words earned Ennan bruises for a week but Ulick did not counter his nephew's agreement. The woman loosed a golden girdle from around her waist and fashioned a halter for Fynnerois from it. Until this day, Fynnerois had never known a halter nor left the fields of Ulick's farm, but she submitted and contentedly followed at the woman's heels.

The fine, red horse stood outside Ulick's house for three nights. He tried to catch it to harness it to a plough but the horse led him a merry chase across the farm. He borrowed a thick-necked, goose-rumped mare from a neighbor, but the fine horse led her off into the forest and returned alone.

On the third day the horse was gone and Fynnerois was returned to them, none the worse for her journeying. Though you would not know that by the way Ulick fussed and fretted over her.

Over the next few months, Fynnerois waxed in size like the moon, her white sides swelling till she could barely fit through the barn doors. Ulick fed her on the best grains and slipped strengthening herbs into her water, shorting his daughter and Ennan's rations in her place. Fynnerois gave birth at night to three healthy calves the color of rich loam: two heifers and a bull-calf. They surpassed their mother. At only a week old the bull-calf sprouted horns and at two he stood taller at the shoulder than Fynnerois.

Ulick looked at him and muttered and chewed his beard.

Ennan feared what his uncle planned.

After three weeks the woman returned to the farm. This time her wild copper hair was loose over her shoulders and she wore white silk thick with blue embroidery. She stopped at the field where Fynnerois nursed her calves and considered the scene: the ivory white mother and the two healthy young heifers.

A weight settled on Ennan's shoulder and he felt like every step he took towards her sank him into the earth. This was not what heroes felt, or if it was, only when they went to meet their doom. Ulick, on the other hand, chortled on his way down from the farmhouse.

"Greetings, Lady," he said. "You see my two fine young heifers, I see. They are the princesses of my farm. A shame that our deal specified that the first bull-calf would be yours."

"And there was no bull-calf?" she asked.

"None," Ulick asserted happily. "Just my two young girls. Perhaps another covering would serve your purposes better."

The woman regarded Ulick with disdain and tapped the butt of her spear three times against the fence.

"Three nights I had your Fynnerois," she said. "So three nights you have to find my bull-calf. Think well on your greed, Ulick mac Fearchair, and think hard on who you try to cheat."

She left without another word and disappeared at the gates to the farm, leaving not a strand of hair or thread of silk to show her passing. Ulick thought he had fooled her.

"Give her the bull-calf, Uncle," Ennan begged hopelessly. "This does our family dishonor and it is never wise to try and trick the likes of her."

Ulick snorted.

"Don't be a fool, boy," he said. "She's just a woman. If she was anything more, do you think she would not have just conjured up the bull-calf?"

He pushed past Ennan and strode back towards the house. Ennan followed him in an attempt to get him to listen.

"She vanished!"

Ulick dismissed that with contempt. "She realized I had gotten the better of her and fled. This is the last we will see of her, mark my words."

That night a storm shook the house, rousing them out of their slumber. Thunder cracked overhead and lightning caged the dwelling. Rain leaked through the ill-thatched roof in dripping streams over their beds. Only Ennan, in his bed in the hay, had a warm night. By morning the house was drenched, half-flooded, and Ulick was more clod-tempered than usual from weariness.

"Give the bull-calf back," Bebin said as they broke their fast. "Things will get worse otherwise."

Ulick slapped her across the face for questioning him, pulled his boots on and stalked out of the house. His furious roar brought Bebin and Ennan stumbling out after him. The fence around Fynnerois' field was broken and one of the two brown heifers was missing. Ulick bent down and picked up a long splinter of wood.

"The bull-calf—" Ennan started. Before he could say anything else, Ulick turned and hit him with the wood. Ennan got his arms up just in time to avoid taking the blow in the face. Splintered edges tore at his forearms. The next blow took him across the shoulders and drove him to his knees. Ulick kept hitting him until his clothes tore and blood dripped into the mud and Bebin threw herself between them. He hit her once, scraping the line of her jaw and cracking her shoulder, then threw the stick down. The effort of beating Ennan had broken a sweat on Ulick's forehead. "Fix the fence," he snapped and stalked away.

Bebin helped Ennan to his feet and used her apron to blot the blood from his face and scalp. Her fingers were trembling.

"He won't listen," she said. "It will only get worse."

"I know."

Bebin twisted her bloodied apron in her hands.

"Stay inside tonight," she said. "I will tell Father it is to guard the house in case any dare try to enter; to stir his fear for his goods and himself. It is not safe for you out here."

That night the small farm house was surrounded by the clangor of a fight: the crash and clash of swords, the moans of the wounded and the shrill screams of embattled horses. It raged through the night, waxing and waning in ferocity. Ennan, huddled by the door and clutching an old cudgel in sweaty hands, heard the battle cries of kings and the death-groans of heroes: Conchobar, Fergus, Cuchulainn. There was no sign of any men in the darkness, but when Ulick drubbed Ennan from the house, he was given rough handling by the emptiness and thrown back over the threshold.

He huddled with Bebin, holding her hand, while Ulick cursed in defiance and drank himself to sleep.

"What will it be the third night?" Bebin asked in a whisper.

Ennan could not answer. He squeezed her hand and murmured comfort against her temple. The sound of battle faded with the sun. The last they heard of it was a harsh, fading whisper through the door.

"You will give her the calf. It is fated."

When Ennan went out to check to the farm, the second calf was gone. Fynnerois stood alone in the pasture, lowing disconsolately for her offspring. He milked her to make her more comfortable and placated her with food. When Ulick woke from his soused slumber he cursed the woman for a thief and a brigand and swore he would have her hung from the crows. Even Fynnerois felt his temper; her mourning driving him to whip her across the field.

Still, he refused to produce the bull-calf.

Once more Ennan fixed the fence, whispering his excuses to the Lady as he did so. He feared she would not hear him, nor care if she did. Her and hers were not known for their kindness.

That night, the third night, a great fête was held on the farm. High, elegant beings danced with capering, chortling things that had trouble holding their forms. Laughter tinged with madness shrilled and the music the beings danced to was plucked on strange instruments that jangled the ear. The few hours of sleep snatched during the night were sour with dreams and portents.

In the morning the pasture was empty: Fynnerois was gone.

Ulick cursed the sun, moon and the gods, hunting up and down the barn for his missing treasure. There was no trace of her. In a fury he snatched up his switch and laid it across both Ennan's and Bebin's back, cursing them for traitors and conspirators. Blood flicked from the slender withy and spattered Ulick's face and clothes.

"You think I am blind to your plotting?" he ranted. "Are my eyes shut; my ears closed when you go off into corners to whisper and conspire? Am I a fool?"

The cool, hard tones of the red-haired woman's voice interrupted him.

"Some would say that to ask the question is to answer it."

Ulick turned, blood in his eye and his chest heaving, and raised the bloody switch to her. She caught the length of wood in her hand before it could strike her face; the meaty thwack making Ennan flinch but the woman's still, shining face showed no reaction. She took the switch from Ulick and her white hands snapped it into short lengths. The pieces fell between her fingers to the ground at her feet. Ulick's hands opened and closed around the weapon he no longer held and for the first time he had wit enough to show fear.

"If you had given me the bull-calf," the woman said. "I would have granted you boons and wealth that kings and druids have begged for. Harm would have bypassed your farm and your beasts would have fattened on stones and sand. Instead, you have lost everything."

Ulick raised his chin and stared at her defiantly,

"You still don't have your calf," he said. "Bring back my Fynnerois and I shall gift him to you. Then we need never have dealings with each other again."

Those flame-lick brows rose.

"You still try to haggle?" she asked.

The young bullock appeared on the road behind her. He wandered up to her and stood, head low and gentle as a spring lamb, by her side. The woman put her hand on his proud skull, between the budding horns. "I am not one of your neighbors to be fooled by gravel amidst the oats or dozed cloth folded under good. These three nights were not a threat but a chance to repent."

The last reserves of Ulick's fool pride were drained. His knees gave way under him and he knelt in the mud, clutching at the hem of the woman's robe.

"And I do," he swore. "I repent, gentle one."

She kicked his hand from her robe. "Too late do you come to wisdom, Ulick. The deadline has passed. You wish to claim your Fynnerois again? Your white queen of cows who you boast is finer than the Morrigan's own? Then go." The woman pointed towards the fence, to the herd of white cattle that grazed there. To Ennan's eyes, it seemed that the beasts had not appeared, more they had been there all along and it was his eyes that were lacking. "If you can find her amidst my herds, Ulick mac Fearchair, then she is yours and your debt to me is discharged. But for each cow you mistakenly claim as her, you must serve me for nine years."

Ulick rose to his feet and stared at the cows in dismay. Each white-flanked, dark-eyed beast was as fine as his Fynnerois but no finer. It was an impossible task, but the woman's command was undeniable. His shoulders slumped and without a second look at farm or nephew or daughter he climbed into the field.

"Fynnerois?" he called. "Fynnerois, my sweet girl. My beauty."

Now the woman's gaze returned to Ennan. He knelt still and felt no urge to rise to his feet. Shame for his part in this bowed his head.

"And you," the woman said.

"He spoke against my father's plan," Bebin said. Her voice trembled and cracked but did not fall silent. "Ennan urged my father to abide by his word and return the calf, but he would not listen."

"And was that enough?" the woman asked.

Ennan raised his head.

"No," he said. "No, Lady, it was not. I should have defied him."

Bebin clutched his shoulder, digging her fingers in. "No! My father would have put him out and where else has he to go?"

"Better that, than to be so dishonored," Ennan said thickly, "Then to bring this down on you and the farm."

The woman's long fingers scratched the bull-calf's poll as a man would a dog's head. Her smile was not cruel, but nor was it kind. It was her smile and as such, beyond understanding.

"What is it you ask for," she said, "punishment or forgiveness? Would you ever decide?"

Ennan put his hand over Bebin's to silence her and looked up at the woman, at her bright hair and her spear and her sharp glory, and he knew her. Dread was the frog in his throat.

"Is there forgiveness in you?"

Her smile widened and she shook her head, raising the spear she carried. Ennan closed his eyes. Some might watch their doom unflinching, but he was not so bold. He heard Bebin cry out and then hot agony lanced through his leg, from thigh to calf to heel.

The scream was wrenched from his throat, harsh as a crow's call, and he would have toppled if not for the spear driven through his leg and into the ground. Her hand was still on the butt.

"No forgiveness in me and my gifts tend to sour. So you have this, Ennan mac Fearchair: a boon that will give you no joy." She wrenched the spear free, shreds of flesh and muscle caught on the barbs, blood dripping from the point. "War comes, Ennan mac Fearchair, and the cream of Ireland's men will die paying their toll to me: My name on their last breath in this life. You heard its ghost the other night. So, I give you your life, Ennan. A cripple will not be called to fight; a lame man cannot keep up with the warbands. You will live long and be content and never know glory.

"Remember me."

"It was when Queen Mebd saw the bull calf born of Donn Cuailnge and the Morrigan's heifer fight Ailill's white-horned Finnbhennach that she set her heart on stealing Donn Cuailnge away for her herd."

I love Irish Mythology, so when Morrigan Books announced that they were publishing an anthology in honor of their patron goddess, the Phantom Queen of War, Death and Sovereignty, I was determined to have my name on the Table of Contents. The question was: what was I going to write about?

In the end, I decided on the 'White Heifer', because I wanted to explore an untold tale from the Ulster Cycle; and because I needed to tell the story of a man who was not a hero, but still had dealings with the gods. Ennan is a kind man, a good person, but neither goodness nor kindness are attributes valued by the Morrigan. Yet, she can be fair, in her own, hard way.

'The White Heifer' is also an exploration of something I have always found appealing about Irish Mythology: that the gods and myths are so intrinsically interwoven into the land and life of Ireland itself. They are not set above, below, or aside, but are an essential part of the world. It was a terrifying wonder to have Morrigan come visiting, but at the same time, it was an accepted one. Her presence in their life was like a storm; something to awe and survive.

Elegant, disturbing prose is Northern Irish author, T.A. Moore's, stock-in-trade. From the decadent, eternally decaying Even City to the worrying charm of Sol in 'A Different Breed', she weaves horror and beauty together to create worlds of dizzying variation and charm. Her first novel, *The Even,* was published in September 2008 and the sequel, *Shadows Bloom,* will be published in 2010.

Elaine Cunningham

She Who Is Becoming

Any man who believes in unchangeable Fate has never stood in the shade of Yggdrasil, nor is he overly familiar with the ways of women.

Three sisters stood beneath the great World Tree, goddesses who spun the threads and wove the tapestry of mortal lives. They gathered around their silver loom and watched in silence as the fabric unraveled from the bottom up.

First, the warriors in the valley faltered and fell. Death continued upward, cresting the hill where a young bard stood. The curved frame of his great battle harp came unbowed. Gold-thread harp strings snapped free and writhed away like worms eager to feast upon unfinished lives.

Urd, the white-haired eldest, sighed and gestured with the distaff in her hand toward a pile of new-spun thread. "Eregar was fated to live long and win great renown as a bard. On this we all agreed."

"I wove such skill into his fingers," said Verdandi, the middle sister. Her round, matronly face was wistful as she ran her own deft fingers over the ruined work. "I fashioned for him the heart of a warrior-poet. Such a man could have written songs that would ring through Valhalla until the end of days."

The youngest sister, Skuld, smirked and brandished the knife that had cut the bard's life-thread.

"The decision was mine to make. If I undo your work, what of it?" She lifted her chin proudly. "I am unchanging Fate. I am Death, which cannot be denied."

"There are three Norns," Urd reminded her.

"She Who Was, She Who Becomes." The maiden gestured to each of the older women in turn. "You may spin and weave the threads, but the future is mine. Only She Who Is Becoming determines the fate of mortals."

The older sisters exchanged a quick glance. Unspoken agreement passed between them.

"Then sharpen your knife, Sister, and get you to Eire," said Verdandi. "It is mine to know what is, and I tell you that as we speak, five Danish warships sail for that green shore."

The maiden frowned. "But those are the Morrigan's lands."

"What of it? Death cannot be denied," She Who Was said mildly.

Skuld eyed Urd suspiciously, but there was no hint of mockery on her sister's time-worn face. After a moment, she nodded and spun away to climb the Great Tree.

It took her less time than that which passes between two beats of a mortal's heart to reach the place where a broad limb arced up into the clouds. Her flaxen braids trailed behind her as she ran, and the raven's cries that burst from her throat soared off to ride the winds.

An answering call came, then another. The clouds parted as Gunnr and Róta, sister valkyries, rode to meet Skuld on horses made of air.

The youngest Norn leaped into the sky and gathered the reins of the wind. They sped toward Eire, crossing silver seas and soaring over awakening villages. If any mortals in the lands below noted their passing, it was only as a keening wind and the distant calling of crows.

Finally Skuld saw five slim ships riding the waves, swiftly closing on the island's southern shore. She and her sister Valkyries circled down for a closer look.

Signal fires burned on scores of hilltops and the swift heartbeat of drums sped the men of Eire as they ran to meet the invaders. Skuld noted with interest the many Northmen among the Celts — tall men with hair as bright as flame or as fair as her own. She'd heard it said that the green island held a magic to rival Annwn's cauldron, for men who came to these shores were soon reborn as sons of Eire.

The ships spilled Danes onto the shore. Eire's sons ran to meet them with axe and sword.

Weapons thundered against wooden shields, battle cries mingled with the calls of gathering crows. Skuld soared above it all, choosing, choosing. Her knife scythed the air, harvesting the souls of heroes. Their blood stained the rocks and ran in rivulets toward the sea.

After a time, Skuld noted that some of the ravens had taken human form. Her gaze went to a woman of middle years standing near the battlefield. A red cloak draped her shoulders, and the long spear in her hands seemed more support than weapon. Gray threads dulled her black hair; lines etched her long, pale face. Perhaps she'd once been beautiful. Now she was invisible — not as a goddess might choose to be, but in the way of women who were neither maidens nor crones.

Skuld's lip curled as she beheld Medb of the Friendly Thighs. Once, Medb had been the mortal queen of Connacht, a temptress to rival tragic Deirdre and fabled

Helen. But long years had passed since men began seeking friendship elsewhere. What immortality could Medb achieve, but to add her faded visage to the Morrigan's many faces?

The thunder of falling sail-cloth stole the smirk from Skuld's face and drew her gaze to one of the Danish ships. The Danes had dropped the square red and white sail, and two men hauled at the ropes that raised the great Raven Banner.

White silk, it was, unmarked as new snow. If the gods deigned to answer, Destiny would be written upon it.

Skuld threw back her head and gave herself up to joyful laughter. She was Death, she was Fate, and this choice was hers to make!

Flinging her arms wide, she gathered the raven to herself and prepared to give the Danes the answer they sought.

A roar of triumph arose from the invaders, for on the white silk appeared the silhouette of a great black bird, wings spread wide and beak open in a silent screech of victory. Fate had spoken; the battle was theirs.

But the men of Eire roared back, louder still, and they fell upon the invaders with renewed frenzy.

And Medb?

The aging goddess dropped her cloak to free arms still slim and hard with muscle. She lifted the spear high over one shoulder and hurled it toward shore. It burst into flame as it flew and tore through the banner, sizzling as it quenched its fires in the raven's silken flesh.

Skuld awoke on the shore, flat on her back, her arms still flung wide in an attitude of triumph. Overhead the Raven Banner still flew, but the silhouette had changed to a bird with folded wings and downcast mien — a sign that the invaders would lose the battle. Strangely, the Danes fought on, paying no more heed to the augury than had the men of Eire.

Skuld hauled herself up, using a broken oar for support, and nearly stumbled over a new-bearded lad who clutched the spear in his gut and in his agony called for his mother.

A stout, gray-haired goddess gathered him into her arms. She wrapped her red cloak around him and crooned softly until he quieted. When his spirit pulled free, she rose with him and gave him a mother's blessing. And she stood smiling while he strode off, as was fitting, without a backward glance.

Nearby a fallen man called his beloved's name. As Medb turned toward him, her face became as young and lovely as Skuld's own. She smiled and extended a hand to the dying warrior. His spirit began to peel free of the battered flesh.

But a keening cry rose over the noise of battle. A girl ran along the shore, heedless of danger, and fell to her knees beside her lover. The spirit faltered, hesitated. Medb nodded and turned away.

"He is yours," Skuld protested.

"Perhaps." The Morrigan shrugged. "He might yet live. He has not chosen."

She Who Is Becoming opened her mouth to protest, but found she could not. She shrugged and tossed a glossy black braid over her shoulder. The new color surprised her, but it seemed fitting. Perhaps goddesses, like ravens, would do well to watch and wait.

And so Death stood in silence, while all around men raised their swords and carved their own destiny, knowing in their blood and bones what gods sometimes forgot.

Afterword

'She Who Is Becoming' grew from several seeds. I started out writing a story about the Norse goddesses in conflict with the Celtic Morrigan, but that story just didn't want to happen. Blending the Norns and the Celtic triple goddess made a lot more sense to me on a number of levels — the universality of certain themes across cultures and belief systems, the blending of Scandinavian and Celtic cultures in Ireland, the ever-shifting face of the Morrigan herself.

Also, the question of personal choice was very much on my mind at the time. My sons bought the book *13 Things that Don't Make Sense* (Michael Brooks) as a birthday gift for their father. One of the essays in it deconstructed the concept of "free will". Their father and I grew up in a fundamentalist church, and free will is a central pillar of that mindset. (How else to reconcile the notion of a loving, omnipotent God and the existence of suffering and evil?)

Religious background aside, free will is such a widely accepted, deeply ingrained cultural assumption that neither of us had ever thought to re-examine it. Our sons, university students studying mathematics and philosophy, grew up with a very different world view. There was much discussion around the household about choice and determinism. Since I tend to think about issues on two levels — real world and implications for fantasy — this got me thinking about the roles of Destiny and Choice in fantasy fiction. Admittedly, I'm not entirely sure how this works in Real Life, but it seems to me that while the concept of Destiny is powerful and enduring, what turns a character into a hero is the choices he or she makes.

Elaine Cunningham is a former music and history teacher with a lifelong fascination for mythology. She has written twenty fantasy books, a couple dozen short stories, and a graphic novel.

About the Editors

MARK. S. DENIZ is a novelist and short fiction writer, who recently turned his hand to screenwriting for a short film, *Silverudden,* which was screened at festivals worldwide in 2007. His published short stories (under the nom-de-plume Sin Deniz) can be found in the Big Finish anthologies: *A Life Worth Living,. Something Changed,* and *Collected Works.* He also features in *FlashSpec: Volume Two,* and the *Black Box* anthology, and will have poetry published in *Doorways Magazine* in 2009.

After a successful year at Eneit Press, Mark started his own dark fiction publishing company, Morrígan Books, closely followed by its imprint Gilgamesh Press, which is to focus on Assyrian topics. More can be found regarding Mark on his blog: http://mark.deniz.wordpress.com.

Mark S. Deniz lives in Norrköping, on the south-east coast of Sweden, with his wife and their two children.

AMANDA PILLAR is a speculative fiction author and editor who lives in Victoria, Australia, with her partner and two children, Saxon and Lilith, Burmese cats.

Amanda has had numerous short stories in print and is also the co-editor of the anthologies, *Voices* (2008), and *Grants Pass* (2009), both published by Morrígan Books. She is currently editing *Scenes from the Second Storey,* due out at Worldcon 2010.

Visit Amanda's website at www.amandapillar.com or read about her adventures at:

http://amandapillar.livejournal.com.

The Cover Artist

REECE NOTLEY was born and lived in Hawai'i until her late teens when her feet grew itchy, and she wandered off to see the world. After chewing through a pile of books, a lot of odd food and a stray boyfriend or two, she eventually landed in Southern California which she believes to be a very nice place but seriously needs more rain.

She has a day job herding pixels for the marketing department of a nice company with a fantastic view of the San Diego seashore and fits in editing *Three Crow Press*, a sci-fi, horror, fantasy, and speculative fiction e-zine (www.threecrowpress.com) in her not-so-spare time.

As of this moment, she admits to sharing the house with three cats, a black Pomeranian puffball, a bonsai Wolfhound and a ginger Cairn terrorist and is enslaved to the upkeep of a 1969 Ford Mustang Grand Coupe, a 1979 Pontiac Firebird and a Toshiba laptop.

The Illustrator

CECILY WEBSTER was born in London, studied archaeology at Bristol and is now drawing things in Orkney. She collects bones, feathers and shiny things, enjoys the company of corvids and believes there's more to the world than can be seen or current science accepts.

"A brilliant premise of horror confined in twelve hotel rooms." - *Australian Horror Writers' Association*

VOICES

edited by MARK S. DENIZ & AMANDA PILLAR

In every room, there is a story.

In this hotel, the stories run to the wicked and macabre.

Well crafted psychological and supernatural horror offerings await you, each written by a master storyteller. Whether you are looking to be shocked, disturbed or out-right frightened, *Voices* will have something to titillate your nerves and make your hair stand on end.

Leave the lights on and brew a strong cup of tea, the voices in this room plan on keeping you up all night.

www.morriganbooks.com

Three Crow Press

MORRÍGAN BOOKS' E-ZINE

Editors

J. LEE. MOFFATT, T.A. MOORE & REECE NOTLEY

Three Crow Press is an online magazine specializing in quality speculative fiction, fantasy (urban, dark and gothic), horror and steampunk, as well as non-fiction pieces and articles.

Well written young adult will be considered if the piece is within the 16+ market.

We are prepared to consider all forms of dark fiction works and are looking for stories that capture the imagination of the *Three Crow* staff. Please check submissions guides prior to submitting.

www.threecrowpress.com
www.morriganezine.com

www.ingramcontent.com/pod-product-compliance
Lightning Source LLC
LaVergne TN
LVHW091030080826
845145LV00002B/425